MAGGIE DOVE'S DETECTIVE AGENCY

SUSAN BREEN

PRESS

For information about this title or to order other books and/or electronic media, contact the publisher:

Under the Oak Press
Irvington, NY

Second Edition

Paperback ISBN: 978-1-7373172-2-7
eBook ISBN: 978-1-7373172-3-4

Publisher's Cataloging-In-Publication Data
(Prepared by The Donohue Group, Inc.)

Names: Breen, Susan (Susan Jean), author.

Title: Maggie Dove's Detective Agency / Susan Breen.

Description: Second edition. | Irvington, NY : Under the Oak Press, [2021] | Series: Maggie Dove ; [2]

Identifiers: ISBN 9781737317227 (paperback) | ISBN 9781737317234 (ebook)

Subjects: LCSH: Women detectives--New York (State)--Westchester County--Fiction. | Rich people--New York (State)--Westchester County--Fiction. | Families--New York (State)--Westchester County--Fiction. | Murder--Investigation--New York (State)--Westchester County--Fiction. | LCGFT: Cozy mysteries.

Classification: LCC PS3552.R36466 M342 2021 (print) | LCC PS3552.R36466 (ebook) | DDC 813/.6--dc23

Printed in the United States of America

For Tom Breen and Lucy Gellman,
two of the most inspirational
people I know (and love!)

Chapter One

Maggie Dove loved her new detective agency. At a time when so many of her friends were grappling with downsizing and gum disease, she felt blessed to have tumbled into an exciting new career. She had a badge. She had an office. She had two partners. She had stationery. The only problem she could see on the horizon was that she had no clients.

Not a one.

Occasionally one of the patients from the dentist's office next door meandered into Maggie Dove's Detective Agency and asked questions, but she suspected they were just killing time until the numbness passed. Cassie Fletcher wanted to hire Maggie to find her driver's license, but it was in her wallet, so she couldn't see charging her. Though she did make up a folder. Old Henry Stample wanted her to do genealogical research for him. That seemed promising, but then he died. Maggie's business partner, Agnes Jorgenson, was hoping to drum up marital-domestic investigation work. This, Agnes claimed, would be a perfect niche for them. To that end, Agnes had put up some discrete flyers at the Darby-on-Hudson Bar & Grill, but so far nothing.

Under other circumstances, Maggie would have prayed about it. She was a Sunday School teacher and prayed a lot, but she couldn't see asking God to bring her business. Detectives thrived on misery: on people whose spouses were cheating or employees who were stealing or family members who were lost. She couldn't bring herself to pray for misery when she'd spent a good portion of her 62-years trying to avoid it.

So, Maggie threw herself into marketing. She sponsored a girl's football team. She sponsored a boy's football team. She gave a class at the library. She gave a talk at one of the bank's Thursday evening soirees. On career day, she went to over to the elementary school and talked to Edgar Blake's first grade class. Edgar was the son of the third partner of the detective agency, and he bounced with excitement at having Maggie visit, though the class was devastated that she didn't have a gun. In vain did she try to explain that she felt reading *The Brothers Karamazov* was as useful to being a detective as owning a firearm. They didn't buy it, and Edgar wept that night, until she let him look through one of Agnes's many catalogues of private detective equipment. He found a teddy bear with a hidden video system. She didn't know when they'd ever use it, but she supposed it fit in with the female-centered vibe of their agency. Still, she paid for it out of her own money.

Now it was the first Monday in October and Maggie was sitting in her office, beginning to feel the prickles of anxiety she associated with waiting rooms. It was four months since they had opened. They couldn't stay in business indefinitely without an income. Agnes was bankrolling their agency, and she had a lot of money, but she also had the attention span of a gnat. Maggie suspected that soon enough Agnes would want to convert their office space into a sculpture gallery, or a donut shop, or whatever else caught Agnes's fancy. Maggie would then have to return to her house and the staid and somewhat melancholy life she'd been living before all these adventures started. She didn't want to go backward. She feared being sucked back into the past, into the grief over losing her daughter that had paralyzed her for two decades. She felt fidgety.

It was a cool blue Technicolor Day that reminded Maggie of the movies of her youth. The sky vibrated blue. The leaves, starting to turn, were so bright as to seem artificial. She could imagine the people in her village suddenly breaking into song and tap-dancing up and down Main Street. Maggie had a panoramic view of Main Street from her office window. She could see all the goings on: who went into and out of the police office, or D'Amici's deli, or the library. She could see who was rushing for the train station and who was meandering by with a cup of coffee, on his way to walk along the Hudson River trails. She noticed the piano teacher Mr. Cavanaugh walking by with his little dog, Fidelio. The Garden Club was out deadheading the chrysanthemums in the flower boxes. The recreation department crew was taping pieces of brown construction paper up on storefronts; later they would be used for the village Halloween poster contest.

Maggie noticed Racine Stern plowing down the hill, her eyes on the ground. It was always easy to spot Racine because she wore a red beret. Never took it off, as far as Maggie knew. She'd gone to France as a young woman and the experience stayed with her. She and her mother, the elderly Madame Simone, were the richest people in Darby-on-Hudson. They lived in the vast Stern Manor in Belvedere Park. They sat three rows in front of Maggie at church, but they never shook hands during the Passing of the Peace. They spoke only to the minister. And God, she supposed. They even brought their own communion cup to church, not wishing to use the silver that was good enough for everyone else.

Now she watched as Racine banged right into Joe Mangione, strolling along with his coffee. She didn't stop. Didn't apologize. Just kept moving forward. Maggie wondered where she was going in such a rush. Not the dentist. Maggie felt sure of that. It was a matter of pride for Racine and her mother that they only went to doctors in New York City. Perhaps the train station then. She was dressed carefully in a black skirt and a black blouse and a black sweater, but then Racine always wore those clothes. People who didn't know her thought she was a nun. She had a sort of Mrs. Danvers vibe, Maggie thought.

Racine kept moving down the hill and then suddenly, and to Maggie's amazement, she stopped right outside the door to the detective agency. Racine paused for a moment, giving Maggie just enough time to check herself out in the mirror that Agnes had hung in the corner. All part of her bid for the women's market in private detection. She'd also had business cards made up in pink. *Do you have trust issues? Hire us!*

And then Racine was there, in Maggie's office.

"You don't have a secretary?" Racine asked.

"Not yet. Agnes is looking for one," Maggie Dove replied. Which was true enough. Agnes seemed to be looking for all sorts of women, but best not to go into that now. Too late Maggie realized she hadn't stowed away *The Brothers Karamazov* and she didn't want to give the impression she'd been sitting around reading, which she had been, though to a purpose. As smoothly as possible, she set the book down by her feet and kicked it under her chair.

Fortunately, Racine was still scanning the office with disfavor.

"Who does your secretarial work?"

"I do," Maggie said.

"Then how do you have time to be a detective?"

"So far it hasn't been a problem," Maggie said, in perfect honesty.

She beckoned to Racine to sit down at the table, which occupied a big part of the office. Agnes thought it would make more sense to have one big table than three small desks, and so she'd bought a huge slab of cherry wood, which was propped up by four sturdy legs, by sturdy meaning that come the next Flood, this table was not going to move. It was more opulent than Maggie would have chosen, and yet she loved it. Turned out the world was full of surprises, if you could just allow yourself to see them. The chairs were best of all. They cushioned you. They embraced your back as you sank into them. Even Racine had nothing negative to say, Maggie noticed, as she settled her slim body into the chair.

"How can I help you?" Maggie asked.

She drew out a pad of paper and wrote down the date. She wrote down Racine's name and the time, for good measure.

Racine licked her lips. They looked chapped and Maggie noticed her wrists were flaked with dry skin.

"I want to hire you," she said.

"Fabulous." Maggie wrote down "hire" and underlined the word three times. She knew there were official New Business Sheets in one of the file cabinets, but she didn't want to interrupt the momentum. She could fill it in later.

"What do you want us to do?"

"I want you to stop my sister from coming home," Racine said.

"Domino's coming home?"

Racine's sister had been away for almost forty years. She'd left Darby when she was just a girl, gone out to Hollywood to be in some movies, married a rock star, and they'd managed to stay married all this time.

Domino's picture had been in *People* magazine. Her husband's antics were often reported on in the gossip sites. Once he'd peed over a balcony, right on to the heads of his fans. Another time he threw his TV out a hotel window and gave a man a concussion.

"She's coming home for my mother's birthday," Racine said.

"That doesn't sound like a bad thing," Maggie replied. "Won't your mother be glad to see her?"

Racine compressed her lips into a tight line. All of Racine was compressed, it seemed to Maggie. She looked worn down, but then while her sister had been gallivanting around, Racine had devoted the last four decades to taking care of her mother. It was an old story. One sister the caretaker, the other one free of care.

"I am going to tell you something which I believe only you will understand, Maggie Dove, because you are a Sunday School teacher."

"Okay."

"My sister is evil," Racine said. "You believe in evil, don't you?"

Maggie remembered a night last April when evil had come close to taking her life. She could still smell the honeysuckle. Cold prying eyes that sought to destroy her. "Yes," she said. "I believe in evil, but I don't know that I'm equipped to deal with it. Can you tell me what scares you?"

"Oh, I'm not scared," Racine said. She ran her finger across her lips. No manicure. "Domino can't hurt me with those witch's tricks of hers. I don't believe in that. But she'll scare my mother, and I don't want my mother upset. She's had enough sorrow in her life, having to leave her country behind, and then being widowed and having her daughter leave her. She does not deserve any more heartache."

She rustled about in her pocketbook and pulled out a small piece of paper. "I have Domino's phone number," she said, setting the plain white paper on the cherry wood table.

"I'll pay you a thousand dollars. Just talk to her and persuade her not to come."

Maggie looked at the piece of paper.

"I assume you've already told her not to come."

"She won't listen to me. She knows I hate her. But I hope she'll listen to you."

"Racine, I know you think your mother doesn't want to see her, but I suspect that she does. After all, Domino is her daughter and your mother is getting on in years and she might not have this chance again. You would feel badly if your mother died with regrets."

Maggie thought of her own daughter, Juliet. Imagined how joyful she'd be if she found out she was returning after having been away for 40 years. Maggie'd always felt a special tenderness for the father in the parable of the prodigal son. The old man asked no questions of his fallen son. He didn't blame him or criticize him for running through all his money and living a dissolute life. Instead, he ran to him and kissed him and threw him a wonderful party. *For this my son was dead, and is alive again; he was lost, and is found.* It always made her tear up.

"You won't help me," Racine said.

"I'd be very happy to help you," Maggie said. "I just feel like, no matter how hard it may be, in the end you will be glad if you welcome your sister home."

Racine stood up and glared at Maggie. She tugged her black sweater more tightly around her. "You have disappointed me," she said, and then left without another word.

Maggie looked down at the sheet of paper on the table, the one with Domino's phone number. She felt her eyes swim. As she looked at it, the numbers seemed to change into claw marks. For a moment she felt dizzy, and then she ripped up the paper and threw it away.

Chapter Two

Maggie just assumed Agnes would agree with her handling of Racine. At worst, she sup-posed, Agnes would joke about it, or tease Maggie for being foolish. What she didn't anticipate was that Agnes would be seized with anger. Not since Maggie saw *The Exorcist*, some years ago, had she seen such fury.

"You did what?" Agnes bellowed.

It was a warm October afternoon. The office win-dows were open; the blinds up. Parents were gathering on the street, chatting while they waited for the school buses to drop off their children. It was a calm and happy scene.

"Agnes," Maggie hissed. "Get hold of yourself."

But Agnes had moved way beyond self-control. She wheezed so hard that the top button of her silk blouse popped open. She always wore clothes a size too tight, whether out of hopefulness or seductiveness, Maggie wasn't sure. She'd had her blonde hair done at a new place and it looked crimped into many small waves. She was all movement and pulse. And anger.

"You turned away a client," Agnes roared.

"Do not talk to me like this," Maggie said. "Sit down and we'll discuss it."

She couldn't understand how Agnes got angry so fast. Since they'd joined together to form the detective agency, four months ago, following the solution of a murder mystery, Agnes had been all good humor and excitement. She texted Maggie all the time. She called her at night to chat. They went out to dinner and she'd even introduced Maggie to her one of her girlfriends, though that particular relationship hadn't lasted. But the point was that Maggie considered Agnes more friend than business partner, a sensation that quickly dissolved under the brunt of Agnes's anger. For just a moment Maggie wondered if she might be joking. But no, the anger coming toward her was real.

"I've been working so hard to drum up clients," Agnes cried out. "I've been developing contacts and taking an online course and begging people to hire us. All the while you sit here reading that *Brothers Karamazov* book of yours and praying."

"That's not fair," Maggie said. "I've been doing a lot to talk up our agency as well. You said yourself it would take a while to get our footing. Darby's a small village."

"This village is ripe with potential work. Do you know how many people here are having affairs? We could be doing surveillance work. We should be checking out au pairs. We could be profitable," she cried out. "Instead, we're sitting here spinning our wheels."

Maggie noticed a woman leaving the dentist's office. She walked into the little tree out front, a tender little ash planted on Arbor Day. It looked like it might fall over under the assault.

Edgar's bus was due to show up in a few moments. She had to go outside and wait for him. She'd promised his mother she'd watch him this afternoon. Maggie'd planned to watch a new Detective Grudge video with him; it was their new favorite hobby. Detective Grudge ran an on-line detective school, Maggie was studying to get a certificate, and every week there was a new Detective Grudge video. This new one was about surveillance and she and Edgar were most excited. She had to fill out a test after each video and she'd already earned two As. Detective Grudge wrote her personally and said she was his best student. *I'm trying*, she wanted to cry out. *I'm trying*.

"A thousand dollars," Agnes cried out. "A thousand dollars."

Maggie felt stunned by her anger. For so many years, decades really, people had treated Maggie with special care because she had suffered so much, and certainly no one had ever yelled at her like this. No one expected anything of her. Simply getting out of bed was an achievement. She felt off balance. *I've lost a child*, she wanted to yell at Agnes. *You can't yell at me*. But she realized that had happened 20 years ago and people had moved on. This was life, this was what Maggie had avoided for so long. This was the world she wanted to reenter. But it was scary.

"I can see how I should have spoken to you first, but I felt my decision was valid. We're just starting to make our reputation and we don't want to be associated with bizarre requests," Maggie said. "We're not exorcists, after all. We're not qualified to take on theological issues."

Agnes slammed her fist against the table, which must have hurt, Maggie thought, as it was a very strong table. "We do what people pay us to do," she cried out. "We are in the business of assisting people. Not judging them. If someone wants us to take pictures of their husband in bed with another woman, we do it. If someone wants us to drop off a subpoena, we hunt them down and do it. If someone wants us to go undercover and pretend to work in a bank so that we can uncover information about a crime, we do it. We do not sit here moralizing about what is right and wrong."

Several of the parents turned to look toward their window. Earlier in the day, Maggie'd pulled up the dark blinds to let in the sunlight, but now she strode over and yanked them closed. She didn't want anyone witnessing this. The room began to smell dank with Agnes's sweat and perfume.

And then, as if things couldn't get worse, the sounds of John Denver singing "Country Roads" began streaming into the office. The dentist had an earphone he gave to his patients to soothe them, but some glitch must have caused the volume to surge. The song horrified Maggie. That very song had been playing at the hospital when she got to it following her daughter's accident and whenever she heard it, innocuous though it was, it made her cry. Her eyes started to tear up, which was bad, because it looked like she was crying about Agnes yelling at her, which she wasn't, precisely. Then the drill started going.

"This is an unsavory business. We deal with people's feelings. You have to wrap your mind around that Maggie. This is not Sunday School. We deal with the dark side of human behavior."

Maggie could have pointed out that she dealt with plenty of unsavory behavior as a Sunday School teacher. One need only think of The Great Chewing Gum Episode of 2012. But she could see that Agnes was not in a mood to be jollied, and although Maggie disagreed with her manner of speaking, she suspected Agnes had a point. Maybe she had brushed off Racine too quickly. She looked at the row of books that Agnes had arranged so carefully on the bookshelf: *The Gentle Art of Interviewing and Interrogating*, *How to Use the Freedom of Information Act*, *Thomas's Pre-Marital Investigations*. All so serious.

"All you had to do was call Domino," Agnes said. "It would have taken five minutes of your time, and then you could have written up a report. That's all. That's all, and then one thousand dollars." Her voice cracked.

"I can see your point," Maggie said.

"How did I even think I could work with a person like you," Agnes said. "Someone who teaches Sunday School. A Puritan. A prude."

"Agnes," Maggie cried out. "You're being a bully. I made a mistake and I apologize, but there's no need to carry on. I can fix this."

Maggie put out her hand, intending to touch Agnes' hand, feeling like she needed to make contact with her on a very basic level. How alone she felt, whereas only moments ago she'd been so happy. Suddenly the office felt so cold and unfamiliar, the table itself a death-like slab, the drilling ominous. She felt like she was falling. How could she have seriously thought she could be a private detective?

"Agnes," she whispered.

But Agnes brushed her away and went stalking out of the room, the second person Maggie had disappointed in less than an hour. She felt light-headed. She wished she drank more. She wished she drank during the day. She looked around at all the books and boxes Agnes had accumulated. She'd ordered so many things from the private detective catalogue. There was the pen with invisible ink, and the TV with the secret surveillance system, and the clock radio that was actually a recorder and the teddy bear with the hidden video system. It had all seemed a bit of a game, Maggie thought. Hard to take it all seriously.

But it was serious. It was serious to Agnes and it was serious to Racine.

She picked up the piece of paper out of the garbage. She looked at her notes. *Evil*, she'd written, and underlined it three times. In that moment she remembered a story about Domino. One she'd completely forgotten about. Domino was seven years younger than Maggie and had gone to a private school, but still, Darby was a small village and stories went around. Domino had liked a boy, she remembered, but he was already taken. Domino was not a person who was used to hearing the word "no," and she told his girlfriend to dump him, but she wouldn't. So, one day Domino put a voodoo doll in this girl's locker.

It had a needle in its neck and Domino announced the girl would die, and several months later she did. She got one of those horrible fast-moving cancers and it began in her lymph nodes. No one seriously believed Domino killed her, but Maggie remembered her mother crying over it. She told Maggie that there were people who brought suffering with them. Maggie realized now that her mother had been frightened of Domino. The memory made her shiver.

Maybe Racine was right, she thought. Maybe her sister was evil. Maggie had got so swept up thinking about the prodigal son, that she didn't think about what Racine was actually saying. Racine was afraid. The dryness in her lips, the agitation, the impatience, were all signs of fear.

She started to type Racine's number into her phone, but right then the bus pulled up. She dashed out to retrieve Edgar. He was usually last off the bus, but this time was first out the door, ran down the steps and pummeled into her stomach. "Ooof," she said.

"He loves you," the bus monitor observed.

"And I love him," Maggie said, though it seemed to her that the people she loved were causing her a lot of pain today.

They went into the office and Edgar went right for the TV, clicking to download Detective Grudge, who would be talking about surveillance today. Then he vaulted over to one of their high-tech chairs, bouncing up and down as he waited for Maggie to accumulate her things. She needed her notebook, and the sheet of questions she had to answer after each episode.

"Maggie, Maggie, Maggie," he called.

"Patience is a virtue," she called back. No point in getting him anything to eat just yet. It would wind up sprayed all over the office. She'd found out the hard way that you could not give that boy popcorn after school.

Finally, they both settled down and Detective Grudge sprang into action, driving onto the scene in a sporty black car. He wore a dark wool coat, dark sunglasses and his thick hair was tightly cropped. He didn't smile. He never smiled. He wore a huge watch that Edgar coveted. "What I'm about to tell you may save your life someday," Detective Grudge said.

Edgar was entranced, and Maggie seized that moment to tuck herself into a corner of her office and press in the number for Racine's phone. Racine answered right away. Maggie pictured her standing by the phone, willing it to ring.

"Hi," Maggie said. "I'm sorry about what I said before. I'd be honored to take on your case."

Racine emitted a low moan. "It's too late," she said. "It's too late."

Chapter Three

The next day Domino's cavalcade arrived. Three long black limousines swanned down Main Street, moving slowly enough that everyone had time to admire them. The entire village was out because it was the day of the Halloween poster painting contest. First prize won a gift certificate at Stan's Pizza. Second prize was a gift certificate at Carvel's. Third prize was a consultation with Maggie Dove's Detective Agency.

Edgar was in the midst of painting a zombie with a spear coming out of his eye, in spite of Maggie's best efforts to persuade him to paint a cheerful zombie, and as the procession rolled by, the lead car stopped right in front of her.

The tinted window came down. Behind it was a face Maggie hadn't seen in a long time. Arched eyebrows, full lips, tufted hair, ageless. Domino waited a beat before speaking. Looked at Edgar, looked at Maggie, looked at the zombie, nodded slightly. "Yummy," she said, and licked her lips. Then the window went back up, the limo pulled away. Maggie noticed the license plate said LUCIFER, which was the name of Domino's husband.

"Was she a vampire?" Edgar asked.

"I hope not," Maggie said, though she felt unsettled. It had all looked too much like a funeral procession. She remembered Racine's words. *It's too late.*

It was fall, but the day felt like summer. The kids wore shorts. The sky was a Mediterranean blue and the houses look whitewashed under the stark sunlight. The air smelled of fireplaces and apples and homely smells. *Yummy.*

"Well, that was a spectacle," a voice thick with a Boston accent cawed behind Maggie, making her jump. It was Joe Mangione, wearing, as he always did, his ambulance corps jacket. He took his job very seriously and last April, when Maggie had found a corpse on her lawn, he was one of the first there. He was generally first anywhere. "Talk about making an entrance. And what have you done here, Edgar Blake? Looks like a piece of roast beef."

"It's a zombie," Edgar snapped.

"Ah yeah," Joe said, tilting his head sideways. "I can see it now. And that's an apple tree."

"That's his mother."

"Ah yeah."

Joe held his hands in front of him, the better to frame the picture in his sights. "Mebbe put in a pumpkin, young Edgar. Break up those colors."

"What do you think?" Joe Mangione asked Maggie, gesturing in the direction of the limousines. "The return of the prodigal son, eh. I hope their story ends better than his."

"Nothing bad happened to the prodigal son," Maggie pointed out. Once you were a Sunday School teacher, it was impossible to stop teaching. "The older son refused to go to the party for his brother, but I've always liked to think he came to his senses. It would be nice to think he got over his resentment and went out and mingled."

"He didn't kill his brother?" Joe asked.

"No, nobody died. Except for the fatted calf."

"What about the mark on his forehead?"

"That was a different set of brothers," Maggie replied. "Cain and Abel."

"Too many brothers in the Bible," Joe said. "Hard to keep straight."

Maggie noticed Edgar began to put a cat in the picture, which was progress, she thought. At least the cat didn't have a spear through his eye. In fact, the cat looked a bit like her own white cat, Kosi, whom she had rescued a few weeks ago, after his owner died. He was an unhappy cat. He missed his owner and was transferring his anger to Maggie and she had the scratch marks to prove it.

"You hear he has a girlfriend," Joe whispered.

"Who has a girlfriend?"

"That Lucifer Raines," he said, gesturing to where the limos had just been. "She travels with them. Her and Domino together. It's a menagerie," he said.

Maggie was tempted to say that the word was "ménage a trois," but decided not to. There were things she didn't want to talk to Joe Mangione about, lovely though he was.

"How do you know that?"

"I heard it at D'Amici's. They say Domino doesn't mind. She always did like to do things differently," he said, and then launched into a story about all the preparations D'Amici had made to get ready for her visit. He'd ordered in high-end cold cuts, because he assumed they'd want quality. He'd stocked up on gluten free bread and fancy bottled water. He'd even made up a "Lucifer sandwich," which had three kinds of meat, Joe said, blushing. The hair salons were offering Domino specials, and the pizza place was selling pineapple-topped pizza, because Domino had said once in an interview that she liked it.

Everyone, Maggie included, expected a lot of activity around this visit. They'd have a genuine rock star in their midst. They'd get to see him up close. And Domino was a fashion icon. The press would arrive. They would eat at all the restaurants. Tour buses would show up. It was all very exciting, except that, nothing happened. Once the limousines turned into Stern Manor, no one emerged. It was as though they weren't there at all.

Days went by. One of the high school kids said he saw a helicopter arriving to drop off supplies. A few people tried to pay a visit, but they were turned away by security. The only person who made it through the gates was Trudi Branch, who owned the town candy store. She and Domino had been friends in high school, and she explained afterward that Domino still had a hankering for one of her old-fashioned candies, a type of soda straw she couldn't get anywhere else. For a while people flocked to Trudi's store to ask her what she'd seen at Stern Manor, but Trudi said she hadn't seen much and so everyone just went back to waiting.

What surprised Maggie most of all was that Racine didn't come to church that Sunday. The Sterns always came to church, a minute before service began, striding through the center aisle as though leading a pageant—often the minister had to hold up the service while they got seated—so it was surprising to see that pew empty. Maggie felt a twist of concern for Racine. She would have mentioned it to Agnes, except she didn't dare raise the subject. Things between Maggie and Agnes had normalized, but there were still bad feelings about the Racine incident, on both sides. There was something electric in the office that reminded Maggie of the charged atmosphere after a storm. She felt badly, and irritated, and guilty, all of which was why, when she was talking to the bank manager during coffee hour after church, she found herself asking if she had any work for her detective agency.

"We're just getting started," Maggie said. "But we're eager. We'll do anything."

Ms. Lancome looked surprised to be asked. No more surprised than Maggie for having asked. Even more remarkable was that Ms. Lancome said, "You know, we just might." And that very Monday morning she called Maggie Dove's Detective Agency to say that they were trying to update their background checks on their employees. She thought it would be about 30 hours' worth of work and she'd pay Maggie $1,000. "That seems to be the going rate," she said. "If you're agreeable."

"I am most agreeable," Maggie replied.

Maggie threw herself into the job, relieved to discover at the end of it that everyone was, for the most part, who they said they were. That Friday afternoon when she got the check, she set it on Agnes' side of the table and waited for Agnes to walk in to the office. Nothing could have been more gratifying than Agnes's response.

She scanned the check, jaw dropping, eyes bulging.

"I can't believe you did this," she cried out. "One thousand dollars. This is fabulous. Just fabulous."

She flung her arms around Maggie and hugged her tightly. Maggie wondered if Detective Grudge hugged his associates, and thought probably not. But this was a nice thing. It was progress.

"I really do want this to work," Maggie said. "I really do want to be a private detective."

"You have made me so happy," Agnes said. "This is going to be the best detective agency ever."

"I hope so," Maggie said. She felt relieved, but exhausted too. She still couldn't quite get used to the idea of being a normal person in the normal world, of being subject to the evaluations and criticisms that most people had to deal with on a daily basis. Only now was she coming to realize what a bubble she'd been in for so many years. In an odd sort of way, her grief had protected her. It had been a shield. Real life took a form of courage she wasn't used to using.

When the Sterns didn't come to church the following Sunday, Maggie began to worry in earnest that something was wrong. First thing Monday morning she called Stern Manor. She decided to make the call from her own house, however, instead of the office. She might have resolved one issue with Agnes, but she had no desire to set her off again.

Maggie settled herself into her living room and scouted out the position of her cat, who sat on Maggie's desk, staring at her. He liked to stand as still as an onyx statue, and then, when you walked by, fly through the air like a bat and claw you.

A woman with a Southern accent answered.

"Stern residence."

"I'd like to speak to Racine please."

"May I have your name," she responded.

"This is Maggie Dove. I'm a friend of Racine's. I'm just calling to say hello."

"I don't see your name on the list."

Maggie began to get annoyed. "Please tell Racine that I'm on the line. She wanted to hire me to do work for her, and she'll want to talk to me."

Five minutes went by. Maggie sat, waiting. She looked at the cat. He looked at her with his amber eyes.

Sometimes at night they seemed to glow. She would wake up and find them surveying her.

She turned away from him, looked out her window at her little oak tree, which was sprouting off acorns in celebration of the fall. Marcus Bender's house was now owned by a young family who had built a playground in the yard for their four children. Her old friend Winifred Bell would have loved that, she thought.

"Hello?"

"Racine," Maggie said, surprised to feel so glad to hear her voice. She wouldn't have said she liked her, but she respected her. She admired her for devoting so much of her life to her mother; she admired anyone who was a caretaker.

"I haven't seen you around. I just wanted to see how you're doing."

"Not so good," Racine whispered. "I had an accident."

"What happened?" Maggie asked. Automatically Maggie reached for a pen and paper. When she was worried, her hands needed to be busy. Unfortunately, Kosi had just decided to unfurl on top of her desk, and so she bumped him and he lunged at her, his claws catching in her sweater.

"Are you all right?" Maggie asked, pulling her cat off her.

"I'm lucky to be alive. My sister tried to kill me."

"What?"

Racine paused, then began to speak loudly. "Yes, I'd love to see you for tea. Let's say in an hour."

"Of course," Maggie said, wondering who might be listening. "I'll be right over."

"Yes, that sounds fine."

Maggie then called Agnes, who sounded like she was at a bar, even though it was Monday morning. There was loud music playing and she heard the shimmer of glass.

"Get over there now," Agnes said, after Maggie told her what had happened.

"Do you want me to wait for you?" Maggie asked. If Domino truly had tried to kill Racine, Maggie wasn't sure she was up to handling that herself.

"Get over there now!" Agnes shouted, and Maggie clicked her phone off. She knew her other partner, Helen, was in the city today. She was on her own. "All right," she said. "All right."

She checked out her face in the mirror and her mother stared back at her. Same white hair, blue eyes and glistening pearl earrings. "I'm a detective, mom," Maggie said. "And I've got a case and I've got to do this right." She looked over at the cat, who scowled at her. Maggie clasped her hands together for a moment.

Then she set out for Stern Manor.

Chapter Four

Stern Manor loomed. There was no other word for it, Maggie thought. It was a massive granite structure that bristled with turrets and cornices and chimneys. There were giant arched windows and scrolled iron balconies, and from the left side of the roof grew a giant tower that looked a little like Jack's bean stalk. At the top was a balcony from which, as Maggie recalled, the late Leonard Stern liked to give speeches. She remembered standing on this lawn after the moon landing and hearing him hold forth on the progress of mankind.

Now Maggie pulled her red Audi TT into the driveway and paused for a moment. It was definitely a house that gave you pause. There were no flowering bushes to welcome you, though there was a massive copper beech tree that Maggie admired. Now that was a tree. It must have been 50 feet tall and it glowed like fire. She felt its benevolent presence behind her as she made her way up the steps to the front door.

The door was surprisingly small for such a large house. Hidden under an awning, it was as though the house itself was saying, *Don't bother me. Stay away.* Maggie hesitated. She was not a person who intruded. She didn't assert. She was a little like a tree, she thought. She just kind of stood there and grew, or occasionally drooped. But Racine was in trouble and needed her help. That gave her courage. She rang the bell.

A maid answered, wearing a black dress and a frilly white apron.

"Yes ma'am," she drawled in a Southern accent.

"I'm here for Racine," she said, and the maid nodded knowingly and then led Maggie into the house.

It was an entry way designed to make you gape, and Maggie did. She followed the maid down a long hallway, paved in patterned tile, at the end of which was a window that opened onto the Hudson River. The view seemed to stretch all the way up to Beacon. Maggie was still admiring the vista when the maid turned right and began going up a winding flight of steps.

Maggie followed, walking across the landing and through a door, and found herself in the most feminine room she'd ever seen. There were frills and gee gaws everywhere. There were porcelain lamps and ruffled chairs and little wooly lambs and all sorts of marble balls, and in the center of it all was a huge bed, draped in salmon-colored silk, and in the middle of that was a little old lady wearing a white peignoir. Maggie had worn something like it on her wedding night. She had a sudden vision of herself and Stuart Dove in a room filled with red roses, a gift from all his college students. They stayed at the Waldorf Astoria, another large Victorian building.

Racine Stern stood alongside her mother, and she looked awful.

Her red beret clung to her like an amoeba. Her black clothes, normally elegant, sagged against her as though that alone were keeping her upright. Madame Simone, however, was all animation.

"Ah, Maggie Dove," she said. "How nice of you to pay us a visit."

Maggie looked over to Racine, who shook her head slightly. So she hadn't told her mother that she believed Domino had tried to kill her.

"You have a lovely spot here," Maggie said.

The view from her bedroom was even better than the one downstairs. The shoreline dipped in, giving the illusion that the room hovered over the water. The leaves were turning and their oranges and golds seeped into the river, so it looked like a rich wash of paint ran through it.

"I am very lucky," Madame Simone said. She cocked her head. "I have nothing to do but enjoy this beautiful view. Not like you and Racine, both of you so busy with your work and me nothing more than a drain on your productivity, as my husband would have said."

"Nonsense, Mama, he adored you."

"Yes," she said, smiling as she looked down at the ring on her finger. It was a large diamond that didn't quite fit with the frilliness of the room, but then Leonard Stern was a man who liked to make statements. "Always marry a man who fears you just a little, don't you think, Maggie Dove? You must never let them get too comfortable. They must never know the power they have over you or they will crush you."

"I can't imagine anyone crushing you," Maggie said. Madame Simone seemed so vibrant at an age when most people were failing. Or most people were dead. Maggie wondered what confined her to her bed and, as though reading her mind, Madame Simone said, "My legs, foolish things." Her wheelchair sat in the corner, alongside a table of silver-framed pictures, atop a plush lime-green carpet.

"But don't tempt me," Madame Simone said. "There's nothing more boring than a woman who complains. Don't you agree?"

"Oh, Mama, you don't complain at all, though you have good reason to."

"What do I have to complain about?" she said dryly. "I am old and ugly, I cannot walk and I am completely dependent on others. And my daughter has come home with this Lucifer and this boy and this…maid."

"It's so unfair," Racine cried out. "All you've had to suffer and now this. It's not right."

Madame Simone settled back into her bed. "See how she fusses over me. I tell her all the time, she should go, leave me alone, put me in a home with the other unwanted, but she will not leave me."

"Never."

"Of course," Madame Simone said, her eyes twinkling, "now that my other daughter is home, Racine has more freedom. I'm sure Domino would not hesitate to take care of me."

Racine stiffened. "Take care of you—I wouldn't trust her to serve you your tea."

"She is fierce, this one," Madame Simone said. "Like her father."

"I am honored to be compared to my father. He was a great man."

Maggie felt touched by Racine's devotion, which felt genuine if slightly over-the-top. She'd always assumed Racine stayed with her mother out of obligation. She'd assumed she would rather have led a different life, to have married and traveled and had children, but she seemed so fiercely devoted that Maggie wondered if she was actually living exactly the life she wanted to live. She'd had a discussion with Helen on that very point the other night, with Helen saying that people wound up with the life they wanted. Maggie had disagreed strenuously. She'd felt that was a dangerous position to take, because it might stop you from ever wanting to help someone. But now she wondered if she'd overreacted. Perhaps Helen had a point.

"Bring her the picture," Madame Simone said. "Show her."

Racine went over to one of the cluttered bookshelves and retrieved a silver-framed photograph. She held it out to Maggie.

"My father," Racine whispered.

There he was, Leonard Stern, with his manly shoulders and strong chin and wavy brown hair, and yet it was

Madame Simone, tucked into his arm, who grabbed your attention. She had the sort of beauty that's startling. You look at it and you can't look away.

"Back when I was a war bride, a thousand years ago, if you can imagine that anyone can still be alive and yet be so old. I met Leonard in France after the war ended. I was only 21. He was quite a bit older, but he knew what he wanted. He married me and brought me here as his trophy."

"He treasured you," Racine said.

Madame Simone nodded. "Poor Domino," she said. "She tries so hard, doesn't she? She's always had to work to keep that man of hers. I would imagine it gets exhausting."

"Exhausting," Racine muttered. "You're charitable. It's degrading to have my sister treated like that."

"I feel sorry for her," Madame Simone said.

"You may feel sorry for her, but you shouldn't give her money," Racine said. "She made her choice."

"My *cherie*, everything that I have is yours." Her voice thickened. She must be very tired, Maggie thought. The old lady leaned back against her pillow. Her eyes flickered.

"You need to sleep," Racine said, as she tenderly brought the coverlet up around her mother.

"You talk to your friend," Madame Simone whispered. "You tell her your secrets. And remember, *cherie*, to bring me my tea at 4:00."

"Of course, Mama," Racine said, and then she guided Maggie into an adjoining room, also decorated in pinks and whites, with plush green carpeting, though the windows were smaller and the lighting more diffuse. As soon as Racine walked in and shut the door, her whole aspect changed. It was like someone had shot her full of Adrenalin. She ripped off the bandage and showed her arm to Maggie. There were two puncture wounds on her wrist.

"Do you know what this is?" Racine asked.

"No."

"The bite of a tarantula."

Chapter Five

Thanks to Detective Grudge, Maggie felt competent to deal with a number of scenarios, from shoplifting to credit card fraud. But tarantula bites were not on the curriculum.

"How did that happen?" she asked.

"My sister put her pet tarantula in my bed. I woke up last night and found it on my arm and when I screamed, it bit me."

Maggie said a quick prayer of thanks that Kosi, her cat, bad as he was, was not a tarantula.

"Domino wants to kill me. She wants my money. She told me so."

"Could we go back a step?" Maggie asked. She could hear Detective Grudge in her mind. There were seven questions he demanded future private detectives memorize: what, when, where, why, how, who and which—though that last didn't seem material to the situation.

"Domino's been here for almost two weeks. What's been happening?"

Racine began to burp, as though coughing up bile, and she tugged a handkerchief from her pocket.

"Acid reflux," she explained.

She gestured for Maggie to sit down on a chair, which, like the ones in Madame Simone's room, was soft and plush. Maggie pulled out a notepad and wrote the date on top of it, and then *Interview with Racine*. This must be where she sleeps, Maggie thought. Right next to her mother's room. There was a thin bed that reminded Maggie of summer camp. It seemed strange that in such a large house she was confined to such an uncomfortable room, but then Racine answered her unspoken question.

"This isn't my regular bedroom. I've only been sleeping here since Domino arrived. I will not leave my mother alone until that woman departs."

"Tell me what happened," Maggie asked, though in truth, Racine needed no prodding. There was no stopping her from telling her story.

"As soon as they arrived, Domino demanded to see Mama. I told her she couldn't; it was her resting time. She could see her after she woke up. I said she would have to wait. Perhaps she was not used to hearing the word 'no.' And that maid…that maid," Racine added, shaking her head. "I said she could sleep in the servants' quarters, but Domino said no. The maid would sleep with them. That this should take place in my father's house!"

She began burping some more. Maggie spotted a pitcher of water and poured her a glass, which she drank right down.

"I left them to their business, but then Lucifer came to me." Here she started to blush. The burps came more and more frequently. "He wanted to introduce himself to me. He wanted to get to know me. I just thought he was being pleasant, and I showed him around the house. But when I got back to my mother's room, I discovered Domino had used him as a ruse. She was in my mother's room with the door locked. I could hear her asking for money.

She told Mama that she'd gone through her entire inheritance, and she just needed $20 million dollars. Just! Because Lucifer has a new tour starting up, but the music company went under and he needs to finance it himself. What is that to my mother? She doesn't listen to his music. I pounded on the door until finally she opened it, and when she came out, she was smiling. She told me that my mother might say no and I might say no, but there were other ways for her to get the money."

Racine crossed her arms. Maggie noticed lines of salt underneath her eyes. She'd been crying and her tears had dried.

"What did she mean?"

"Under the terms of my father's will, our money must stay in the family. If I'm dead, when my mother dies, the money would go to Domino."

"She was threatening you?"

"Yes," Racine said. "Yes. And then last night I woke up to the tarantula."

She looked exhausted, and no wonder, Maggie thought. She probably hadn't left her mother's side since

Domino's return. Outside the weather was a cool gauzy blue, all so beautiful, and yet inside it was overheated. Maggie pictured people going by on the Circle Line, admiring grand Stern Manor and envying the people who lived inside. A spring inside the chair poked at her. Like ghost's fingers, Maggie thought, and she remembered rumors she'd heard that this house was haunted. Just then she noticed a hauntingly beautiful boy walk by on the back lawn. He had pale white skin and dark hair and he walked with an athlete's grace.

"Milo," Racine said, clenching her knees tightly together. "Domino's son. He will eventually inherit all the money. After my mother dies, and if I die."

"I'm not a lawyer," Maggie said. "But it cannot be legal to make threats against someone like this. I think you should go to the police."

"No," Racine said. "I can't bring the police into this. We have a reputation to uphold. The Stern name was very important to my father."

"He wouldn't have wanted you to be killed."

"No," Racine said. She looked at a picture of Leonard Stern, hanging on the wall. There was a red rose in a vase underneath it. "But I don't want to involve the police. I want you to talk to her. Now that you're here, and you've heard the story. You can tell her to leave me alone."

"You want me to threaten your sister."

"Yes, I'll pay you a thousand dollars."

Again with the thousand dollars, Maggie thought.

"You must talk to her and make her leave me alone."

Maggie wanted to tell her that she couldn't do it. She couldn't even get her six-year-old ward to stop hurling himself into her stomach. She couldn't get her angry cat to stop hissing at her throughout the night. But then she thought of Agnes and Detective Grudge and how serious they both were. Private detective work was like life in that it required you to do things that scared you. She would have to try to frighten Domino into leaving Racine alone.

"Where is she?" Maggie asked.

"She's in the cellar," Racine said, "With the ghosts."

Chapter Six

The stairs to the cellar were located by the front door, through an opening that looked like a closet. Following Racine's directions, Maggie tapped on the door and then went down the steps, toward a light she could see emanating from the bottom. There she found Domino sitting in a lotus position in the center of a white circle. Around her, at the compass points of the circle, stood a spray of dried flowers, a statue of a voluptuous woman, a statue of a horned man, and a dark green candle.

As Maggie watched, Domino inhaled deeply several times, then exhaled quickly, as though she were panting. Then she pinched her right nostril shut, and breathed in through the left. She did that five times, and then pinched her left nostril shut, and breathed in through the right.

"The light is my presence," she whispered. "The light is power. It fills me until I am presence, until I am power."

Then she opened her eyes and sighed. "Maggie Dove."

At that moment, Maggie noticed, in the corner, a cage that housed a tarantula. It was a large creature, furry and dense, and Maggie shivered thinking of what it would be like to have that touch you.

"They're such beautiful pets," Domino said, "So beautiful, so loyal, so misunderstood." "I understand she bit Racine."

"Of course, she did. Poor thing was terrified. How would you feel if someone looked at you and started screaming?"

Domino stretched over and reached into the cage, pulling out the creature and holding it closely against her. She wore a thin black yoga outfit that was more of a second skin than a piece of clothing.

"They're so delicate," Domino said, rubbing her hand against the spider's legs, which opened and closed against her touch, in a manner Maggie found disturbing. Which was irritating, because she knew Domino was trying to disturb her.

She noticed Domino wore a delicate antique ring that didn't seem in keeping with her personality. "Thank the gods she wasn't hurt. Their bellies make them heavy and when they fall, they can explode."

"Racine thinks you were trying to kill her."

"I didn't put Charlotte in Racine's bed. She got out on her own, and she must have had something she wanted to communicate to my sister. She is a very insistent little girl," she said, holding the spider up to her lips.

"She would never have bitten her if Racine hadn't made so much noise. I suppose Racine is not used to finding anything in her bed. Anyway," Domino said, putting the spider right over her heart, so that it clung to her like a brooch, "there's nothing dangerous in her venom. Her bite could no more hurt my sister than a bee's sting." She closed her eyes briefly as the spider moved across her breast. Only then did Maggie notice Domino had a scar on her arm. It was a white zigzag against her tanned skin.

"Unfortunately, Racine didn't know that. She was terrified."

Domino arched her back slightly, the better to position the tarantula on her breast. It was true what Madame Simone had said about how hard Domino worked, Maggie realized. Every gesture carried intention. Everything she did was to be observed. Everything for show. She wondered if Domino ever just kicked back and read a book.

"You look different," Domino said, finally tugging the spider off her and putting it back in her cage. "You've gotten old."

"We've both gotten older," Maggie snapped.

"Not me," Domino said, looking at the mirror across from her. "No one would think I'm 55."

"When are you leaving? "Maggie asked.

Domino laughed. "You've lost your sense of tact, Maggie Dove."

"I don't like playing games, Domino. You've asked your mother and Racine for money and they've said no. What more do you want? What do you think will happen?"

Domino leaned back and stretched her right leg, stretching, stretching as far as it would go. "Just because somebody says no once, doesn't mean they'll say no forever."

"You think Racine's going to change her mind?"

Domino tipped her tongue against the bottom of her teeth. She looked like a snake, Maggie thought. Then she shook out her right leg and began stretching out her left.

"Have you ever been to a coven meeting, Maggie Dove?"

"No."

"You might enjoy it more than you think, once you get over your archaic Christian principles. It's all very life-affirming. I assure you that Christians have done more harm to witches than we have to you."

"Domino, I do not want to have a religious debate right now. I'm fond of my archaic Christian principles. What I would like to know is when you are going to leave?"

Domino ignored her. She stretched and stretched her left leg and then she sighed, let go, and assumed a straight-backed sitting position. She breathed in deeply, then picked up the candle that shone in front of her, and held it close to her right hand. Closer, and then closer.

All Maggie could think of was Thomas Cranmer, who'd dipped his own hand in fire when he was burned, back in the time of Queen Mary, because he was a Protestant. He'd had a moment of cowardice beforehand, had signed a recantation to try and save himself, but as he burned, he put the offending hand in the fire as a way of atonement. Maggie had always thought that such a horrifying and great act of courage. But she hoped Domino did not intend to reenact it.

"In the years of the burning," Domino whispered, "no one was safe. They went after children. They burned them right alongside their mother, because they knew the magick could be inherited and they wanted to wipe us all out. Your kind forced us all to go underground, but we survived. We developed ways of getting poison to each other to end our suffering. Some of the torturers became angry because, they said, you could put a witch on a rack and she wouldn't even cry out. Our magick is very strong."

"You've made your point," Maggie said. She couldn't bear to watch the flame, but didn't dare to turn away either. Domino frightened her. Domino might well have special powers, but Maggie suspected she was also working quite hard to play on Maggie's fears. It wouldn't have surprised her to find out Domino had read up on Thomas Cranmer. There was something not quite real about the whole thing, and it felt like a monumental distraction. Maggie felt her anger starting to rise up, and she was gearing up to knock the candle out of Domino's hand.

But suddenly the door flung open and the maid came scampering down the steps. "My lady," she called out, and then stopped when she saw Maggie. Finally, Domino set down the flame.

"Oh, pardon me," she said. But Domino looked at her with those hypnotic eyes.

"Never apologize, Passion. I told you that."

"I didn't mean to interrupt."

"You've met Passion, Maggie Dove?" Domino said.

Maggie looked more closely at the maid. She was young, but not as young as Maggie first thought. Twenty-five perhaps.

"She takes care of us, doesn't she? Passion, Maggie Dove is a Sunday School teacher. And now a detective," she added, sounded bemused. "She's investigating me." She turned back to Maggie. "Oh, you'll appreciate this. My son wants to go to Sunday School. He'll be at church this Sunday."

"He'll be welcome there," Maggie said.

"I'm sure."

Domino directed her gaze back at Passion. "Maggie Dove thinks I've been threatening my sister. She doesn't understand that I want nothing but happiness and joy for my sister. Isn't that right?"

Passion giggled. "Yes, my lady."

"Come here," Domino said, putting her hand on the young woman's head and tugging her to her, reaching up to kiss Passion on the lips. Passion kissed her back until suddenly Domino bit down hard and broke skin. Passion pulled back, and for just a moment something dangerous flashed over her face, and then she giggled and stepped back. "Punishment," Domino said. "For interrupting. Now go tell my husband I'll be ready for him soon."

"Yes, my lady," she said, and ran up the stairs.

Domino watched her go. "So hard to find good help."

Her eyes narrowed then as she looked at Maggie. A little blood still clung to her lip. "This has always been my favorite space. My sacred space. I spent most of my youth down here. Closer to the spirits."

"It seems somewhat dank to me," Maggie said. She felt like her skin was crawling with invisible vermin. She wanted to get out of there.

"You feel it, don't you? They're always so strong this time of year, as we get near Samhain, and the veil between the seen and the unseen is at its thinnest. I feel them strongly—their lives were ripped from them. They wanted to live, and now they want to talk to the living. They speak to me. Some of my kind like to go outside, under the trees, but I like to do my worshipping here, among the dead.

"The dead are so powerful. I don't need to tell you that though, do I, Maggie Dove? Juliet's here, you know. Death is not the end. I could show you how to talk to her. I feel like she's very close by. Perhaps in the mouse that scurries beneath my feet, or perhaps even in Charlotte. Is that possible?" she whispered, lifting the tarantula's cage.

She was a bully, Maggie thought. Always had been, except that now she was a bully who claimed to have supernatural powers. But she was also a middle-aged woman worried about her looks. She feared losing her grip on her husband. She needed money. She was human, fallible, vulnerable. Maggie could deal with her if she thought of her like that. She tried to look kindly at Domino, and had the pleasure of seeing her falter just a bit, she hoped.

"What is it you want, Domino?"

"I want money," she said. "And I will have it."

"Not if it means hurting Racine," Maggie said.

Domino picked up the statue of the horned man. It was an ugly face, a leering face. "I have no plans to hurt Racine. Nothing I do can will work if it isn't in alignment with her highest good."

"What do you mean nothing you do will work? What do you propose to do?"

"Don't you worry about that, Maggie Dove."

But Maggie had enough. She hated being manipulated. Part of why she was so religious, she supposed, was because she approved of honesty. *This is who I am, this is who we are, this is what we believe.*

She stood up. "Domino, your sister is a good woman. She's devoted her life to taking care of your mother. If you want to come back here and rejoin the family, I'll be happy to help you, but if you're just going to terrorize your sister and mother, then you'll have to go."

Domino looked at her. "Are you suggesting your gods are stronger than mine?"

"What I am suggesting is that if a tarantula or anything else shows up in Racine's bed, I will call the police. Listen," Maggie said. "You have one sister. Family's important. You're more likely to get what you want through kindness."

Domino smiled. "Throw myself on the mercy of my mother and ask for forgiveness?

"Yes, something like that."

Domino started to laugh. The sound twisted around Maggie like a tornado. She had to get out of there. She walked toward the steps, forcing herself not to run, but once she was out of Domino's sight, she ran for the front door.

Left without even saying good bye to Racine. Just raced out the door and across the front lawn, toward the copper beech, which almost seemed to be waiting for her. Maggie settled herself down under its welcoming branches. Immediately the air felt cleaner. She always felt redeemed by a tree. Once outside she could feel the darkness of that house wash off her.

She wondered if she should go talk to her minister. They had a new one, a woman from Ghana. Maggie didn't know her well though, and she'd rather not come across as a nut, showing up at her office and blathering about witches. Perhaps she should talk to Walter Campbell. She'd told Racine she wouldn't bring in the police, but she needed to talk this over with somebody. Agnes was still a wild card and Helen had not been at work in a while, so Walter seemed like the best option. She hoped it would not be too much of a violation of her promise to Racine.

Still, she felt a flutter of something strange in her heart at the prospect of talking to Walter Campbell. She'd not really spoken to him since that horrible night in April in the park, when he'd hugged her and whispered to her and she'd felt a closeness she hadn't expected. She was just getting ready to go when she noticed a man, one tree over. He was staring at Stern Manor. He looked at it with hatred, she thought.

He had an unusual face. It looked like someone had grabbed his chin and wrenched it. She didn't want to draw his attention, so she stayed under the tree, watching him. He spoke to himself, muttering. Then he turned to look right at her, and left.

Chapter Seven

The Darby Police Station was a small building, tucked next to the library. Maggie'd always approved of the location; she liked to think that some child had looked at the jail and then looked at the library and chosen a different path. Hopefully it hadn't worked the other way as well.

Now she walked into the police station, which was divided from the public by a tall barrier. Maggie could barely see over it, and she always felt like she was in a production of *A Midsummer's Night Dream* when she entered, though, hopefully not playing the part of the ass.

"Hello, hello," Maggie called out.

In the past it would have been Peter Nelson who answered her. Maggie's favorite Sunday School student, her late daughter's fiancé, a man who had a knack for getting into trouble. Unfortunately, he'd been forced to leave the police and had moved to California, where he seemed to be thriving with a new wife, and a baby on the way. She missed him, but felt so relieved he'd found a safe haven.

"Hello," she tried again, and this time a young black woman stepped up to the barrier.

"Yes?" she said.

Maggie smiled at her. "My name is Maggie Dove," she said. "You must be the new police officer."

"Mercy Williams," she said. "I was just transferred here from the Bronx."

She looked like a very neat person, especially if you compared her to Peter Nelson, who was mess. Her hair was almost completely shaved off, she wore no jewelry. Maggie suspected she would have a beautiful smile.

"Well, I'm a Darby old-timer. Welcome to our village."

"Maggie Dove," Mercy said. "You drive that red Audi TT."

"That's right," Maggie replied, surprised.

"I noticed you parked illegally by the fire department last Saturday."

"Oh I know," Maggie said, blushing. Over Mercy's head hung a poster of the ten most wanted criminals in the United States. "That was wrong of me, but I needed to run into the deli to pick up a platter for the church, and I couldn't find a spot. I couldn't risk being late, you see."

"Twenty minutes," she said. "I wrote you a ticket, but Superintendent Campbell told me to rip it up. He said you're someone special here."

"Yes," Maggie said, feeling worse and worse. "Funny you should mention him. I'm here to talk to him right now. Could you buzz me in?"

"He knows you're coming?"

"Yes," Maggie said, because she was feeling irritated with this young woman, because she didn't want to explain herself anymore, because she was feeling upset that Peter was gone and everyone always seemed to be mad at her. She'd been yelled at more in the last week than in the last twenty years.

She would have just turned around and left, but she did want to hear Walter's opinion. She didn't always like him, but she trusted and respected him. She was also curious to see whether she still felt the connection with him that she had. She had no plans for throwing herself on his desk, as she had with her late husband, so many decades ago, but she did feel a pleasant sense of anticipation.

"All right," Mercy said. "Go ahead."

Walter's office was down a dank corridor, past a jail cell, past an interrogation room, at the end of the hall. She felt something was off even before she walked into the room. Did she hear giggling? That was not a sound she associated with Walter Campbell. She kept moving forward, unable to stop herself, which was how she came to surprise Walter with his arms around a woman. They sprang apart. That was an expression she'd read in romance novels, but had never actually seen until this warm Monday afternoon: They sprang apart.

"Maggie Dove!" Walter cried out.

Maggie blushed. She wouldn't have felt so awkward except that he was so awkward.

"I'm sorry," he said. A tanned, trim woman stared back at her puzzled. "This is my wife," he said. "This is Heather."

She was so young, Maggie thought. But of course she was. His children were young. His oldest daughter was ten years old. This woman looked to be around 45, which made her twenty years younger than Walter and almost the same distance from Maggie. She looked very fit. She looked a woman who ran and lifted and cycled and swam.

"You're the lady Walter helped last spring," she said.

"Yes, I am that lady."

"Was there something you wanted to talk to me about?" Walter asked. He looked like he was boiling, she thought. She'd never seen him off balance before. He looked like he was trying to telegraph her something with his eyes, but she was damned if she knew what it was. It was so much easier when people said things instead of clutching you and whispering them, as he had in the park last April.

"Can I help you?" Walter said.

"If you could give me a few minutes of your time."

"Of course. Of course. Heather, I'll meet you at home."

"Pork chops?" she asked.

"Please."

Maggie sank down into a chair. She crossed one hand over the other, rubbing at the wedding band she'd never taken off, and never would.

"Heather's moving to Darby," Walter said. "She wants to give things another try. Feels we owe it to the children."

"I'm happy for you, Walter."

"I guess it's the right thing to do," he said. "I have to put my children first. I have to seize this opportunity."

"Of course, you do," she said. And she believed it. So why did she feel so glum as she launched into her description of what happened at Stern Manor? The whole thing seemed so flimsy in the light of day, or in the light of Walter. The tarantula on Racine's bed, Domino's strange manner. The malevolent man she'd seen staring at Stern Manor.

"Domino does have a genuine reason for wanting Racine dead," Maggie felt obliged to point out. "She wants that money."

Walter nodded. "And she's threatened her?"

Maggie shook her head. "She hasn't come out and said she's going to kill her. Domino doesn't do things like that. She hints and prowls and insinuates."

Walter scratched his head. She noticed a picture of his wife and children on his desk and she wondered if it had always been there. On the wall he had a Russian icon that she believed was real. A museum piece. He had a lot of money. That's how he came to have this job. He'd been a hedge-fund trader, had made a fortune, but walked away from it all to get a better life. In the process he'd pushed Peter out of his job, which had caused some bad feeling, but she believed he was committed. He was a man who couldn't bear to do a poor job.

"If she actually threatened Racine, then we could bring her in for questioning. We could charge her with harassment. But it sounds like she hasn't done anything explicit."

"No, and in any case, Racine doesn't want to bring in the police. She's concerned about her family's reputation. I just came to you because I wanted your opinion." Or to be perfectly honest with herself, which she tried to be, because she wanted an opportunity to talk to him.

She stood. "I've wasted your time."

"Not at all, Maggie Dove. You're never a waste of time."

He walked her over to the door, and she stopped for a moment, so that he almost walked into her. Up close he was even taller than she realized. It was like talking to a copper beech. "Walter, what do you think I should do?"

"You've done what you can do, Maggie Dove. You've alerted the police. You've spoken to Domino. The fact is, this sort of family squabble is not that unusual. But sisters do not generally kill each other." He smiled gently. She walked out the door.

But most sisters are not like Domino Raines, she thought.

Chapter Eight

After she left the police station, Maggie headed down Main Street toward her detective agency, but as she got close, she had to stop. She still could not see that building without admiring it. It wasn't an impressive building—simply a sturdy- looking blue structure with a signpost out front from which hung a large plastic tooth. Underneath the tooth, in smaller letters, was the sign for her detective agency. But it was hers, and she was ridiculously proud of it. She imagined her mother and her daughter standing alongside her. *Will you look at what I've done*, she said.

Fabulous, they answered.

When she got inside, she was glad to see both her partners there. Helen was on the phone. Her fingers were constantly scrolling, scrolling, and Agnes was talking to some named Cherrelle, though when Maggie walked in, she said, "Got to go, babe." Edgar ran right into Maggie's stomach.

"Oof," she said.

"So where have you been?" Agnes asked.

"Where haven't I been," she answered, and told them about everything that had transpired.

"Did Racine write you a check," Agnes asked. "When she hired you to threaten Domino?"

"No, but she's the richest person in Darby. I'm not worried about her paying."

"The rich are the worst about paying. That's how they get their money. The poor person doesn't want you to think he's poor, so he'll pay you right away. But the rich person doesn't care what you think, so she'll stiff you."

Maggie thought about how Racine had looked: frightened and worried about her mother, and she thought the last thing on Racine's mind was surely the bill from Maggie Dove's Detective Agency.

"I don't think Racine intends to stiff me."

She could see Agnes beginning to boil. She was wearing a blue jump suit and stiletto heels. The skin under her neck was turning red.

"But I'll go tomorrow and talk to her."

"Bring a new-client contract with you," Agnes said, as she stalked to the office door. "And make sure she knows that she has to pay half up front. No exceptions, I don't care who she is. Don't screw this up, Maggie," she said, slamming the door.

"What is wrong with her?" she asked Helen. "I can't say anything without her getting mad."

"New romance," Helen explained. "She's under stress."

"The lady from the bar?"

"No, this is Cherrelle Watson. She works for the county in the records department. Agnes was trying to develop some undercover sources and, it looks like she developed Cherrelle."

"That sounds encouraging, on several levels," Maggie offered hopefully.

Edgar climbed on Helen's lap. She was wearing her standard outfit of Gap jeans and a button-down white shirt. Her eyes always closed when she talked, as though she were so exhausted it was impossible to stay awake. She had numbers written on her hand, which could have been the code to a nuclear missile, or the combination to Edgar's locker at the YMCA. Or both. Maggie had yet to figure out what she did for a living. She just knew it was important enough that one phone call from Helen got them a detective license, something that would have taken hours of apprenticeship otherwise.

Helen sighed. "She's worried Cherrelle's too good for her because she has a master's degree. And then, she's married, and that's a problem."

"To a man or a woman."

"Does it matter?"

"I suppose not," Maggie said, though she was curious. "How long has she known her?"

"Two weeks I think," Helen said, which reminded Maggie of Racine's first visit around the same time, and the day Agnes lost her temper.

"It seems very early on to be so serious," Maggie said.

"Don't look at me. The last man I went out with… Well," she said, stopping herself as she drew Edgar more closely to her, "enough said."

"We live in complicated times," Maggie said. "When I was young—Oh never mind. I hate conversations that begin 'when I was young.' How are you?"

Edgar had fallen asleep on her Helen's lap. He was like a dog. He had the gift of being able to fall asleep in any position, in any place, at any time. The sun was setting, the sky a brilliant orange over the water. Across the way Maggie could see Edgar's poster hanging on Iphigenia's hair salon. She suspected Iphigenia would have preferred a poster with flowers, but she was a good sport. She'd root for Edgar to win.

"How am I? I'm okay," Helen said, "for someone likely to win the Worst Mother in Darby-on-Hudson Award."

"I doubt that," Maggie said. "You're a devoted mother."

Helen shook her head. "Not according to the teacher I met with today. She's concerned that Edgar refuses to skip. I told her I didn't care if he skipped. I've never had to skip a day in my life, but it's something to do with a Phys Ed requirement and she wants me to impress upon him that he should skip, and so I said that I was damned if I was going to force my son to skip, and so I got sent to the principal's office."

"Well," Maggie said, looking down at Edgar, who twitched even in his sleep. "You know he can run."

"Yes, that was another problem. I know these things are important, Maggie Dove. I know he has to learn to play by the rules and be an upstanding citizen, but I like his wildness. He's free now in a way he'll never be again. Do I have to be the one to rein him in?"

"No. But then you have to accept the fact that you have a lot of parent-teacher conferences in front of you."

Helen grimaced. "I bet you didn't have these problems with Juliet."

Maggie started at the sound of her daughter's name. It was true. Juliet had caused her no difficulty in school. She'd loved learning, had counted off the days in August waiting for school to begin. The highlight of Juliet's year was going to Staples and stocking up on school supplies.

"That's true," Maggie said. "She was always good, but I think it was just her disposition. She liked rules and order. I don't think I can take credit for that. Had I had another child, she might have been a terror."

"Did she ever get in trouble?" Helen asked.

"Oh yes," Maggie said. It was fun to think about her daughter as a troublesome child, as opposed to being a tragic figure. "One time she removed a book from the library without checking it out. The librarian found it and suspended her for a week."

Helen looked at her solemnly and then she started to laugh. It was nice to see her laugh. She didn't do it often. "Oh, Maggie Dove. She does not sound like a terror."

"I suppose not," Maggie said. Edgar began to rustle. Soon he would launch himself back into the world. "You are an amazing person, Helen. All the things you do. Flying here and there and solving global conflicts and talking to the President."

"Just once," she said.

"You're a great mother. You don't need to be like everyone else. You love him, that's what matters."

"You think that's enough."

"I think that's everything. Listen, I miss Juliet every day of my life, every hour, but the great comfort I have is that I loved her. I loved her with all my heart."

Helen leaned over and put her hand on Maggie's. "Hey, listen, I have something to tell you and I hope you like it. I mean, I hope I'm not being pushy, but the school is having this Senior Friends Day and Edgar doesn't have any grandparents, or none that I'm speaking to anyway, and I wondered… we wondered… if you'd like to be Edgar's surrogate grandmother."

Maggie was touched, but she was afraid to speak because she thought she'd cry, so she just hugged Helen, kissed Edgar, and went home to her evil cat. Even he seemed a tad friendlier, and she went to bed and dreamed of Edgar and children on a playground and she woke up to find Kosi staring at her. There was something of Domino about him with his predatory glare. His tail twitched.

Maggie carried him out of her bedroom and shut the door, but Kosi scratched the door, which was even worse. It was as though he was trying to claw his way back to her side. Eventually she opened the door again and went downstairs to her living room, where at least she could sit in her chair and look out at the rising moon and not worry about Kosi lying across her face. She must have dozed off at some point, and when she woke up, she had an idea.

She knew how to help Racine.

Genius, she thought, and then she fell back asleep.

Chapter Nine

When the new day finally dawned, Maggie awoke and unfurled her cat from around her neck. Then she showered and put on her work outfit, which was exactly like her casual outfit. Black slacks, a white shirt, pearl earrings and a gray sweater. Maggie liked to think she was perennially underdressed for formal moments or overdressed for casual ones. Then she set out for the office, stopping off at the bakery to pick up a scone.

They made a different one every day of the week, but Thursday was her favorite because that was the day they made cranberry and walnut ones. She also picked up some coffee. For a long time, she thought the bakery made the best coffee in the world and she was always trying to duplicate it, without success, and then she realized that the reason it tasted so good was because they put cream it. Thus armored, she set out for the office.

Maggie intended to get there early, before either Agnes or Helen showed up. Her plan was to give Racine the teddy bear with the video camera. That way she could watch what was going on and evaluate whether Domino really was sneaking into Racine's room. But she wasn't sure how the teddy bear worked, and Maggie was not a technological sort of person, and so she figured she would get in early and read the directions. She wanted to have it all set up to avoid having someone, mainly Agnes, yell at her.

Turned out the bear was not that hard to operate. It was an unhealthy looking, hairless bear that had a transmitter and antenna concealed inside it. You just needed to hook up the receiver to a DVR, and it would transmit the picture and sound. That was all well and good except that Maggie hadn't used a DVR in several years, but fortunately she'd stored her old one in her garage, intending to donate it to someone for something, and so now all she had to do was remember how to use the DVR.

She was feeling rather triumphant when she got everything working, except that the range for the receiver was only 100 meters, which was 328 feet, which wasn't far enough. She wouldn't be able to get that close to Stern Manor without being noticed, and she did not like the idea of being discovered by Domino and her tarantula. No, she'd have to stand on the other side of the iron gate that surrounded the manor and in order to do that she'd have increase the range of the receiver significantly. *I can do all things through Christ who strengthens me,* she whispered. Her favorite prayer. And at that moment she noticed the Walking Club go by.

The Walking Club consisting entirely of the three Faraday sisters and Richard Strauss, who was looking for a wife. He was 90 and no one was eager to take him on, but he hovered around the Faraday sisters hopefully.

Too late did Maggie realize she should have pulled down the blinds.

The three sisters collided into a sudden stop. Then they pushed their way through the door and arranged themselves in front of Maggie.

"There's trouble," Leona Faraday said. She was the eldest of the sisters. She was also the tallest, the best-looking and the spokesman. She planted herself on one of Maggie's high tech-tech ergonometric chairs, and the other two sisters flanked her. Mr. Strauss stood. He was a man who would always stand in the company of ladies.

"What's happened?" Maggie asked.

"There's a revolution. No one in the Dining Out Club wants to go to that restaurant in the Bronx."

"They have to. That's the one Reverend Sunday picked."

"No one's going to come. Do you know what it's like driving around in the Bronx in the dark?"

"That will be insulting. She wants to share her culture with us. We should be honored."

Their new minister came from Ghana. She'd moved to the United States as a health care worker, had tended to one of the elderly parishioners. That woman died and left Sunday enough money to go to school. She'd gone to divinity school, got her doctorate, and after their most recent minister left to go on a year-long yoga retreat in Costa Rica, Reverend Sunday was hired to fill the position.

"I'm not disagreeing with you, Maggie. I'm just saying that no one's enthusiastic, and I can't force people to come."

"Listen, I have put up with Margot Hunter's tuna casserole every Christmas Eve for the last twenty years of my life," Maggie snapped. "We can go to the Bronx, we can try this food. Maybe we'll all love it."

The youngest of the Faradays began fiddling with the teddy bear. Her name was Hortense. Or Horty, to her friends and family.

"What's this?" she asked.

"Oh, it's my genius idea come to nothing," Maggie said. She explained the issue with the range and Horty began nodding. Then she opened up her pocketbook and began rummaging around.

"It's going to be dark," Leona pressed on. "There are going to be a lot of stoplights, and you know how Mildred Taylor is with stoplights. They make her nervous. She drives through them. Remember when we went to see the Rockettes? You don't want that to happen again."

"What type of range do you want?" Horty asked.

She was a very soft-looking woman, with the pallor people got from spending a lot of time inside. "I guess I would need 300 meters. That would do it."

She began thumbing through the directions, looking at the DVD, fiddling around with the wires. The room was quiet except for the sound of Hortense muttering and Leona breathing furiously. Maggie understood her friends were nervous about driving to the Bronx, but she also knew that it was important to Reverend Sunday to have them go. She'd hate to insult her.

"What about this?" Maggie said. "One of my former Sunday school students runs a limo business. What if I ask him to drive us? I bet he'd give us a good rate."

Suddenly Hortense pressed a switch and a picture popped up on the TV of the five of them sitting in the office.

"There," she said. "I changed the range."

"How did you do that?" Maggie asked.

Leona looked at her younger sister proudly. "She's a genius," she said. "She set up our home entertainment system."

"You're a lifesaver," Maggie said to Horty.

The three sisters stood up and moved toward the door, which Richard Strauss held open for them. On their way out, Leona stopped. "Don't forget that limo driver," she said, and the four of them swanned out of the office.

Now that the teddy bear was operational, all Maggie had to do was go over to Stern Manor and give it to Racine.

Once again, she parked her red Audi TT in the driveway and went to that strange small door, but this time it was Racine who answered the doorbell with a smile.

"Maggie Dove," she said. "So glad to see you."

She wore a lime-green pantsuit and a yellow scarf. She still had on her red beret, but she also had on eye shadow and lipstick. In fact, if it weren't for the beret, Maggie wouldn't have been sure it was her; she would have thought it her cheerful twin sister.

"You're looking well," Maggie said.

"Oh I am," Racine cooed. "I'm feeling better than I have in years."

Even the bandage was gone, Maggie noticed. There were just two little red marks where the tarantula bit her.

"Is that for me?" Racine asked, clutching at the teddy bear. "You brought me a gift? How cute! No one's given me a doll in years."

"No," Maggie said. "It's not that type of doll. It's more of a spy camera."

"A spy camera? Why would I need that?"

"Remember you told me you thought your sister was trying to kill you? Remember the tarantula?" Maggie asked.

"Oh," Racine said. She held up her arm to the sunlight. "That was a misunderstanding. Charlotte's bite could no more hurt me than a bee's sting."

It was odd, Maggie thought, that she was using the same language Domino had.

"So things are good between you and Domino?"

"Very much so. I'll tell you, Maggie. I didn't realize how wonderful it was to have a sister. I've been foolish. You were trying to tell me something similar, weren't you? You were trying to get me to understand the importance of family when I first met with you. You told me that it was a blessing for my mother to have Domino come home and you were so right. I was so caught up in my own self-righteousness that I didn't see the big picture."

"I'm glad you're happy," Maggie said. "But there did seem to be some real cause for concern."

Racine laughed. Maggie didn't think she'd ever heard the sound. "Oh, how silly of me. I know what you're worrying about," she said. Then she reached for her pocketbook. "Your fee. I don't want you to think I cheated you. I know we agreed on $1,000, but that doesn't seem right. Would a check for $5,000 do it?"

"Racine," Maggie said, as she watched Racine write out the check, her letters swirling in large flourishes. "Are you sure you're all right?"

"Oh yes," she said. "Never better."

Maggie struggled to know what to do. Something about this didn't sit right with her. "Would you just humor me, Racine? Would you just take this teddy bear and put it in your room? There's no harm, is there? It will only work if someone comes into your room. I don't even need to check on it, but it will give me peace of mind."

Racine hesitated, but then she gave Maggie a wide grin. "Of course, Maggie Dove. Anything for you!"

Chapter Ten

The invitations arrived the next day. They went to every single citizen of the village of Darby-on-Hudson. They were printed with gold lettering on heavy black stock. "Come celebrate the return of Domino Raines and her family at a special Halloween celebration on the grounds of Stern Manor. Costumes required."

Immediately the village sprang into action. Costume consultants began arriving from Manhattan to set up shop. Two hundred dollars for a consultation. People began to form teams. Five of D'Amici's regulars planned to go as a giant Italian sub. Joe Mangione planned to tag along as a pickle. A fight broke out between two men who wanted to be Harrison Ford in *Star Wars*. Some of the high school students refused to dress up out of principle, though Maggie wasn't sure what the principle was.

Agnes wanted the three of them to dress as detectives, with trench coats and hats and business cards. She planned for Cherrelle to dress up as a sultry detective agency secretary. She planned to introduce her around. Edgar wanted to go as a zombie with a knife in his eye, but Helen said no, and instead he dressed up as Detective Grudge.

Everyone was excited except for Maggie, who felt that the whole thing was wrong. It wasn't natural for Racine to be happy. People didn't change overnight, did they? Not that way. Of course, Maggie had changed overnight herself, but that was because disaster struck. Maggie'd gone from being a normal, friendly person to a person clenched with grief, and it had taken her decades to get back to any form of normalcy. But that was different, surely.

Something was wrong, and she felt certain Domino was behind it.

She kept seeing Domino as she had looked in the cellar. *Just because somebody says no once, doesn't mean they'll say no forever.* Was it possible that Domino put a spell on Racine that caused her to change her personality, and if she could do that, could she also bilk money out of Racine? Could she get her to give her the inheritance?

Did Domino's witchcraft actually work? Maggie didn't want to think so, but she was a religious person. She believed in a God she could not see; could only feel and love. Was it such a stretch to go from believing in one set of unseen forces to another? This was the exact reason Racine had come to her, Maggie realized. Racine knew it would take a believer to believe what she was afraid of.

"She gave us $5,000," Agnes said, when Maggie raised her concerns. "You're not thinking we should give that back."

"Seems sort of hard to prove, Maggie Dove," Helen said, but she couldn't say more because there was a crisis in Syria and she had to write a report.

Maggie would not go to Walter Campbell about it. That much she knew.

After puzzling over it a bit, Maggie decided her best plan of action would be to go to the library. She could research witchcraft there. But not at the Darby library. It would be all over town in fifteen minutes. Instead, on Thursday afternoon she went to the big, anonymous library in Yonkers. Almost immediately, she found the book she was looking for: *The Only Book of Wiccan Spells You'll Ever Need.* She flipped through it.

There were spells for everything. Spells to relieve digestive complaints, and spells to quell the common cold. There was a weight-loss chakra. She flipped through to the chapter on spells for hard times. There was a courage spell and a quick cash potion. Then there was a spell to overcome obstacles. That required a statue of an elephant and a knife. There were no statues mentioned that looked like the ones she'd seen on Domino's circle. None of the spells seemed anything but innocuous, and the book assured its readers that white witches believed it was unethical to try to change someone's will without their consent.

But that implied there were black witches, and black spells. The book was silent on that score. She looked through all the books on witchcraft, each one more life-affirming than the last. Invariably she would find a sentence suggesting another type of witch existed, but nothing more was said. She decided the best thing to do would be to take out the books and read through them more carefully and then perhaps go through the bibliography.

That Sunday, the minister preached a sermon on evil. Surprising how often it happened, Maggie thought, that she heard a sermon on the very topic she'd been worrying about. Maggie had not heard a minister preach about evil in years, and yet here was Reverend Sunday Nkrumah tackling the subject. She looked somber. She wasn't a large woman, but she had presence. She exuded power, and she started to speak—so softly that everyone had to lean forward—about what the word "evil" meant today.

"We have become so preoccupied with forgiveness and grace, that we have forgotten about the word that's at the heart of it all," she said. "Sin!"

Then she began to talk about the prodigal son, and that the reason the father forgave him was because he confessed his sin. He atoned.

"If we abandon the language of sin, then when the devil appears in our midst, we will be speechless before him," she said.

Afterward, Maggie kept thinking about what the minister said. She knew she had felt something dark in the cellar with Domino. She believed that hatred carried its own power, and she sensed Domino was a woman who hated. At the same time, she felt out of her league.

She was just a Sunday School teacher. Nothing more. She had no superpowers. She had no weapons. But she knew what she believed and she knew there was right and wrong, and she believed Domino was on the wrong side of things. Maggie feared what would happen at the party next Saturday night. She felt she owed it to Racine to protect her as best she could.

Chapter Eleven

Stern Manor was transformed on the night of the party. There were pumpkins everywhere. Some were carved to look like gargoyles or monsters. Others were stacked on top of each other to look like dinosaurs. Others looked like celebrities, and every single pumpkin glowed with light. The constant flickering made Stern Manor seem alive, beating with a thousand hearts.

Thousands of people poured onto the lawn. People from the village, people Maggie had never seen before, people she couldn't recognize because of costumes. Edgar ran off the moment they got there to watch the magicians doing tricks, Helen chasing after him. There were roving fortune-tellers and women dressed as maids serving an extravagant selection of hors d'oeuvres: bacon dipped in chocolate and chili-covered snapper and seared steak lettuce cups and crab beignets. Everything oozed the moment you put it in your mouth, so it seemed like the whole village was oozing and dripping and everyone seemed overexcited.

Almost immediately Agnes got into an intense phone call with Cherrelle, who had not yet turned up.

Cherrelle couldn't find the manor, she couldn't park, she had a migraine and she had to go home. Agnes's insistent voice throbbed underneath all the other mayhem. "You've got to take care of yourself better, babe. You have to take care." Finally, Agnes charged off and Maggie was alone.

Not really, because she was surrounded by a whole village worth of people she knew, but her stress separated her from them. She was worried about Racine. Couldn't really focus on anything else, and she just wanted to find her and reassure herself that Racine was all right.

Every so often Maggie caught a glimpse of Domino in white, with her husband at her side. Honestly, it was hard to know if they were in costume or not. Mercy was there, dressed as a police officer, which Maggie assumed was also not a costume. She noticed Milo Raines lope by, also not in costume, followed by a group of girls and Billy Kim on a hover board. She waved. She couldn't help herself, and Billy waved back and gave her that crooked grin of his. She hadn't seen as much of him since Agnes stopped paying him to follow her, but it was always a treat when he cropped up, and she was absurdly touched that he waved at her. She remembered riding on his dirt bike with him. She remembered how he saved her life last spring.

Finally, she spotted Racine. Or she spotted her beret, anyway, and Maggie made her way in her direction. Racine was dressed as an artist, in a white smock.

Maggie was relieved to see Racine standing alongside her mother. Her devotion hadn't changed, whatever was going on with her sister.

"How are you?" she asked.

The old lady seemed much frailer than she had two weeks earlier. She wore a flapper outfit costume that looked like she might have worn it in the 1920s, and she had a soft white blanket draped over her.

"Who are these people?" she asked. "I don't know any of them."

"This is Maggie Dove," Racine said. "You remember her. She came and visited with us."

"I don't know who these people are," she said. "Why are they all on our lawn?"

"It's a celebration, Mama," Racine said, tucking her hand against her mother's cheek, stroking her softly. "We're celebrating Domino's return."

"They look disheveled," she said. "These aren't our kind of people."

Racine nodded at Maggie. "I think I better get my mother back. She's exhausted."

"Of course," Maggie said.

Maggie watched the two of them head back to the house. The crowd parted in front of them, but no one spoke to them. They were in their own world. A sharp bolt of lightning suddenly lit up against the sky. Everyone oohed, assuming for a moment that it was a light show. Anything seemed possible right then.

Time to go home, Maggie thought. She'd done what she could. Checked in on Racine. There was not much more to do.

Maggie turned toward the exit and found herself face-to-face with Domino. She wore a sweeping white cape, tight white pants, and she'd dressed Charlotte in a little matching outfit. Around the spider's midsection was a diamond studded chain. It looked as though Domino had got access to some of the money.

"Maggie Dove," she said. "I heard you were doing research on witchcraft at the Yonkers Library."

Maggie felt herself blush. The lightening speared overhead.

"How on earth do you know that?" she asked.

"Don't you suppose that there are librarians who are witches?"

Maggie considered the possibility. Was it possible that some rogue witch librarian had reported her to Domino? She thought it unlikely. She believed that librarians were forces for good, and while she was willing to consider the possibility of a white witch among them, she could not imagine one reporting her to Domino. Whatever Domino was, witch or otherwise, she was not a force for good.

"I was researching spells," Maggie replied.

"And what did you learn. Did you determine whether or not I've put my sister under a spell?"

Domino was the same height as Maggie, and yet she seemed to loom so much larger. She was like a spider, all her parts moving, ready to bite. Maggie wanted to take a step back, but felt she shouldn't.

"I learned that it violates your code to put someone under a spell against her will."

Domino laughed at that. She had one of those loud, attention-getting laughs. Always the center of attention, Maggie thought. One of those people who crave it, no matter the reason.

"Against my sister's will? I don't think she's a good judge of what's good for her or not. Look at how she's spent the last forty years, taking care of my mother. If I put her under a spell that gets her out of that, I would think she'd be grateful."

"Lucky for you, she is so devoted. You haven't had to spend much time looking after your mother."

"No," Domino said, eyes suddenly softening. She turned down her lips a little bit. "Now you've made me feel guilty, Maggie Dove."

A bright shard of lightening split against the sky. For a moment it seemed it would hit Stern Manor. It ratcheted right over the tower.

"The gods are so strong," Domino said, reenergized. "It's time for me to get my part of this party going."

She leaned forward and Maggie thought she might kiss her. She pulled back sharply, and Domino laughed, and then she walked away.

Now Maggie really and truly was done. As she set off toward the exit though, she ran into Walter Campbell, dressed as a spruce tree.

"It's the perfect costume," she said, in all honesty. "Are your children little spruces?"

"They're not here," he said. "They had to go visit their grandmother.

"You mean to say you dressed up as a tree and you don't have any kids around to witness it."

"I wanted to get into the community spirit."

Suddenly she could see him so clearly as tall, earnest boy, bullied horribly, and she felt the strongest tug of emotion for him. Maybe she could tell him what she feared. Maybe she should give him more credit.

"You seem troubled," he said. She stared into those caring brown eyes that looked so ridiculous shrouded by green leaves. She had to try, but how do you tell a respectable man that you think someone put a spell on your client?

"Walter, this is really hard to say. I feel like a fool. It's just I have something I need to tell you and I know you're going to think I'm insane, but I—"

"Stop," he said, putting his hand out to her cheek, brushing it softly. "There's no need to say anything else. I feel exactly the same way, but it's not right. It just can't be."

Then he turned around and left.

"Oh my God," Maggie muttered. "Oh my God."

At that moment, the crowd seemed to vibrate with Maggie's consternation. The whole assembly began to murmur and hum. Turning in the direction of the crowd's gaze, Maggie saw Domino walking out onto the tower. The tower had always looked high, but with

Domino's slight figure on top of it, it seemed even higher. A spotlight picked out her face.

"My people," she said. "My village. Thank you so much for coming out to celebrate my favorite holiday. Halloween."

Everyone cheered.

The noise reverberated and the sound of the thunder got louder. Sudden cracks of lightning flickered over the water and acted like a strobe light. Maggie felt the hairs on her arm prickle. Everything felt off. Domino was so exposed up there. What if she got hit by lightning?

"I think she's drunk," Tim Harrison said. "She's slurring her words."

"I'm happy to announce that I will be moving back here permanently. We will be living in Stern Manor with my sister and mother. My dear sister is welcoming us with open arms.

"Come here, Racine," she said, beckoning toward a figure in the hallway that Maggie could now see was Racine. "Come on," she crooned. Racine shook her head. Didn't want to move. But Domino held her arms over her head. She began chanting. Maggie couldn't hear what she said, but she could feel it.

Suddenly Maggie knew what Domino was going to do. She was going to force Racine to jump. She'd bewitched her. Maggie started to push through the crowd toward the tower, when she heard a sharp laugh. She looked up in time to see Domino hurtling toward the ground.

Chapter Twelve

For just a moment, there was complete silence. Then all was movement and there was Walter Campbell, rushing toward the body, tearing off his costume as he ran. Joe Mangione pushed his way forward as well and the rest of the ambulance corps assembled. More quickly than Maggie would have believed possible, the police began arriving. They cordoned off the body and asked people to fill out statements, setting aside people they wanted to talk to further.

Maggie, being one of the last people to talk to Domino, was asked to sit for a while, but in the end, she didn't have much to say. Everyone had seen the same thing. Domino walked toward the balcony, she gestured toward her sister to join her, she laughed and fell over. It was her laugh that haunted Maggie. A triumphant laugh. It echoed over and over in Maggie's head. She dreamed it in her sleep, and the next morning, when she woke up, she thought she still heard it, except that it was the telephone.

"They've finished the autopsy," Agnes said.

"That seems fast. How do you know that?"

"Cherrelle told me. She works for the county and has access to the coroner's records. They're calling it an accidental death."

"I guess that makes sense." Maggie kept reliving the sight of Domino seeming to flip right over the railing.

"There was one surprise," Agnes said. "She had LSD in her system. Cherrelle thinks the family wants to suppress that information. They want to bury her quick, hush it all up. The lawyers are talking to the coroner now. Welcome to America."

"Agnes, maybe they're just ashamed of how she died. Maybe they don't want people talking about it."

"Right, and if you and I had somebody die and we were ashamed about it, I imagine they'd listen to us too. This is why the rich are different than you and me. They have influence."

Maggie thought Agnes was right, but then Agnes was also rich. The only person in this discussion that didn't have much money was Maggie.

She wasn't actually shocked Domino had taken LSD. In fact, she would rather think Domino was possessed by drugs than witchcraft. But she couldn't stop thinking about what Domino said about the afterlife. She wondered if she was in heaven now, or if she had been transformed. Had her soul perhaps moved in to Maggie's cat?

That she could believe.

And what about Juliet? She thought of Domino's words; in truth, she'd never forgotten them.

How many times had she had the sense of Juliet right near her? Especially on birthdays and holidays, she sometimes found herself turning around quickly, expecting to see her daughter there. She felt unsettled. Domino was dead, but the story didn't feel over.

The next day was Sunday and the Sterns came to church. They walked down the center aisle, staring straight ahead, Racine pushing her mother in her wheelchair, Milo walking alongside them. Each was dressed in black, Madame Stern with a bit of gauze covering her eyes. The minister paused the service to come down and hug them, and Maggie went over and tried to offer her condolences, but Racine was brittle as a twig. She wouldn't even make eye contact.

"I'm sorry," Maggie said.

Racine looked like what she had been before. The smiles were gone. The color was gone. Once again, she was downtrodden Racine Stern in her black clothes and her red beret. Maggie wondered if she even remembered how she had changed.

During the service Maggie noticed several strange men and women file into the church. It was always nice to see young people in church, of course, but these didn't seem to have a religious aspect. They all clustered behind Racine's pew and Maggie noticed during the Passing of the Peace that one of them grabbed on to Racine's hand and wouldn't let go.

"Leave us alone," she shouted. "Animals."

They all began taking pictures then and Racine went tearing out of the church, pushing her mother's chair, shouting at the reporters to leave her alone. Four of the ushers surrounded her to try to offer protection, but Maggie could hear the reporters clamoring: "What are you hiding? When will the autopsy be made public? What do you think of the rumors that you killed your sister?"

The next day was officially Halloween, and yet the town was quiet. No one had the heart for much celebrating, except the little kids, who didn't know what was going on. From her office window Maggie could watch them darting around, little fairies and elves with their heavy bags full of candy. Reporters wandered around also, talking on their phones, darting into stores.

There were brief accounts of the preliminary autopsy in the newspapers and on-line, but there was no new information. Domino Raines died of multiple head injuries after plunging over the balcony at Stern Manor. She had LSD in her system. Death was ruled accidental.

Maggie thought that was the end of it, but it wasn't.

The first person to stop by her office that day was Betty Springer, who wandered in after having a root canal. She said it was shocking that Racine got away with murder. And could she have some water.

"What do you mean she got away with murder?" Maggie asked. She gave her the water in one of the cups Agnes had encouraged her to use, a pink one with their slogan on it.

"It can't be coincidence that she was up on the balcony with her sister. She had to have done something. The rich play by different rules, don't they? You throw enough money at a problem and you can get away with anything."

Maggie thought Betty was just suffering from the ill effects of anesthesia, but throughout the morning, people kept coming by and murmuring about Racine's guilt. Joe Mangione said he was sure Racine had a mechanized robot push Domino over the balcony. "Like one of those Roombas. But with lethal intent." He told her about how the reporters were coming into D'Amici's and buying up all the sandwiches. They couldn't get into Stern Manor, but they were camped out on the lawn, assaulting everyone who came by. They really wanted to talk to Lucifer, but he hadn't emerged from the house.

"Maybe he set the whole thing up as a publicity stunt," Joe suggested.

Not until Maggie went to judge the poster contest with Hal Carter did she finally realize just how serious Racine's position was. Hal had, up until a year ago, been considered the most romantic man in town. He'd devoted his life to his mother, a difficult woman. But after she died, he married his beautiful young girlfriend. Then it came out that he'd been carrying on with his young wife's mother, and in a short period of time he'd gone from being revered to vilified. Maggie had never been that fond of the saintly Hal Carter, but she found herself enjoying the demoted one. He seemed more honest, more real. He was gentler. She used to think he had a bad temper, but suffering had softened him. She supposed in that way she could actually relate to him. It was depressing, but suffering did seem to make people kinder. She thought of a line from a poem by Naomi Shihab Nye that she liked so much:

Before you know what kindness really is you must lose things…"

Now Maggie and Hal wandered up and down Main Street, looking at the different posters. She was relieved that Edgar was not the only youth who had violent zombies, but one thing did surprise her, as they looked at the posters: all the monsters shared one particular feature. Whether zombie, ghost or witch, each one wore a red beret, and on Tuesday morning, when Maggie saw a familiar figure in a red beret striding toward her office, she had a pretty good idea of what Racine wanted.

Chapter Thirteen

"Have you heard what they're saying about me?" Racine asked. She stormed into Maggie's office as though she owned it. She slammed herself down into one of the ergonomic chairs, which snapped up around her like a Venus fly-trap. "Have you heard that filth?" In her right hand she clutched one of the posters Maggie had seen only the day before, with the red beret on top of a witch.

"They're calling me a monster. They're saying I murdered Domino."

Maggie felt slightly relieved to see Racine back to looking normal. She wore black, she had on no make-up, and she wore her usual lace-up black shoes. Whatever had taken hold of her was gone, and that was a good thing.

"It's just kids," Maggie tried to reassure her. "It's a Halloween prank. It will pass."

"They are accusing me of murder." Racine grasped the table with her hands. She leaned forward. Maggie could feel the blast of heat coming off her. "They're saying that I pushed her somehow. And it's not just kids. Those reporters. They won't leave me alone."

"Racine, everyone in the village could see you didn't go near Domino. It's not like you're going to be arrested. The reporters will go away when nothing happens."

Outside, one of the dental patients was taking a selfie in front of the ash tree. People seemed to feel a need to send a picture of their clean teeth to loved ones.

Racine pulled back her head and for a moment she looked just like Domino. Same blazing eyes, same certainty of expression.

"Would that be enough for you, Maggie Dove? Would you be satisfied to have your reputation damaged thus? They are saying I'm capable of murder. Whether I did it or not, they are saying that I could have. Me!"

Maggie sank back into her seat. She looked out the window at Main Street. She remembered the terrible night last April when she found Marcus Bender's body on her front lawn. She'd known no one would seriously think her a murderer, yet she'd felt diminished by her anger for him. She remembered how ashamed she'd felt when she heard his widow railing about her to the police on her front lawn.

"No," she said. "I wouldn't be happy about that."

"*Exactement*," Racine said. "This is exactly my point. They are mocking me, these people who don't even know me. They shred my name." Her face assumed a look of disgust as though she'd eaten something bad. She puckered her lips and Maggie noticed long dry lines on either side of her mouth.

"I want to hire you," Racine said.

Maggie was on the brink of saying, *Again?* She wondered if the detective agency could maintain itself if they had just one client, who kept rehiring them.

"I want you to prove I did not kill my sister."

Maggie didn't see how she could prove something didn't happen, when no one thought it did happen. But people did think it happened. That was the thing.

"Racine, what were you doing out there on the balcony?"

"What?"

"Last I saw you, you were taking your mother to bed. But then all of a sudden you were on the balcony."

She clutched at her beret. "I don't know. I don't know. I don't understand." She leaned toward Maggie as though trying to tell her something without speaking. Maggie thought of how cheerful she'd been, how afraid Maggie'd been that Domino would hurt her. Had Domino hypnotized her into going onto the balcony.

"If you could just prove my sister killed herself. That would clear me."

"Did she? Do you have proof?"

"Yes, I have proof—in my heart!" Racine said. She pounded her chest with the flat of her hand. Maggie tried to imagine Detective Grudge dealing with a client who felt something in her heart. She suspected he would want firmer proof.

"She didn't seem like a suicidal sort of person," Maggie pointed out.

"Pull down the blinds," Racine said.

"Okay." Maggie went over to the window and lowered the blinds. Immediately the room darkened and silenced.

"What I am going to tell you, I have not told to anyone else. I did not tell this the police." The drawn blinds cast her face in a reddish light. She looked like she might burst into flames. "I did not want to drag our family's name through the mud with talk of suicide, though I never imagined that it would get worse. That people would call me a murderer." She pulled a handkerchief out of her bag and dabbed her lips. Maggie noticed a tiny bit of blood on the white fabric.

"She told me she was going to kill herself."

"Domino told you that?"

"Yes, right before she died, she told me she was going to kill herself."

Maggie rocked back in her chair. "Forgive me, Racine, but it seems a little convenient. Do you have any proof?"

"Are you calling me a liar?"

Just then the door banged open and Agnes strode in. She wore a purple silk blouse that flowed around her arms like wings. There were two little cutouts that exposed her shoulders. She'd been frowning when she walked into the room, but at the sight of Racine, her face broke into a politician's wide smile. "Ah," she said. "Another client. And who is this?"

"This is Racine Stern," Maggie said.

"Ah," Agnes crooned. She looked like a purple balloon, ready to float into air. "What a pleasure to meet you at last. I'm very sorry for your loss. Can I get you something to drink? Has Maggie offered you refreshment?"

"No," Racine said. "No, thank you."

"You must be parched," Agnes said, walking over to one of the closets and plucking from it a bottle of white wine.

"It's only 11:00," Maggie pointed out.

"It's after 5:00 somewhere. Will you get us some ice, Maggie? Now."

"From where?" Maggie mouthed. They had no freezer.

"From our friends next door," she said, nodding toward the dentist's office. "They're all so helpful," she said to Racine. "We professionals have to stick together."

Maggie dashed next door and retrieved some ice from the dental hygienist, who wrapped it in a gauze pad, and when she got back to her own office, she found Agnes with three glasses. She handed over the wad of ice. Agnes grimaced, but pitched a cube into each glass, popped the bottle and poured the wine. Then she went to the closet and pulled out some Girl Scout cookies, which she put on a little pink platter.

"Now," Agnes said. "What can we do for you?"

Racine swigged the wine right down. Then she burped softly. "As you know, my sister died. Everyone in town seems to be blaming me, and I would like you to prove it was a suicide."

"Of course."

"I was just trying to explain to Maggie Dove that my sister told me just before she died that she planned to kill herself, but unfortunately I don't have any proof."

"How could you?" Agnes said, leaning forward—as she did so, knocking her knee into Maggie's so hard, she thought it would bruise. "Pardon me," she said. "So clumsy. You've come to the right place, Racine. We're not the police. We are not bound by rules. We can do whatever our client wants us to do, and if you wish us to prove your sister a suicide, we can do that."

"Ah, thank you," Racine said. "This has all been so terrible. Domino's death, the horror, and my dear mother so devastated, and then these rumors about me, and the posters. All I can think of is my poor father and how he worked his whole life to build up his business. He told me over and over again that nothing was more important than your reputation. To think of losing it, after forty years of devoting my life to my family…Well, it's unbearable."

"Why do you think Domino would want to kill herself?" Maggie asked.

"That's exactly what we're going to find out," Agnes said, planting her hand firmly on Maggie's shoulder.

"Now," she said to Racine, "you've given us a lot of money already, and I don't want to pauperize you." Racine tittered a bit at that.

"However," Agnes said, "we do have an additional service that might interest you. A special one."

"What's that?"

Maggie felt curious herself. She didn't know they had a special service.

"It's our gold star service. For an additional $5,000, we guarantee that the full services of our agency will be dedicated to your project. We will take on no new clients until such time as you are satisfied. We'll also give you daily updates. Naturally," Agnes went on, "our regular services are superior, but this is the type of service we've geared toward a special clientele used to getting special attention."

"That does interest me," Racine said.

"Maggie, go get the gold star contracts out of the cabinet."

"Where are they?"

"Under G," Agnes said impatiently, and lo and behold, there they were. Regular contracts with a gold star at the top, which Maggie felt fairly certain had been stolen from Sunday School. She used them to mark attendance. Maggie wasn't sure whether to be appalled or impressed. It occurred to her that she didn't really know Agnes Jorgenson at all. Although she'd worked with her for four months, and considered her a friend, there were depths to her that defied Maggie.

"Now," Agnes said, wresting the contract out of Maggie's grasp, "let's just sign this and then we can get started."

Racine opened her pocketbook, pulled out her checkbook, and wrote the check without hesitation.

"Make sure to write *gold star service* on the subject line," Agnes said. "We wouldn't want it to get confused with anyone else's."

Racine stood. She smoothed down her black sweater, breathed in deeply. "You can promise that I will have your full attention."

"I can guarantee it," Agnes said.

"Where are you going to start?" Racine asked.

Agnes pushed out her lips. "I think the best place to start would be with the police. Maggie has a special relationship with the superintendent of the Darby police force, and I'll send her to get the inside scoop."

"Then you'll report back to me," Racine asked.

"Of course," Agnes said smoothly, though even she jumped when the door banged open again. This time it was Helen rushing into the office. Her pale face was flushed, her kerchief askew. She looked like she'd been running.

"Maggie," she cried out. "I have an emergency."

Then she noticed Racine, and started. "Oh, I'm sorry, I didn't know anyone was here."

"No, I'm sorry," Racine said. "I can see this is a very busy office and I don't want to interfere. You'll be in touch with me soon," she said to Maggie.

"Of course."

"I'm one of your new gold star clients," she said to Helen. "You must be the third partner."

"Yes," Helen said. She put out her hand. "I'm Helen Blake."

Racine peered at her closely and seemed to like what she saw.

"Gold star client?" Helen asked after she left.

"I feel so guilty I can't even speak," Maggie said. "What's the emergency?"

"Oh," Helen said. "I told Edgar I'd go apple picking with him tomorrow but I can't. Would you be willing to fill in for me?"

Maggie started to laugh. Agnes began laughing too, and then Helen joined in. It was a nice feeling, the laughter pulling them all together. Maggie felt something hard within her dissolve.

"Of course," Maggie said.

"Just make sure to go to talk to Walter Campbell first," Agnes said. "In fact, you should go to him now. You're going to have to write up a report."

Walter Campbell, Maggie thought, whom she had last seen on the grounds of Stern Manor, whom she had apparently left with the impression that she was about to declare her undying love for him. Now she had to interview him for her gold star report.

Chapter Fourteen

Once again Maggie tangled with the new police officer when she went to the station. "I saw you in the handicapped spot the other day," Mercy Williams said as soon as she saw her.

"Well, yes," Maggie conceded, "though in fairness, I was picking up a meal for Maureen O'Shea and she is handicapped. I couldn't find a parking spot and I knew she was waiting for me."

Mercy Williams eyed her without mercy. "Superintendent Campbell said you'd have a good reason," she said, sniffing. She was as tidy as she'd been the last time Maggie saw her. Closely cropped hair, uniform carefully pressed, shoes shined. Maggie knew this young woman had had to struggle to get to her position, and she wanted her to feel comfortable in Darby. Fact was, Maggie admired her ferociousness and honesty. Maggie shouldn't have parked in the handicapped spot. Maggie suspected she took an awful lot for granted.

"I wonder if you'd like to go to dinner," she tried.

"What?" Mercy flinched, as though Maggie had just punched her.

"Not with me. I mean not just with me. But a bunch of us from the church are going. Not that you need to be a churchgoing person to go. The restaurant's in the Bronx. It's called Kumasi and it serves food from Ghana. Ghanaian food."

Mercy crossed her arms. "I go there all the time, but why are you?"

"Our minister is from Ghana."

"Oh," she said. Maggie saw indecision play across her face.

"I suspect the superintendent will be coming too. And his wife," she added. She thought, she hoped, she saw Mercy softening just a little bit. She truly did want her to feel welcome, and so Maggie was smiling when she went into Walter Campbell's office.

"Maggie Dove," he said, smiling as well. There was definitely something alarming about having Walter Campbell smile at you. He was so large and his smile so big. It was hard to escape the thought that he planned to eat you. He put out his hand and she shook it and then he took her hand with both of his and sat down. She noticed he'd put up some of his children's art. There was a drawing of apples. Oh God, the apple picking trip was tomorrow. She had to remember to buy Dramamine. It would not do to throw up on a bus with Edgar.

"This is a pleasure," he said.

She sat down at his desk. It was one of those big aluminum desks that reminded her of ones her elementary school teachers used to have. Maggie was always the girl who brought in an apple for the teacher. Back then it wasn't an ironic statement.

"Racine has hired my agency to look into her sister's death."

"Oh."

He clenched his hands together. The word "lockjaw" popped into her head, and she remembered suddenly a friend of her mother's who got bit by a rabid dog and had to have shots in his stomach for the period of a year. "There's no mystery to her death. The autopsy report was quite clear. She died of multiple head injuries."

"Racine thinks she might have committed suicide," Maggie said cautiously.

"No, "Walter said, shaking his head.

"Surely you can't be 100 per cent positive, Walter. There's always a little doubt in any situation."

He'd painted his office, she noticed. Hadn't it just been white? Now it was more of an eggshell white and she wondered if his wife had come in to spruce things up. He looked neater too. Tidier. His hair more carefully brushed.

"No," he said. "We were most thorough."

"The whole report was done in less than 24 hours," she pointed out. "How thorough could it have been?"

"It was thorough," he responded.

She noticed he had a copy of it on his desk. He drew it toward him, shielding it with his arm. She suspected he'd not be happy to know that Cherrelle had called them with the preliminary data.

"There was no indication of suicide," he said, scanning the report.

"Walter, I don't understand how you can be so confident. Surely a person who takes LSD before going out on a high balcony is looking for some trouble. Knowing Domino, it's not hard to believe that if she was going to take her life, she would do it in a very public manner. She'd been under a lot of financial stress. And her husband had a girlfriend. There were things that might have made her suicidal. Anyway, didn't I read that most suicides are impulsive?"

"She didn't take LSD," he said.

"I thought that's what the news said."

"The news got it wrong. She took lysergic acid, but in a different form. She used ergot."

"What's that?"

He stood up and retrieved from his book shelf a large book, and began flipping through it. It was a chemistry textbook. He got to the section on ergot and showed it to her. Ergot, she read, was the fungus from which LSD is derived. It grew parasitically on rye, and on other types of grain and wild grasses. Kernels infested with this fungus develop into brown pegs that pushed forth from the husks of the grain. There was a picture attached, which showed yellow grains on a field and little brown stalks sticking out from them. She read on. "In 1938, the Swiss chemist, Albert Hoffman, looking to develop new medicines from ergot, happened upon lysergic acid, and accidentally transformed that into the hallucinogenic, LSD."

When Maggie finished reading, he took back the book and put it on his shelf.

"So what does that mean?" Maggie said. "LSD or ergot—it still sounds like the same thing? One way or another, she took a hallucinogenic that caused her to fall to her death."

Walter seemed to struggle within himself. She didn't understand what the problem was. Whether or not she believed Domino killed herself, she thought you could make a case for it. The more she thought about it, the more sense it made. Domino was under a lot of stress.

"Ergot has a peculiar history," Walter Campbell said. "In the Middle Ages, in large doses, it was used as a poison. But in smaller doses, it was a hallucinogen. It caused visions and euphoria. Over time, people began adapting it, using it as a drug. It became popular in some forms of witchcraft, at covens, because it expanded the witch's consciousness. In the grips of a hallucination a witch could see more clearly into another world. Or so they believed."

He straightened his tie, which was regimental. No surprise there.

"Domino was merely excited, Maggie."

"How can we know that for sure?" Maggie pressed. "Don't we have to follow up on this, for Racine's sake if for no other reason? If we can't prove definitively that she wasn't murdered, the accusation will hang over Racine for the rest of her life."

Walter hesitated, shifting uneasily. She couldn't understand what he was so nervous about. The man was so tightly wound. Then he cleared his throat and began to speak. "One thing people noticed was that swallowing the ergot led to unpleasant side effects. Nausea, vomiting and so forth, and so they began experimenting with putting it into lotions."

"What are you saying? Domino smeared ergot on herself?"

"No," he said, looking uncomfortable. "She inserted it." He lowered his gaze to his desk. "We found…a broomstick on the balcony, with ergot residue on the tip, as well as…something else." He glanced quickly at Maggie before looking away again. "It appears she put it on the tip of her broomstick, and then…"

"Oh," Maggie said in a small voice, stunned.

"She was excited, Maggie. Things were going her way. She planned to announce she was moving back to Darby, and Racine had just given her a great sum of money. Domino must have inserted a fair amount of ergot into herself and lost control. She probably thought she was flying. It was an accident, Maggie Dove. Pure and simple."

He stood up.

"Leave this alone, Maggie Dove. There's nothing here for you or your client. This was a tragedy, but it was no one's fault but Domino's."

He paused to make his point clear, just in case she hadn't understood him. "Leave it alone."

Chapter Fifteen

Maggie hated being told what to do, but in this case, she thought Walter had a point. Domino's death did not sound like suicide. It sounded dramatic and vulgar and slightly nauseating, which was consistent with Domino. She remembered Domino biting Passion's lip. Yes, this was exactly the way she would have expected Domino to die.

Under normal circumstances, Maggie would have gone back to the office and conceded. But although that was a temptation, she didn't want to do it. First of all, she knew Agnes would kill her. They had one client, and she did not propose to be the one to lose her.

But it went deeper than that.

Maggie was a private detective. Her job was to investigate. Walter had presented compelling facts, but she doubted that was all there was to know. She'd been hired to gather information about Domino and she planned to do it. She could hear Detective Grudge's instructions in her head: *Don't take anybody's word for anything.*

She'd also learned, over the course of her life, that people often liked to do what was easiest. A tragedy had occurred, the woman was disliked. She was strange. She was downright demonic. Why push it?

Because it's the right thing to do.

So, what to do?

She was on Main Street, not far from Doc Steinberg's office. She would stop in and ask her what she knew about ergot. At the very least she would confirm what Walter Campbell said.

Doc Steinberg's office was busy, but Maggie'd brought along her book. She figured she could sit and read *The Brothers Karamazov*, and sooner or later Hannah would fit her in. She was on the part about Zosima's decaying body, which was both hysterically funny and mind-bendingly sad, like most of life, Maggie thought, and she was so engrossed that she didn't even hear Doc Steinberg calling her in.

"When you're ready, Maggie."

"Sorry." She tucked her book back into her bag and followed Doc Steinberg into her office. It was a room that always made Maggie feel anxious. She was conscious of all the bad news handed out in that office, some of it to herself. But she also trusted Doc Steinberg as much as she trusted anyone in the world. Doc had gone with Maggie to the hospital the night Juliet died, holding her hand while she talked to the people at the organ donation bank.

"As you know," Maggie said, "I have a detective agency now. I've been hired to examine the state of mind of Domino. To be blunt, her sister thinks she killed herself."

Doc Steinberg nodded. She was a strong woman, big boned, but she always wore bright red shoes. She also liked dangling earrings that she'd got in India when she spent a year there.

"Do you think that's possible?" Maggie asked. "I assume you know the details of how she died."

"A broomstick." Doc Steinberg rolled her eyes. "I've been practicing medicine for a long time, and there's one thing I've learned. Nothing is as creative as a person planning their suicide. I suppose it's the ultimate opportunity to tell your story. Some people want to do it quietly and not have any bother. Other people…I read about a man who purposely crashed his car in the middle of a busy intersection. He wanted people to see him die. He wanted to shock them. Then I've read about cases where people wanted to cast blame on someone else, and they arranged the whole thing to make someone look guilty."

"So, you…"

"Then there was the guy who put a noose around his neck, tied the other end to a tree, got in a car, and accelerated. Not pretty."

Her phone began to ring; Maggie didn't want to take up too much of her time. "So, you wouldn't rule out a suicide? she asked quickly, getting straight to the point.

"Maggie Dove, I don't rule out anything," she said and turned her attention to her phone call.

"Well, that was successful," Maggie said when she got back out on Main Street. Automatically she looked around. Not a good idea to start talking to yourself, she supposed, though it was habit she'd gotten into in her long years of mourning. Sometimes she was the only person she could stand to talk to.

Joe Mangione walked by just then. "Good for you," he called out.

She needed to think this all over. She felt exuberant. She hadn't given up and she'd learned new facts which validated her position, even if they were awfully flimsy. The sun was warm. The leaves were fluttering around her feet, and Maggie thought that instead of going to the office, she'd head up to the woods to plan out what to do next. The woods always cleared her mind, and she was especially partial to them this time of year, when the acorns were falling and the squirrels were chasing one other around. There was something mournful yet hopeful about fall that she liked.

She trudged up the hill and walked past the large rock that marked the entry to the woods. She took one of the less accustomed paths, feeling a need to lose herself. She could hear the Saw Mill. She knew she was near civilization, if in fact a parkway equaled civilization, but it was nice to wander where there was nobody else about. She tried to think about what to do next. Detective Grudge said that the primary job of a private detective was to gather information, so that was what she would do.

She needed to start setting up appointments with people. She would talk to Lucifer Raines and Passion and Milo. Perhaps she would see if she could find the coven Domino belonged to. She kept walking farther and farther, deeper into the woods. She thought about the man she'd seen at Stern Manor. She could try to track him down. If nothing else, she would get a better picture of who Domino was. She knew she'd gone to a private school. Cranston. Maggie began thinking about Juliet then, which she always did, when she'd been solitary long enough. It was like a sudden cloud settled on her. She didn't want to push it away; she would never push her daughter away. But her steps slowed.

She thought of something Racine had said about a reputation, which had been burbling inside her since this morning. She thought about it because it had affected Juliet too. She'd been a good girl, never giving Maggie trouble. But on the last day of her life, she'd gone to a party and she'd had something to drink. She was only 17. She shouldn't have been drinking. It was a miniscule amount—she might not even have felt it—but it showed up on the autopsy. Immediately people blamed her, even though the accident took place while the car was parked. The truck came at her head-on—nevertheless she had alcohol in her blood. Maggie'd felt ashamed, and angry. To have her lovely daughter remembered for this one fact. Over time, over decades, her anger had dissolved, but she still understood what Racine meant when she said she felt accused. Maggie too had felt accused. Of being a bad mother, of not teaching her daughter well enough.

Just then Maggie stumbled across a rock with strange markings on it. She traced her finger over them. They looked like hieroglyphics. Turning around, she realized she was in the middle of a large clearing. Someone had scratched a circle into the earth. She also realized she'd spent an hour walking. She'd been so caught up in her thoughts that she wasn't paying attention. No longer could she hear the Saw Mill Parkway. The ground was wet; she'd wandered into the wetlands. She still had an hour or so daylight left. She had her phone. There was no reason to panic, but she felt unsettled. That was when Maggie heard a twig break.

It was the distinctive sound of a heavy animal.

Maggie remembered a night last spring when someone had been after her, but surely no one chased her now. She hadn't done anything, had she? She felt afraid. She closed her eyes and whispered a prayer, but then she thought perhaps God would rather she took the initiative and get moving, and so she started to do, and at that moment something flew at her. She screamed until she realized who it was.

Agnes howled with laughter.

"You must be deaf, Maggie Dove. I've following you for an hour and you didn't notice."

"If I have a heart attack, let it be on your conscience."

Agnes kept laughing and laughing until she couldn't breathe. Then she started wheezing and collapsed onto a log. "Sorry, Maggie," she said. "But you are hopeless. You have to practice your surveillance skills."

"Why are you following me?" Maggie felt hot pains shooting down her arm. A squirrel screeched as it flew overhead.

"I've been following you since the police station."

"All afternoon? Why?"

"Because I wanted to see what you were going to do," Agnes said. She began fluffing up her hair "Now that we have a client, we want to make sure we give her our best effort."

"You were checking up on me?"

Agnes had on the same bat-like outfit she'd worn in the office, but she'd changed her shoes, Maggie noticed. She had on black sneakers with silver highlights. She'd put effort into this.

"I just wanted to be sure you were on track."

"That is incredibly insulting," Maggie said. "I'm the one that got the client, let me remind you. She came to me in the first place because of who I am, because I'm a Sunday School teacher. What clients have you brought in with all your carousing. I talked to Walter. I have a plan. But this is no partnership, Agnes. Partners do not treat other partners like this."

Agnes rocked back on the log.

"In fact," Maggie said. "I have half a mind to quit right now. You really could have given me a stroke. Look where I'm standing, Agnes. Doesn't this look like a witch's circle to you?"

Agnes didn't speak, just looked down at her sneakers.

In fact, while I've spent the whole afternoon doing billable work, you've been completely wasting your time. Following me."

"You're right," Agnes mumbled. "You're right." She began to cry. "I don't know what's wrong with me."

"Agnes, you have to take it down a notch. All this hysteria is killing me—and probably you. You're yelling at me and then you're hugging me and then you're sad and then you're happy. Do you think it's possible you should see a doctor?"

"I did," she said, "and the doctor prescribed Xanax."

"Well, could I suggest then that if you feel one of these mood swings coming on, that you take a pill?"

"Yes, Maggie Dove. Absolutely. I'm sorry. Can we hug it out?"

"Of course," Maggie said, and they hugged and she felt better, sort of, and then Agnes said, "Hey I know you're angry and all, but do you know how to get out of here?"

"No," Maggie said. "No, I do not."

"That's okay. I have a compass," she said. "All we have to do is figure out which way is north. What side of a tree does moss grow on?"

Three hours later, Maggie stumbled into her house. She made avocado toast, her latest obsession, for dinner, ate it; and then went to bed. The cat leapt alongside her.

"Don't even start," she muttered and pulled a pillow over her head.

That night she dreamed of Stern Manor. She was trapped once again in the cellar. She tried to get out but she couldn't. She woke up late at night, panting, only to find her ghostly white cat staring at her. She looked into his tiger eyes. She felt he wanted to talk to her, but didn't have any idea what he wanted to say, except she felt the strongest sensation of contempt. That cat looked down on her and she didn't like it.

Not until she woke up at 7:00 did she remember she'd forgotten to buy the Dramamine. Oh dear. And so, the new day began.

Chapter Sixteen

Maggie had an issue with school buses, the issue being that she couldn't sit on one without feeling sick to her stomach. At sixty-two years old, she'd figured she'd probably go the rest of her life without having to ride on one again, but she had not anticipated the unexpected devotion she felt for her young friend Edgar. The problem was that now she had to make it through a forty-five-minute ride without doing anything embarrassing to herself or Edgar. But it was a real struggle, all the worse because the day was so warm, the bus so bumpy, her stomach so unsettled.

Hoping to trick her body into a healthier frame of mind, Maggie invited all the kids to sing along with her in a rendition of "The Wheels on the Bus." wheels on the bus. That went well for about fifteen minutes, but then Edgar began spinning his arms round and round and he hit Lester Kozcak in the head. Fortunately, Lester's mother was Sybil, the real estate agent who Maggie liked so much, but it was impossible to talk to her because every time she tried, Edgar grabbed her hand and said, "Look at me. Look at me. Look at me."

Then the bus driver announced there was a traffic accident ahead blocking four lanes, which just seemed cruel to Maggie. There was never traffic on this section of the Thruway. She tried to close her eyes, but Edgar pried them open with his fingers. "Are you okay, Maggie Dove? Are you okay?"

He smelled of Swedish fish and sweat and she felt something prickling at the back of her throat, but she forced herself to imagine the embarrassment on Edgar's face. She would not be sick. She would dissolve into a puddle of acidic stomach juices before she would throw up on her favorite child.

Maggie was, however, first off the bus when they finally arrived at the orchard, narrowly beating out Ambrosia Fletcher, who did throw up. And then, finally, they were surrounded by rows and rows of apple trees. The air smelled fresh and sweet.

Sybil, the real estate agent, offered to take Edgar with her son and get them started. "Give you a little time to catch your breath, Maggie D."

The woman was a saint. One of Maggie's favorite people in town. A big-hearted friendly girl who drove a Bentley and seemed to sell all the real estate in Darby. But Edgar wouldn't go with her. "I won't leave, Maggie Dove," he said, and so she staggered forward, praying for help. She hated to bother God with issues of nausea, but this one was important. Finally, she began to feel better, and she began to enjoy wandering among the trees.

Maggie liked the apple trees, which seemed so unobtrusive and low to the ground, and yet burst with this miraculous fruit. She'd always wished Adam and Eve got into trouble over a chestnut tree, leaving the apple out of the picture. Of course, all Edgar wanted to do was climb the tree and throw the apples to the ground, and they were only half an hour into this trip and she was feeling exhausted. Had he been her own child, she would have tugged him into a corner and hissed at him, but you couldn't yell at someone else's kid, could you?

"Come, let's stand like soldiers," she tried, which didn't work exactly as she had planned, but got him off the tree.

"Edgar," she said. "You're killing me. Could you calm down just a little bit?"

"Maggie Dove," he cried out, barreling into her.

Just then a cluster of kids came over and Maggie hoped for a moment they were going to join him. Beyond Ambrosia Fletcher, who he abused, he didn't seem to have any friends, she realized, but now one of the group stepped forward and said, "Is this your grandma?"

"Yes," Edgar said.

Maggie didn't correct him. There was nothing worse than a fact-checker in a conversation. So many good conversations were built around lies, she thought.

"How come she has a different name?"

"I'm on his mother's side," Maggie said, which was the truth.

"How come your mom didn't come?"

"She has to work," Edgar said, but she noticed he stepped back toward her. His normal bravado had vanished. The parents were all off chatting a few trees away.

"My mom works but she was here today," one of the girls said. "She always tries to make time for me when something's important."

"Prioritizing," another kid said.

"Where's your dad," a different kid asked. Edgar didn't answer. He just leaned back against her.

"You don't have a dad, do you?"

"Now that's enough," Maggie said. "All of you. You're being unkind."

But they were relentless.

"You don't have a dad. You just have a grandma and she's not even your grandma."

Maggie tugged Edgar away from there, suddenly understanding why he had been so eager to get off the school bus. It hadn't occurred to her that he would be a child kids would tease. She had always worried that he would be the bully, what with all his energy.

"Oh Edgar," she said, crouching down, hugging the poor little chick whose eyes were filled with tears. Then, swooping onto them was Sybil, tugging along her son, who'd been in the back of the pack. "You apologize now," she said to him; he looked down at the ground.

"Come on," she said. "Don't be this type of boy."

"I'm sorry," her son said.

Sibyl then linked her arms with Maggie's. She was a big, strong woman and Maggie suspected she could have carried her through the orchard, which she sort of wished she would have done. "Come on, we're going to pick these apples together."

Soon enough Sibyl's good nature lifted everyone. The boys got on together well, and Maggie and Sibyl stood there watching them play.

"I'm sorry," she said. "I've spoken to Lester about this teasing."

"I wasn't even aware it was going on."

"You know how it is. Anyone different."

Maggie did know how it was, she just hadn't realized that Edgar fell under the category of different, and there was a lesson for you. He seemed so smart and cute and energetic to her, and she loved him for all those qualities. It hadn't occurred to her that other people might not feel the same. She supposed she also hadn't realized how rambunctious he was. Put Edgar next to a bunch of other six-year-olds and you realized his wildness.

"I don't know how they figured out that not having a father here bothers him so much. There are plenty of kids who don't live with their fathers, but they only pick on him. They have a sixth sense. Monsters."

"I had no idea. I'll talk to Helen. Maybe she can arrange for his father to come on a field trip." Though even as she said it, she realized she had no idea who Edgar's father was. Helen never spoke about him.

Fortunately, the teachers began teaching the kids a lesson, and Maggie and Sibyl were left alone for a bit. They began talking about the party at Stern Manor and

Domino's death. Sibyl had been there too, of course, and had seen Domino fall.

"I didn't want to go. That place is cursed."

"How do you mean?"

"Don't you know, Maggie? To think you're a lifer. I guess it's one of those things everyone assumes people know and so no one talks about it."

Sibyl patted around her shirt absentmindedly. Maggie remembered how she'd stood on street corners when she was a young woman, smoking cigarettes. Old habits were hard to break.

"That house has a terrible history. Haunted, and I don't mean just on Halloween. I mean the real deal."

She brushed back her blonde hair and smoothed down her shirt. She was a laughing girl, a person who brought joy.

"Why?" Maggie asked. "What happened?"

"You know how a lot of people in Darby were connected with the Underground Railroad?"

"Of course," Maggie said. "I have a hiding spot in my house where the escaped slaves hid on their way to Canada."

"Right, right, right, I forgot. Well, Stern Manor, or as it was then, St. Clair Manor, was built in 1843. Some woman with a lot of money. I don't know how she got it, but she built an extensive cellar in the house and became involved with the Underground Railroad. However, the railroad was built on trust—secrecy doesn't exactly breed responsible oversight—and this woman was evil.

She took the slaves in, then she held them. In her basement. For years. Until one day, one of the slaves set a fire. I guess he figured he'd rather burn to death than live in that cellar any longer, enduring God knows what went on down there."

Maggie remembered the scar of black smoke in the basement. Surely Domino knew the cellar's dark history and yet she chose to sit down there.

Sibyl shivered. "Supposedly there's the ghost of a slave who stays in that house. She wears a white shroud and cries for her daughter. Oh, Maggie, why would someone do something like that—and why would anyone want to live there? That house has been cursed. I can't tell you how many suicides took place there. Quite honestly, I think that's why the Harrison family sold Leonard Stern the house. They never had much joy living there. The oldest son died and the wife got sick. Terrible place."

"Hold on a bit. What do you mean the Harrisons owned it? I thought that house had been in the Stern family for generations."

"No, Leonard Stern wanted people to think that. All lord of the manor."

Sibyl bit into an apple. Juice ran down onto her shit and she laughed. Maggie thought if she bit into an apple like that her teeth would fly right out. "No, Stern didn't buy that place until after World War II. My father sold it to him. Harrison had fallen on hard times, with his son killing himself and all. Started gambling. He needed the money, but I think he was glad to get out of there."

"How did he kill himself?"

"Cyanide, I think. Anyway, there he was and there was Stern with his new war bride. So, Harrison moved out, and he got the family settled in a nice, small place he could afford, but things kept going wrong for him, and then young Tim ran into trouble with the law and fast forward…here we are."

"Tim Harrison, the garbage man, grew up in Stern Manor?"

"He was quite a hottie," Sibyl said. "He and Domino had a thing, actually. But she was ambitious. She didn't want to marry a home-town boy."

"Domino and Tim Harrison dated?"

"In high school. Yes."

Tim Harrison, whom she ran into all the time at D'Amici's deli, was a nice quiet man who always had a dog tucked under his coat. He rescued strays and carried treats for dogs or cats. Maggie'd never actually spoken to him. He had the damaged look of a man who'd seen too much trouble when he was young. But she thought him kind.

"Is he the one the whole voodoo doll incident was over?"

"Crazy, right?"

"It is crazy," Maggie said, though she wasn't that surprised. That was the thing about living in a small village, so many connections. People changed and evolved over time, but their roots went deep.

The boys started running toward them. Sibyl sighed and stood up. "I'll tell you the truth, when I saw

Domino falling, and I saw that woman in white, even though I knew it was Racine, I thought it was that ghost come to take its revenge. I thought the house itself killed Domino."

Chapter Seventeen

Maggie Dove went home and took a long hot shower. She needed to wash all the apple juice off her skin, and hair. When she was done, she changed into a fresh pair of black pants, a white shirt and a soft gray scarf. She put on some blue eye shadow and pink lipstick. She thought, when she examined herself in the mirror, that she looked thinner. She hoped being sick all morning had worked off a few calories. She was considering the possibility when Kosi jumped on the counter, knocking over her bottle of skin cream.

"It's not bad enough," she pointed out to him, "that you're vicious, but you're also emotionally needy. It's a bad combination."

Offended, Kosi jumped off the counter and bolted downstairs, his tail twitching as he ran. Maggie followed him, heading toward the kitchen, thinking that so long as she'd lost weight, she might as well have some bread pudding. But before she got to the kitchen, she stopped to look at the spot under her staircase that had served as a hiding station for people on the Underground Railroad.

It had always been a source of pride for her that her family, the Civil War-era Leighs, had helped with the Underground Railroad. She'd felt proud thinking of how they'd hid fugitive slaves right in this very house, helping them journey on to Canada. Part of why she had stayed there after her daughter died was because she felt the house had good karma. Brave people had stayed there. To think of someone imprisoning those slaves who had already been through so much was horrifying. It was evil.

She kept coming back to that, the evil that wound its way through Domino's life. Why would she choose to sit in a cellar where such hateful things had been done? What dark passions did she draw on? One of the joys Maggie had always felt in her faith was that she believed it brought her into contact with goodness. She associated with people who wanted to do good with their lives. Sometimes they succeeded and sometimes they didn't, but they always inspired her.

She couldn't understand the pleasures of evil, and yet she knew they were all around her. Not long ago, she'd seen a bus with an ad on it that said, *Tap into your dark side*. Why? she wondered. Why would you want to?

Was it possible that Domino had tapped into something evil that had come out and killed her? Could the house itself have drawn Domino to her death?

Houses did have atmosphere. She remembered once Sybil decided she should consider moving into another house and the two of them spent a day visiting places. You could tell the moment you walked into a home whether people had been happy there. Maggie's own house, she thought, had a sort of weary happiness to it. She hoped people who visited felt happy here, in her home with all her books and maps and comfortable seats. What comforts did Stern Manor offer? Could it be haunted? And if it was, what was she supposed to do about that?

Detective Grudge was silent on the issue of investigating ghosts who might have commit crimes.

An image came into her head of that broomstick and all that implied.

Maggie settled herself on her couch, and opened her computer. It was only early afternoon. She figured she'd watch a half hour of Detective Grudge and then head to the office. She clicked on the video and the sound came up, the jazzy trumpet and shivering symbols. Detective Grudge arrived in his Maserati, got out of the car, looked into the camera and said, "To understand the present, you must know the past."

Dear God, she thought. How had he managed to express the exact thought she'd been having? It was like the way her minister had spent years preaching about forgiveness and neighborly love throughout her whole siege with Marcus Bender, and the moment he died, she stopped talking about that. Maggie had noticed something similar when she wrote mysteries, a long time ago. When her mind was focused on an issue, it cropped up everywhere.

He went on to talk about how important it was to understand everything about a suspect. "Your ability to delve into a suspect's past and uncover secrets will be key to how successful you are as a private investigator."

He made sense, she thought.

She had to believe that whatever caused Domino's death had its roots in the past. Couldn't be coincidence that she was only home a brief time and then she died. Some hateful spirit from the past. Or some hateful living person. Had Domino not died in such a public way, Maggie would have been positive she'd been murdered. She had enemies, her sister first and foremost. Maggie couldn't imagine Racine arranging such a spectacular death. Though the bottom of the balcony had been obscured from view by the railing. She thought Joe might have had a point when he said a Roomba caused Domino to fall. But that brought her back to Racine, and Maggie knew that she could not accuse Racine or murder. No matter what happened. They had one client who kept hiring and rehiring them. She could not go to jail. Agnes would murder Maggie, in that event.

No, she had to find another candidate and figure out how he did it. Lucifer, for example. He might well want to get rid of Domino.

She'd start by calling Lucifer, though the idea of it gave her pause. Phones made her nervous. There was something presumptive about them in the way a text wasn't. Plus, Lucifer was a rock star. She'd never spoken to one. But she had his number. Racine had given it to her. She tried to think of positive things as she waited for him to pick up. She thought of her cherry wood table, which she loved.

"Hello," he said. He had a slight British accent.

"This is Maggie Dove," she said. "I'm a private investigator and I need to talk to you."

Chapter Eighteen

Stern Manor looked sullen. The pumpkins had begun to melt and spread. Their smiling faces had stretched into grimaces. The balcony was boarded shut, crime scene tape whipped around in the wind. The temperature had dropped 30 degrees, the sky was gray, and the river behind it was gray too. Little brown waves rippled through it like sharks. Maggie parked her TT, got out. The instant she closed the door, Racine came running out of the house.

"You're here," she said. She seemed to be getting thinner and thinner, Maggie thought. Her eyes were actually sinking into her head.

"Don't let him manipulate you," Racine said, as she beckoned Maggie into the house. "You have your questions prepared? You're ready?"

"I'm ready," Maggie said. She'd spent the whole night preparing for this interview. She'd read up on his Lucifer's background, which was surprisingly unremarkable. His mother was a school teacher and his father a builder. He grew up in a small town in England, but even as a young boy he'd felt drawn to the dark side of things. She'd found an old school photo of him from when he was Edgar's age, and he looked like a young version of his Gothic self. He formed a band called The Shards. They had a hit and another hit. He married Domino, and their antics always seemed to keep them in the news. Maggie was curious to talk to him because he seemed more persona than person, but then Domino had been like that too.

"Remember," Racine said, "he's not going to think it's a suicide. He certainly wouldn't want the world to think she was unhappy. He's going to try to convince you that it was an accident. Just remember that. And you'll write up a report later, right, since I'm a gold star client?"

"I most certainly will," Maggie said. "How is your mother doing?"

"Not well. Not well. She's taken to her bed. She won't be satisfied until this is all resolved. We're depending on you." Racine's eyes glowed with a furious light. Could these be a killer's eyes, Maggie wondered? Perish the thought.

"Where is he?"

"He's in the library," Racine said, and led her down the long hallway she'd been through before, but this time they went left. The same tile pattern carried through on the floor, and looking at it more carefully now, Maggie could see it was a throne interlaced with a star. The walls were richly paneled, every single detail of the house carefully chosen, she thought, and underlying it all, the screams of the people who had died here.

They came to a heavy wood door, closed. Racine knocked.

"Maggie Dove is here, Lucifer," she called out, and then she darted away, as though frightened.

Maggie stepped into the library, which was stunning in its opulence. It smelled of leather and old paper. Light shone in through the window in beams, picking up the dust, like a searchlight. The cherry wood shelves were lined with books, but they weren't the sort you would actually read. They looked like they might shatter if you picked them up. And there, in the middle of it all was Lucifer Raines, rising gingerly from a leather chair, an old copy of *The Brothers Karamazov* in his hands. The gold lettering on the leather cover glinted.

"Ha," she said without thinking. "I'm reading that too."

"Are you?" he asked, in a gentle British accent. "Which translation?"

"I don't know. The one you get for 99 cents from Amazon."

"Sorry," he said. "I'm a bit of a snob when it comes to my Russian translations. A purist you might say. But it does make a difference."

"I suppose so," she said, sitting down in a leather chair across from him at his invitation. Her feet did not quite reach the floor, but she crossed them and hoped he wouldn't notice. He had a cup of tea next to him, and he'd draped a shawl across his legs. He did not, on the face it, look like a man who would stand on a balcony and urinate onto a fan's head.

He asked if she'd like some tea, but she didn't want to put him to any trouble because she could see he was shattered. She recognized the stance of grief so well. The rigidness in the jaw, the shoulders clenched, the tentativeness of the gaze, as though not quite certain what was coming next. It brought her back to her own deep grief, to a memory she'd forgotten of how her friend had given a gift certificate for a massage soon after Juliet's death. The masseuse, after working on her, asked if she'd been in a car accident.

"No," she'd answered, puzzled.

"That's the only other time I've ever seen a spine so clenched," the masseuse had explained.

Whatever Lucifer had done or not done, Maggie thought, his grief was sincere enough.

"Someone told me once that everyone has a favorite brother."

His eyes gleamed a little. "Ivan, of course. How could I not like the brother who talks to the devil?"

"The one who argues that evil is subjective."

"Yes, that people do what they wish without any regard for morality. And let me guess, Maggie Dove. I imagine that your favorite character is Alyosha."

"Of course," she said. "How can I not love someone so pure hearted. Though to tell the truth, I love them all. Sometimes when I'm reading it, I imagine they're all my Sunday School students."

How funny, she thought, how books could connect you to another person. She'd gone there expecting to dislike Lucifer, and yet it was impossible to dislike someone who read the same books you did.

"Even the father? Lucifer asked. "You could imagine him in your Sunday School class?"

"Perhaps not him. And not Grushenka either. She scares me." For much the same reason as Domino had, she supposed. Such unbridled passion.

He laughed. "I had a Sunday School teacher like you when I was a boy. Not one of her successes, I'm afraid."

"Sunday School teachers are a forgiving lot. After all, we're all sinners."

"Do you really think that?"

"I had a minister once who liked to say that the only people who went to church were sinners. I've always liked that."

He was quiet for a moment. She wanted to speak, but held back. Detective Grudge said that silence was the most important part of an interview. Their silences were when most people spoke most eloquently.

"This book belonged to Domino," he said. "I felt I needed to read something she enjoyed. I can't let go of her yet."

"There's no reason you should. You hold on to her for as long as you can."

He ran his hands through his hair. His long hair was pushed back off his head and dyed dark black, and he had a dramatic widow's peak. He should have been ugly, Maggie thought, but there was something in his expression that drew you in. There was something vulnerable about him, in just the same way Edgar seemed vulnerable when he got into trouble. Something childlike. A man who needed to be protected.

"I'm sure Racine told you that she hired me to find out more about what happened. She feels like there are people in this village who believe she killed Domino."

Lucifer shook his head. "That's ridiculous. No one killed Domino. I read the autopsy report. It's quite clear her death was accidental. Unless you're suggesting I gave her the ergot, that I put it on the broomstick."

"Even if you did," Maggie said, "I don't know how you could know she would go over the railing." She paused, thinking that if he was guilty, he'd feel compelled to offer an explanation. But he didn't.

"Do you think it's possible that Domino wanted to kill herself? Could her death have been self-inflicted?"

"No," he said. "She was happy."

He ran his finger up the spine of the book. Long fingers. Was he a witch too? she wondered.

"She was happy in her marriage?"

"Yes, very."

"It was an…unusual marriage," Maggie said, feeling a need to be diplomatic. She supposed "unusual" was as good a word as any to describe living with your wife and your mistress.

He looked up at her. He had the face of angel, she thought, the same sweet details, the soft eyes and the thin lips. But there were also parts of him that made her think of the devil. Just like Ivan. Good and bad.

"She was an unusual woman," he said.

"She never felt jealousy?"

"About Passion?" he asked. "Why should she? I wasn't going to leave her. There were no boundaries between us. What I wanted, she wanted. What brought me pleasure, pleasured her."

He said it as though he were saying that he would have milk with his tea.

"That flies in the face of everything I know about human nature," Maggie said.

He laughed. "Perhaps you know the wrong humans."

Leaving aside the mechanics of the whole thing, she simply could not imagine her husband, Stuart Dove, coming home and saying he wanted to bring another woman into their relationship. She would have been terribly hurt. It would have suggested to her that she alone wasn't good enough for him. She would have felt embarrassed. Plus, she simply could imagine how that conversation would begin. "*By the way…* "

"Are you planning on marrying Passion now?"

"No," he said decisively. "I'll never marry again."

He shrugged. His eyes closed slightly. She thought of what Detective Grudge said in his episode on lying, that it's almost impossible for a liar not to give himself away. He will blink, fidget, sweat, have dry mouth. Lucifer was doing none of those things. Oddly enough, as she thought about it, the only person who had exhibited that behavior was Racine.

"Does Passion know you don't plan to marry her?"

"Yes," he said levelly. "I never lie. I've been very open about my expectations."

The house suddenly shook with the rattling noise of a train going north. The only disadvantage to living on the Hudson River. Washington Irving, who'd lived only a mile or so north, had fought hard to stop the train from coming, but hadn't succeeded. Always hard to stop the onslaught of a train. She thought of Domino again. Of the way she'd kissed that girl and bit her lip. Of the look on Passion's face when she left the room. Whatever expectations Lucifer had of Passion were not necessarily the same ones Passion had of him. There were parts of human nature you couldn't eliminate no matter how much you wanted.

Suddenly Lucifer seemed to slump. All the energy went out of him as though he were a balloon losing air. The exhaustion of grief, she thought. The weight of being upset all the time.

"You must be tired," she said. "I won't keep you much longer, but there is one bit of information you can help me with. Is there anyone Domino was having an argument with?"

He smiled at that. "There were many people. Domino had a strong personality."

He looked down at a ring on his hand, a striking black onyx ring.

"Maybe somebody who cropped up when she came back to Darby," Maggie asked. "Someone she hadn't seen in a while."

"There was Grant Winfrey," he said.

Maggie started. She hadn't actually expected him to come up with anything. She wrote down his name in her notebook.

"Who is he?"

"She knew him from school. I think they were having an argument about the coven. She told me not to worry about it, but he came by the house."

The man on the lawn, Maggie thought.

"Do you have any idea where he is?"

"He's a doctor, I know that much."

"Okay, I can find him," she said.

Always ask one last question, Detective Grudge said. You never know what may turn up.

"Just one last thing. When was the last time you saw Domino?"

He leaned back in the leather chair. "I saw her just before she started up the steps to the tower. She was magnificent," he said. "She was beautiful. We…," he cleared his throat and looked at Maggie. "We were intimate and then she gave me Charlotte and went upstairs."

"Why did she give you Charlotte? Why didn't she bring Charlotte upstairs with her?"

"I don't know," he said.

"Didn't she take that tarantula everywhere with her?"

"Yes," he said, closing his eyes, keeping them closed for a moment. "That's true."

"But she might not have wanted to take Charlotte with her if she thought she was going to kill herself. She might not have wanted to kill her too."

"Yes," he said, frowning. "That's true."

"Where is Charlotte now?" she asked.

"I don't know."

"How do you mean?"

For the first time in their conversation, Lucifer looked disconcerted. He began running his hands through his hair.

"Domino gave Charlotte to me, and I was holding her, but then Domino fell and I must have put Charlotte down. I forgot all about her."

"You mean to say that there's a tarantula roaming around Darby."

"Yes," he said, and bit back a laugh. "Domino would have loved that."

He was right, Maggie thought, after she ended the conversation, as she tiptoed outside, watching very carefully where she planted her feet.

Chapter Nineteen

"There's a tarantula wandering around Darby?" Walter Campbell sputtered.

"Unfortunately," Maggie said, and went to hang up the phone.

"Just a minute. Did I not make myself clear? Did I not tell you to leave this situation alone?"

"It's not a situation, Walter. It's a case. My case. This is my job. And I suspect your job is to find that tarantula."

"But…" he started to say, and this time she hung up the phone. She truly did not want to deal with any more angry people, and she had to write up her first gold star report for Racine. She noticed then that the red light on the VCR was blinking. The teddy bear video camera must be picking up movement in Racine's room. Probably Racine. She hadn't had a chance to look at the tapes yet, but she made a note to watch them later.

Maggie pushed Walter out of her head and focused on writing a detailed account of what she'd done, and she added in an action plan for the next day. She would hunt down Grant Winfrey and see what he had to say. She even added in Detective Grudge's quote about the past. She was just about to send it to Racine when the phone buzzed. It was her minister.

"Maggie Dove. Would you come up here please? I'd like to talk."

Oh God, Maggie thought. What had she done? She'd not been called to the minister's office for ages. Not since setting the church on fire, but that was long ago and a complete accident and had more to do with the state of the church's oven than anything else. She supposed this time it must have to do with the upcoming Dining Out Club. She wondered if Reverend Sunday was concerned about the logistics, or perhaps worried people might not come. Maggie was worried people might not come.

The Bronx was unfamiliar, the Ghanaian food was unfamiliar and Reverend Sunday was unfamiliar. A few people had switched churches since her arrival, trans- ferring membership to churches they described as tradi- tional. Maggie had no plans to switch churches, but she was getting her bearings herself. The minister played such an important part in her life that it was always an adjustment getting used to a new one, and Reverend Sunday was different. No question.

But Maggie did want to get to know better and she certainly wanted to help her, and so she dropped everything, brushed her hair, brushed her teeth, put on lipstick, and headed up the hill to the minister's office. On the way she passed Tim Harrison at D'Amici's and made a note to herself to stop and talk to him later. She passed by Trudi at the candy store and waved. How she wanted a Snickers bar, but she knew once she gave in, that would be the end of it. Every day was a struggle with her weight. She wasn't fat, but she could stand to lose a few pounds, and every so often she did lose a few pounds, and then she got so excited she had a big meal and she gained it right back.

As she always did when she saw her church, Maggie felt comforted. Here had her parents been married; here had she been baptized and then her daughter baptized, and then buried, as well as her husband and someday she would rest here too. This was where she belonged. Automatically she looked up at the steeple, which was always a beacon for her. How different it was than the terrible tower from which Domino fell.

She found the minister and the church secretary reviewing a box of donuts that D'Amici delivered every day. That man was providing nourishment to the entire village, though he was also engorging them with calories.

"Ah, Maggie Dove," Reverend Sunday said. "Chocolate glazed?"

"Thank you," she said. It was pointless to resist, and she felt slightly relieved. Nothing too terrible could be coming if a chocolate glazed donut was on the table.

"Come into my office."

The reverend wore a soft gray suit that hung loose on her. Her hair was tightly pulled back into a braid that twisted around her head, and she wore stockings and sensible pumps. She always wore suits, always looked ready to go to the hospital or lead a funeral service. She was ready, Maggie thought. A woman who was ready for anything.

The room soothed her. On the desk was a picture of a beach that she assumed was from the reverend's home country of Ghana. She knew, only because the reverend often referred to it in her sermons, that Ghana was a beautiful country located in sub-Saharan Africa. It was also a country struggling with the AIDs crisis and Reverend Sunday had left there after most of her family died of the disease.

Maggie noticed Reverend Sunday was reading *The Screwtape Letters* by C.S. Lewis. She smiled at the sight of that old red book; one she'd not picked up in a while.

"No one has ever spoken more profoundly on the topic of evil," her minister said.

"I haven't read it in years" Maggie said, as she settled into a hard-backed chair across from the reverend's desk. She supposed the reverend didn't want to encourage too much conversation or she'd be at it all week.

"You should." Sunday opened the book to a passage she'd underlined. "I've always liked this: 'She's the sort of woman who lives for others—you can tell the others by their hunted expression.'"

Maggie laughed. It wasn't what she was expecting. "I hope I'm not one of those horrible women. I always worry."

"Not you, Maggie Dove." The reverend flipped forward. "This is the passage I think of when I think of you: 'Courage is not simply one of the virtues but the form of every virtue at the testing point, which means at the point of highest reality.'"

Maggie felt profoundly touched. She barely knew this woman, and here she was giving her one of the nicest compliments she'd ever received. "Thank you," she said. "Though I have to confess, I had no idea how much courage life would require. I certainly didn't choose this path. Anyway, I don't know if I've done anything as courageous as leaving my country behind and starting a whole new life somewhere else."

"Of course you have, Maggie Dove. Isn't that exactly what you've done with your detective agency? Isn't that a new country for you?"

"I hadn't thought of it that way, but I like it," Maggie said.

A chocolate glazed donut, a wonderful compliment and spiritual support. She felt energized. She felt empowered. She was ready to go. She would call Grant Winfrey. She would talk to him. She would not be afraid. She got to her feet, and was just about to leave when Reverend Sunday said, "Sit back down, Maggie Dove. There's something I wanted to talk to you about."

"All right," Maggie said, sitting.

"What do you think of Walter Campbell?" the reverend asked.

It was the absolute last thing Maggie would have expected her to say and she suspected her jaw dropped.

"As a man?" she answered. Was it that obvious, she wondered? She liked him, but she certainly had no intention of having an affair with him.

"As a Sunday School teacher."

"I've never seen him teach," Maggie said, "but I would assume he's very serious and thoughtful about the subject."

"Yes," Sunday said. "Serious and thoughtful. You describe him very well."

She sat quietly then.

Maggie glanced across the desk at a photo of several people who all looked like Sunday, standing on a vast plain, which must be in Ghana.

"This is a delicate subject. I hesitate to raise it, but I believe I can trust your discretion. We've had some complaints from some of the parents about Walter Campbell."

"I see."

"No one doubts his seriousness, of course. But he is not always sensitive to the children's needs." She sighed. "We live in strange times, Maggie Dove. When I was a girl, I was expected to listen to the minister. I was to memorize the verses of the Bible. I was not to question. But now, here, in America, we expect our children to be more outspoken. We want them engaged. Not to put too fine a point on it, there are parents who are threatening to leave the church is Walter continues to teach the class. Walter's struggling and I would like you to help him."

"You want me to teach the confirmation class?"

"I'd like you to co-teach it. You don't mind working with Walter, do you? My understanding was that you are friends."

Maggie had been raised to believe that if a minister asked you to jump, the only possible response was to ask, "How high?" So, there was no question in her mind that she would do what the reverend asked. But she had to voice a mild protest.

"He's not going to like this," Maggie said. "He's a proud man and he's going to feel betrayed."

"I know," the reverend said. "That's why I've chosen you. If anyone can do this tactfully, it will be you, Maggie Dove. I'll call him later today and explain."

That's going to have to be one heck of an explanation, Maggie thought, as she trudged out of the church. Walter would be so upset, and she couldn't blame him. He was not a man who bent with the times. Not a man who bent, period. But he was a good man, and that should count for something. She felt awfully low as she headed toward Main Street, and she was surprised to find Mercy Williams walking toward her, scowling.

Automatically Maggie smiled. "How are you?"

"You think it's funny, do you?"

"What," Maggie asked.

"It's you," Mercy said.

"Yes?"

"You're the one who told the superintendent that I should be looking for a tarantula. You're trying to get me killed, Maggie Dove."

Chapter Twenty

Maggie sensed disaster was about to rain upon her head, but meanwhile she had a job, and the only thing she could think to do was go back to her office and figure out how to find Grant Winfrey. He was her great clue and she wanted to pursue it. Detective Grudge had all sorts of advice for tracking down suspects, but Maggie thought she'd try putting his name into 411.com. There he was, on Broadway in Yonkers.

She jotted down the address and phone number, and wrote down a list of questions, starting with, *How did you know Domino?* Building up to, *Why were you skulking on her lawn?* She'd come up with five questions when she saw Agnes walking down Main Street, holding a heavy box. Maggie got up to open the door, and when Agnes entered, she saw the box was filled with bowling trophies.

"Are we sponsoring a league?" she asked.

"No," Agnes said. "I want to have some gold in this office. People are more likely to hire us if they think we're winners."

"Winners at bowling?"

"People don't care what you've won, Maggie. They just want to know you can win." She set three of the trophies on top of the bookshelf, and turned them slightly, so that the bowling ball was less obvious. "What have you been doing to keep us solvent?"

Maggie told her about her interview with Lucifer and how Grant Winfrey's name had come up and that she was planning to call him. She explained that she'd seen him lurking at Stern Manor and that Lucifer said he and Domino had argued. She went on to say that she'd come to think that the answer to what happened was in Domino's past, and she wanted to research it.

"When are you going to call him?" Agnes asked.

Agnes was not a person who believed in giving a lot of positive reinforcement, Maggie thought, but perhaps that was only natural. Agnes had worked for a superstar corporate mogul, who had married her and then died, leaving Agnes all her money, but Maggie suspected the mogul had also left Agnes with an understanding of the harsh rules of corporate America. She demanded perfection, which was fine, if you were perfect. Maggie would have to learn to deal with this attitude. She couldn't get upset every time Agnes yelled.

"Call him now," Agnes said. "Let's get this show on the road."

So Maggie called, and got his receptionist, and asked if she might speak to him. Maggie told the receptionist that she was a private detective and wanted information about Domino Raines.

"Just a sec," the secretary said. "I'll connect you."

She put Maggie on hold. Classical music came on. Maggie waited for a minute and then the receptionist was back. "He said no," she said, and hung up the phone.

Stupidly, Maggie sat there. She noticed streams of high school students heading down Main Street. There must be a program at the park.

All Maggie could think to do was call the number again, but this time the receptionist said that he was busy and couldn't talk.

There was no point in calling back.

"What are you going to do," Agnes demanded.

Maggie considered stopping by the bakery and getting a scone and then going home and to bed, but she suspected that was not the answer Agnes was looking for.

"I could go down there. To his office." She looked around at all the bowling trophies, which seemed to mock her. "Though it seems sort of late. It's past four o'clock."

"In what country is that late?" Agnes said. "Get going and you'll get there before they close."

"But they know my name now. The moment I say it, he'll clam up." She shouldn't have been so direct, Maggie thought. She should have just gone down there in the first place.

Agnes sat across from her at the table. She clasped her hands together and locked Maggie into her gaze.

Heat seemed to come off her. Agnes didn't have big eyes, but they were focused. Concentrated.

"We're private detectives, Maggie Dove. We're not bound by the same rules as the police. They don't know what you look like at the doctor's office, and there's no reason you have to tell them your real name. You can make up a name. Tell them you're someone else. Why don't you pretend to be Estrella Watson and say you're with a pharmaceutical company and you want to sell him drugs? That will get you in."

"But I don't have any drugs to sell."

"All you need is to get in the door. Once you have him alone, then you can ask him what you want."

Just then Helen slipped in. She had a knack for appearing out of nowhere. You thought she was in Syria and next thing you knew she was sitting right alongside you.

"What do you think would be a good undercover name for me?" Maggie asked.

"Estrella Watson," she replied.

"What?" Maggie said, startled. Things were getting too spooky. There were tarantulas in town and ghosts at Stern Manor and Helen could read her mind.

Helen laughed. "The window was open. I heard you two. Pick something that feels natural," she said. "What about Mary?"

"Maybe a little obvious," Maggie said.

"If you don't' want to say you're a drug rep, why don't you say that you're with the FBI?" Agnes suggested.

"You're doing a background search on someone. People will always talk to you if you're with the FBI."

"Won't they want to see a badge? Isn't it a crime to say you're with the FBI if you're not?"

"Now you're just thinking of problems," Agnes said. "Your job is to think of solutions."

She had a point, Maggie thought. She didn't want to be negative. She tried to think. "I like the idea of saying I'm doing a background search. Maybe I can say I'm with the IRS. That wouldn't be a crime, would it?"

"Now you're talking," Agnes said. She began rustling around in her bag and pulled out a billfold. Then she snapped it open to reveal a silver badge. "Use this if anyone questions you. If they want ID. No one looks at these things too closely."

"Okay," Maggie said, putting it in her own pocketbook. A fake identity, a fake badge. Oh God. "Then I think I'm going to go."

She hoped someone would stop her, and tell her this was all too much for her and she would be better off going home and reading. But no one did. "All right then. I'm off."

Helen was on her phone, but she gave her a thumbs-up sign. Agnes smiled. "Don't screw this up," she said.

"Love you, Mary Dove," Helen called out as Maggie walked out the door. "Hey, why are there bowling trophies here?"

"Okay," Maggie said to herself. She was about to go on her first undercover mission.

Chapter Twenty-One

I n her previous life, when she was young and hopeful and foolish, Maggie wrote mysteries. She'd had
some success. She'd had to come up with charac-
ters, of course, and as she drove south on Broadway,
she thought that coming up with an undercover identity
should be no different. If she was going to go undercover, she would do it right.

There was no need to be Estrella Watson. Why not
choose a name she liked. Beth. She'd always thought
a pretty name. Beth Hawke. She would be 61-years-
old, because why not make herself a year younger? She
would be with the IRS, but the head of a division. She'd
give herself a nice cat, one of those fluffy ones that sat
on your lap and purred. She piled on backstory as she
drove south on Broadway. Perhaps someone in her family had won a lottery a few years ago. There was bad
feeling. Relatives jealous. Beth tried to be a peacemaker.

Maggie drove south, past the construction that had
been going for ten years, past the quaint houses of north
Yonkers with the incredible views of the Palisades,
sheer cliffs of rock that dropped off into the Hudson.
No vegetation grew on them, and there was something

hypnotic about knowing they looked just the same as they had for centuries, when the earliest inhabitants lived here. Soon enough, Broadway became congested. The views were blocked by apartment buildings, pawnshops, check cashing places, and then blocks of brick apartment buildings, and in one of them was Grant Winfrey's office.

She parallel parked and got out of her car. Two men were standing by the adjoining gas station.

"Nice job," one said.

"Thanks," she said. Beth Hawke was a good parker. Her brother raced cars and he taught her how to park.

Maggie strode into the doctor's office and there she found a scene out of *Dante's Inferno*. Patients were everywhere. They were sitting and standing and crouching and kneeling and reading and whispering. Most of them were old. Most of them looked like whatever was going on with them was bad. At the hub of it all was a receptionist, and Maggie walked up to her. This must be the woman she'd spoken to.

"Hello," she said. "I'd like to speak to Dr. Winfrey."

"Do you have an appointment?" She was a middle-aged woman with a stain on her shirt, not something you usually saw at a doctor's office. There were Post-it notes all around.

"No," Maggie said. "But I'm happy to wait."

"What is this about?" the receptionist asked, but then the phone rang, and she grabbed up a Post-it note and began writing things down, and then a nurse came by and waited, arms crossed, and the receptionist got flustered and hung up. "Did you get the information?" the nurse asked her.

"Yes, yes," the receptionist said. Maggie figured every office had an Agnes, and she thought she might do better sitting for a little bit and waiting for things to calm down. An older woman limped off and Maggie swooped into her seat. She looked around, wondering, as she did so, what you could deduce about a man from looking at his office. *Pay attention*, she could hear Detective Grudge muttering.

This doctor had a lot of magazines. More than usual. Maggie was of an age where she spent a fair amount of time at a doctor's office and she knew the general list they had, and this far exceeded that. But what did it mean? Grant Winfrey had varied interests or he had Boy Scouts in the family. He overbooked his patients, that was for sure. Was that because he was greedy or compassionate?

There was a water stain on the ceiling. She had the sense that the doctor was overwhelmed. She'd noticed that often receptionists were the face of the doctors. The receptionist had a photo of three children on her desk. They looked young, and Maggie saw no wedding ring on her hand. For a moment she was tempted to go home and leave this poor soul alone. She remembered how overwhelmed she'd felt when she had a young child and she didn't have to go to work…but right now there was Racine to think about. Racine had concerns. Plus,

Maggie was a private detective. She went back to the desk.

"Yes," the receptionist said, clearly not recognizing her at all. "How may I help you?"

"I'd like to speak to the doctor," Maggie said.

"What's your name, please?"

She was on the verge of saying *Beth Hawke*, when all of a sudden, a different idea occurred to her. "Would you tell him my name is Mary Stern? I'm a relative of Domino Raines."

She almost shivered with the thrill of it. Saying a name that was not your own felt heretical, and exciting. She remembered the look on her husband's face when she wore a red dress one afternoon, pushed the books off his desk, and pounced.

"Mary Stern," the receptionist repeated.

"Yes, and please tell him I'm related to Domino."

"You don't look like her," the receptionist said.

"You knew her?" Maggie asked, before realizing how foolish the question was. Domino had been a celebrity.

Behind her a crowd of patients watched her in that half-awake state people go into when they're at the doctor's. No one was reading through the magazines. No one was on their phone. This was a serious sort of doctor's office. One of those places where you were not going to get a happy diagnosis. The phone started to ring again and when the receptionist picked it up, her whole face went red. "I told you not to call here," she said, and slammed down the phone, and then the nurse

popped her head and asked where were the charts, and
the receptionist looked at Maggie and snapped, "If you
were related to her, wouldn't you know if I knew her?"

Maggie didn't get upset. She could see the poor
woman was under stress, and there was no point in
adding to her burden. Maggie fell back on a trick she'd
learn to use in Sunday School when she had an unruly
student. She forced her eyes to twinkle.

"I work with someone like that," she said. "She's on
my case all the time. No matter what I do, she finds fault
with it."

That was actually true, Maggie thought. Always
best to draw on the truth. Maggie noticed her nametag
read Tami.

"They should really hire an assistant for you, Tami.
This is more than any one person could do."

"Right," the receptionist said. "Nobody could be
expected to stay on top of this. The patients just keep
coming and coming and I ask for help. They say they
don't have enough money. But how is that possible if
there are all these people here."

"Malpractice insurance?" Maggie tried, which was
something she knew doctors talked about a lot.

"I don't know," she said. Her phone started to ring.
She looked around, lifted the handset and slammed it
back down.

Tami took a breath, wiped her nose with her hand
and looked at Maggie. "She was here. Your cousin,
Domino. A few days ago. She was a piece of work."

"What did Domino do this time? I'll tell you, she wasn't easy to have as a relative. Always doing something."

"Right."

One of the patients wandered up. "Do you know when the doctor will be ready?"

"Just ten more minutes," Tami said, waving him back to his chair. "First of all, she came slamming in here. Didn't say a word to me, just went right into his office. I got in a lot of trouble for that. Thought I'd lose my job right then and there."

"They couldn't possibly fire you," Maggie said sympathetically. "What would they do with all these phone calls?"

"Right," Tami said.

"What day was that?" Maggie tried.

"Last week. Let me see. It was the day of the audit. No. It was the day they had spinach on special and it was $2.99. No, that was Thursday. No. no. no." She wagged her finger. "It was Tuesday. Because that was the night Dylan got the Tic Tac up his nose. You wouldn't have thought that was possible. Yes, it was Tuesday."

"Did they start to argue? I know they were having an argument about something, and my cousin has a temper."

"No, she stayed pretty calm. It was the doctor who was yelling."

"Excuse me."

They both jumped. Maggie peered into the eyes of a woman who looked like she'd seen it all and hadn't approved of most of it.

"May I help you?" the nurse asked.

"I was waiting to speak to the doctor," Maggie said. "My name is Mary Stern."

"Mary Stern," she repeated. Maggie felt confident she knew it was a made-up name. "I'll tell him you're here," she said. Then she looked at Tami. "Would it trouble you to answer the phones?"

"No ma'am," she said and rolled her eyes and Maggie went back down to sit. She hadn't been sitting long when she noticed a man wearing a white coat walking quickly by the window, presumably to his car.

She ran up to Tami. "Is that the doctor?"

"Yeah," Tami replied. "Hey, where's he going?"

"Thank you," Maggie said, and dashed off. She wasn't fast enough to catch him. He got into a Hyundai, and without even thinking about it, she ran to her car and pulled out after him. A day of firsts, she thought. Her first undercover assignment and her first surveillance. Anyone would think she was a private detective.

Chapter Twenty-Two

Maggie followed Dr. Winfrey up Warburton Avenue. It was a two lane-road, the traffic slow. She made sure to keep a few cars between them. She was doing okay. Even the lights were going her way—fresh green after fresh green. Only one stale red light, and it didn't last long. Best thing was that she was familiar with the area, so if he turned and confronted her, she could tear out of there. She kept an escape route in her mind at all times.

Her only concern was that she was driving a bright red Audi TT. There was no question it was the type of car a person might notice, which was why she bought it in the first place. The detective in her mystery series, Inspector Benet, was the sort of man who liked flashy cars and she absorbed his habits. Some of them.

Maggie figured Dr. Winfrey was heading home. She planned to follow him to his house, then ring his bell. She couldn't imagine he'd slam the door on her. One of the advantages of being Maggie Dove was that people did not slam the door on her.

But to her surprise, he veered off on to the Saw Mill Parkway. Now the pursuit became a little trickier because the road was empty. She trailed back as far as she could. There weren't many exits, so she didn't have to worry that he was going to disappear. She kept following until he turned onto the Cross Westchester Expressway. Now she began to feel more flustered. Following somebody onto a major highway felt like more of a commitment than following them onto a road. She began to feel nervous, but excited too. She wondered where he was going. What if he was going to Canada? How far would she follow him?

To her relief, he got off at exit 5. Maggie was on familiar territory here. She followed him past the bowling alley, which was surprisingly expensive. Maggie once had a birthday party there for Juliet and was stunned when the final bill came to $300. Some little friend had insisted on ordering French fries for everyone, which had added $100 to the total. It was a great party though. Now that she thought about it, she might still have trophies from that party. Then past the County Center and into White Plains proper and past the sign for the DMV, and then she followed Dr. Winfrey to a small parking lot tucked into one of the side streets.

He got out of his car. He was a tall man, with graying hair and he bent forward slightly as though pushing a weight. Fortunately, he didn't turn around. Maggie waited a beat for him to move on ahead. She wasn't concerned. This was a place she knew.

There was a bookstore right near here where she used to buy Sunday School supplies. She hadn't been there in a long time. Just ordered it all online now, but she'd spent many happy hours in that store, looking for presents for Sunday School teachers and treats for kids. So many stickers! She followed Dr. Winfrey through the passageway, walked out on to Mamaroneck Avenue, and he was gone. She saw lots of people, but no Dr. Winfrey. He had to be here! There had to be a reason he'd driven to this spot.

There was the Sam Ash store, where her daughter had bought a guitar a long time ago. A Mexican restaurant. A bar, another bar. Maggie kept walking. It was getting chilly. The sky was darkening. It was past 5:00 and the sun was starting to set. The end of Daylight savings time was only a few days away; one of the most depressing times of year, as far as Maggie was concerned. She felt tired. A day that began with interviewing Lucifer Raines and hunting for a tarantula and ended with following a stranger was a long day. But she kept walking, hoping to see him. Once she started a task, she liked to finish it. She walked past the bookstore and was surprised to see it had changed its name. Now it was called Celestial Delights. It was a pagan bookstore.

She paused for a moment to look in the window. There were all sorts of books laid out dealing with witchcraft. There were shimmering wind chimes and a little black cat that peered out at her. And as she looked more closely she noticed Dr. Winfrey, talking to the clerk. They both turned toward her, and then away. Maggie took a deep breath and went inside.

Chapter Twenty-Three

The store smelled of incense. Maggie jumped when the door slammed shut behind her, the bell jingling loudly. The clerk and Dr. Winfrey both nodded at her, and she nodded back. Then Maggie walked to the rear of the store. She figured Winfrey would walk back there and she could talk to him then. A perfect location for a brief interview.

There were more candles than she'd ever seen in her life. Narrow candles with strange words on them. She picked up one that showed an angry face. "Orisha" it read. "Enforces divine justice." The next one was yellow and red. "Burn for fertility," it read. Maggie imagined Domino browsing there, looking for what? Was there a candle that could make someone do what she didn't want to do? Was there a candle that could make Racine give her money?

The door chimed and she saw Dr. Winfrey had left.

She was about to chase after him again, but stopped. He knew she was following her. He'd nodded to her. Maybe she would do better to get information here. The sales clerk could tell her about Domino. She might be more talkative.

So Maggie picked up one of the candles and headed toward the counter. It was a green candle with black writing on it, larger than the other ones there.

"I'd like this one," she said, setting the candle on the counter.

The sales girl started. "No, you can't have this one."

She started to pick up the candle, but Maggie got her hand on it first. "This is the one I want."

"It's not for you," she said. She looked frightened. Maggie looked at the candle, which looked innocuous enough.

"This is a store that sells candles and I want this candle."

The young woman began tugging at her necklace. Maggie noticed a name on it. Perhaps she should try a different tack. "Lily, is that your name? I mean you no harm. Why can't I buy this candle?"

"I'll get you a different one," she said. She yanked the candle out of Maggie's grasp and put it in a cabinet and locked it, and then she led Maggie back to the candle section. She scanned them for a moment and then picked up the red and yellow one. For fertility. "This is a good one," she said.

Maggie saw no other candles there like the green one.

"I thought I saw a candle like that green one at Domino's house, when I was there."

"You knew Domino?"

"Oh yes," Maggie said. "For a long time."

"I've never seen you at the meetings."

"I go to different meetings," Maggie said. Well, that was true enough. *Always keep a lie as close to the truth as possible*, Detective Grudge had cautioned.

"I saw her burning a candle very much like this on the night she died."

Lily began shaking her head. *"An' it harm none, do what thou wilt,"* Lily mumbled. She had long bangs that made it impossible to see her eyes.

"Did Domino want to harm someone?"

"That would violate the main law of our faith," Lily cried out.

Maggie remembered what Domino had said at the party; that there were white witches and black witches. That there were people who wanted to impose their will on others, and people who felt that wrong. It made sense, Maggie supposed. There was no community of people that existed without disagreement.

"Did Domino want to do something she wasn't supposed to do?"

Lily began gnawing at her lips, and just then the cat jumped next to her. Her face softened a bit. Maggie bent over to stroke the cat, relieved that, unlike her own cat, it didn't scratch her.

"What's his name?"

"Issbia," she answered, elongating the word as she spoke, so that it came out more of a soft hiss.

"I have a cat too. His name is Kosi. Not as friendly as this one, though."

"Is he a familiar?" she asked, peeping up at Maggie, curious.

"What's a familiar?"

Lily looked taken aback. She brushed her hair out of her eyes.

"You don't know?"

Another customer walked in, nodded at Lily and went over to a corner table to look around. Lily seemed emboldened by his presence, spoke a little louder.

"It's a spirit that takes the form of an animal. Issbia was given to me by my grandmother after she died. She gives me advice. She helps me when I'm in trouble. She's always with me."

"How could I tell if my cat was a familiar? As opposed to just a cat?"

"Does he assist you with your work? Does he speak to you in your dreams? Is he there when you need him?"

"No," Maggie said. "Quite the reverse. He's more of a hindrance, I'm afraid. I don't think he likes me."

"Someone may have sent him to spy on you, then. Do you have an enemy?"

Maggie puzzled about that. Did she have an enemy? She'd had an enemy last year, when a man had tried to kill her, but he was in jail. She would have considered Marcus Bender her enemy, but he was dead. She supposed Domino was her enemy. It was hard to say. She'd felt hatred coming off of Domino but wasn't sure it was directed at her. Was it reasonable to suppose that Domino had inhabited her cat's consciousness? The thing was that Kosi was miserable long before Domino entered the scene.

"I might," Maggie said.

"I can show you a candle to help keep peace in the house."

She noticed the other customer had moved toward a curtained area in the back section of the store. Maggie caught him staring at Lily, nodding slightly, and then he slipped behind the curtain. He had a crooked face, and a sharp beard. Something more was going on in that store, Maggie thought. Something sinister, but did it relate to Domino?

Maggie knew she had to press this girl, though the idea didn't come easy. She didn't like to force people to do what they didn't want to do. She favored more of a slow and steady approach, though that generally took about fifteen years. She'd have to be more assertive.

"You know, I think I'm just going to stand here and think for a moment," she said. "There are so many choices. I want to choose wisely."

Lily looked at her closely. Maggie assumed her most innocuous gaze. She fluffed up her hair a bit, tried to channel Miss Marple and look wooly. It must have worked, because Lily left her alone and went back to the counter, and then the man came out from behind the curtain. He looked at Maggie for a moment. He was not so easily duped by her Miss Marple imitation, she suspected. She could almost feel him looking right into her soul. He gazed at her fiercely. But then he moved on.

He stepped up to the counter and began whispering at Lily.

This was the only moment she'd have.

Quietly as she could, Maggie headed in the direction of the curtained door.

She looked toward the counter. She couldn't see them, so she hoped that meant they couldn't see her. There might be security cameras, but this store seemed decidedly low tech. Quickly as she could, she stepped into the room. In front of her were an array of green candles, just like the one she'd tried to buy. There was no time. She picked one up and stuck it in her bag, and then she stepped back outside the curtain, almost slamming into the man who'd watched her before.

She couldn't move. But she had to. She pressed forward, toward the counter, and dropped two twenty-dollar bills by the cash register.

Then she dashed out the door. She walked as fast as she could toward her car, looking back every so often, terrified that she might see that crooked face looming behind her. She got into her car and raced back to her house, but she left the candle outside. She would figure out what it meant, but she didn't want it in her house.

Chapter Twenty-Four

Maggie didn't want to be alone in her house that evening. All this darkness was making her jittery. She wanted light and laughter and someone congenial. She decided to call Helen. Perhaps she could stop by and show Helen the candle. Helen spoke several languages. Perhaps she'd see patterns in these letters. If nothing else, she'd listen to Maggie's story.

It was past dinner hour, and dark outside, but Maggie suspected Helen would not be bothered if she called. And in fact, the minute Helen answered the phone she said, "Maggie, I've just been thinking about you. Why don't you come over for dinner?"

"Now? Don't you need time to prepare?" She couldn't help herself. Sometimes she sounded like her mother. "I mean," she added, "I always need to psyche myself up before a party."

"It's not a party, Maggie. It's you. Just come on over."

"Of course," she said.

Helen laughed. "The times they are 'a-changing.'"

Maggie laughed. "And not a minute too soon."

"I'm making fajitas," Helen said.

"Even better."

Helen was a surprisingly good cook. She didn't have a huge repertoire, but the things she made were always tasty and unique. She'd toss in an unusual ingredient that you'd never think to use. Cinnamon in beef stew, or chili peppers in a meat loaf. One small change made a huge difference. Another life lesson, which, reminded Maggie, as she drove over to Helen's, that she needed to talk to her about what had happened at the apple orchard. She'd been trying to find the right moment, but there was always a commotion. Plus, it was not an easy conversation, asking a person who the father of her child was, especially when the person so clearly didn't want to say.

Helen lived in a small gatehouse on a big estate. It was a sliver of a house, made of stone. In fact, Maggie thought, as she pulled into the driveway, the stone could have been cast off from the granite used on Stern Manor. Maybe the original owner had given it to some of her workers. That didn't exactly fit with what Maggie knew of her character, but people were complicated. The cruelest were capable of great kindness, and the other way around. The odd thing was that although both homes were made of the same material, the vibe was completely different. Stern Manor was cold and imposing; Helen's house warm and inviting.

She kept electric candles in her windows and they glowed all the time. She had a wreath up on the door with sprigs of heather in it. She still had her Halloween pumpkins out. Somehow, she'd managed to stop Edgar from smashing them, and they were neatly carved with faces of bunnies and cats and dogs.

Maggie had to pause for a moment to admire the house and to say thanks that this was a place to which she was invited. *I'm loved here*, she said to herself, and to Juliet, who she always imagined listening along. Whether the thought was true or not, it was a comfort. No sooner had she said her prayer that Edgar came blasting out of the house.

"Maggie Dove. Maggie Dove. I'm working on a LEGO space ship. Will you help?"

"Of course, she'll help you," Helen said, coming out to kiss her hello. "Maggie Dove is always there to help a desperate mother."

She wore her trademark black sweater and jeans and she had a kerchief around her hair. But Edgar must have put his hand in the flour as Helen made dinner, because she had two white handprints on her shirt. "He's up to step 133," she explained. "But there are 600 more to go."

"I would love to," Maggie said, because she did truly love LEGOs. "But first I have to tell you about what I've done."

She told Helen everything, about how she'd followed Grant Winfrey to the pagan bookstore and then talked to Lily and then took the candle. Maggie grew more and more impressed with herself as she kept talking and Helen's response was everything Maggie could have hoped it'd be. When she drew the candle out of the bag and put it on the table, Helen clapped with pleasure.

"Oh, Maggie Dove," she said. "You are invincible."

"I know," Maggie said, sipping some of the wine Helen handed her. "I feel ridiculously proud of myself. Never could I imagine doing such a thing."

"You're a natural private detective," Helen said. "You're good with people and you're curious and you're brave."

"I'm curious anyway."

"I'm serious, Maggie. That took bravery. I do a lot of things." She looked over toward Edgar, who was making piles of red and white LEGOs. "I see a lot of bravery and cowardice and I want to tell you that was brave."

She clinked her glass with Maggie's.

"I will accept the compliment," Maggie said. "Now, would you look at this lettering? Does it mean anything to you?"

"Maggie Dove," Edgar started to wail. "Maggie Dove. I want to build LEGOs."

"Hold on treasure, I'll be right there."

"They're runic," Helen said, running her finger over the lettering, "but I don't know what they mean. Tell you what I'll do. I have a friend who's a cryptologist. I'll ask him to look at this, if you don't mind lending this to me.

"Thank you," Maggie said, "but I don't want to distract your friend if he's trying to discover the secret to world peace, or some such thing." Helen never talked about where she worked, but Maggie knew it was something serious. One call from Helen had gotten them their private detective license, and one time Maggie had googled Helen's name, and the minute she clicked on it, it disappeared. But now Helen just laughed.

"Not to worry. Edgar has time on his hands. Not young Edgar, I mean. Old Edgar."

Maggie looked over to Edgar, who seemed to have fallen asleep, using the LEGO instructions as a pillow. "Is that who you named your Edgar after?" Maggie whispered.

Helen's eyes sparkled. "You can't work your magic on me, Maggie Dove. My secrets stay with me."

"I'm good at keeping secrets," Maggie said. She wished Helen would confide her. This young woman was holding a lot to herself and Maggie worried it was wearing her down. She had no family she spoke about, and no friends that Maggie could see. She certainly had made no friends among the first-grade parents.

"Sorry Dove," she said, but there was no harshness in her voice. Still, Maggie couldn't help but wonder what it was about Edgar's father that troubled her so. She wondered if he could be someone famous. She assumed Helen hadn't married him and she wondered if that was the source of her hesitation. Maggie wasn't a prude, but she knew she came across that way.

"Helen," she said, looking again at Edgar, who looked like an angel when he was asleep. "You don't need to tell me anything. But you should think about talking to Edgar. He might need to know."

"He's being bullied, you mean."

That surprised Maggie. She'd just assumed Helen didn't know. "The teacher called you?"

"Yeah."

Helen drank some more of her wine. "I'm sorry for that, I know it's tough being bullied. But he'll have to deal with it. There are bullies in this world, and you have to learn to be strong."

"That's a hard lesson for a little boy."

Maggie looked over to Edgar, who snored gently, mouth open. Helen got up and covered him with a blanket.

"Life's hard. I don't need to tell you that, Maggie Dove."

"No, though I've always been appreciative that I had people like you, to soften things a bit."

Helen poured the last of her wine into the sink. Then she sat back down at the table with Maggie.

"You asked me, when this whole thing began, if I believed in evil. I didn't answer you then, but you should know this about me: I do believe in evil."

She looked over at Edgar and smiled slightly.

"I grew up Holcomb, Kansas. Does that ring a bell?"

"That's where *In Cold Blood* took place."

"Correct. My mother was friendly with the Clutter family, with the older of the sisters, the one who survived because she wasn't home when the murderers came. Not that it mattered. It destroyed her life. I was fascinated with that murder growing up. Maybe because it touched people I loved. People came up with all sorts of explanations for why those two men did what they did. Broken home. Sexual orientation." She shrugged. "I'll tell you what I believe. I believe they were possessed by the devil. No normal human could have done what they did, and because of that, I decided to devote my life to fighting evil. All over the world. It's a hard road, Maggie Dove, and it's lonely and the sooner you get toughened up for that, the better.

"I love Edgar with all my heart, but he is not going into this world defenseless. "

Chapter Twenty-Five

That night Maggie's dreams were violent. She dreamed of blood and witches. She kept seeing Domino falling and then rising up and then falling. After the third time jolting herself awake, Maggie decided she'd be better off sitting in the living room. She'd have a cup of warm milk and sit and read. Except that in *The Brothers Karamazov* she was up to the scene in which Ivan talks to the devil, and she was feeling inundated with witchcraft, and so she set the book aside and just looked out the window.

Most of her view was taken up with the oak tree on her front lawn, which had had a growth spurt. There was a metaphor for you. It had been savagely attacked last spring, and now it bloomed and flourished. Unfortunately, right now it sounded like it was clawing at her window. A sharp breeze had come up. The oak tree kept tapping. Kosi was restless, roaming around, pouncing into corners. A train went north, screaming on the brakes. She could see a bit of the rising moon above the tree, hovering.

Maggie pulled a blanket up around her and tried to rest, and then her phone rang. She jumped, grabbed it.

But no one was there. She pressed star six nine, but it said the number was private. She looked at the phone, waiting for it to ring again, but it didn't. Still, her heart kept pounding. She imagined the man with the crooked face, knowing that she would be up and waiting for his call. Trying to frighten her.

All the events of the day swam before her. Her meeting with Lucifer. She'd come away from that confident that he was truly grieving, that he was not involved in Domino's death. But now she wondered if that was so. She thought of Dr. Winfrey, who seemed too inept to be truly dangerous. Though there was something going on at the pagan bookstore. And then there was Helen, who she loved like a daughter, who was keeping an important secret from her son. Maggie knew there was nothing worse than getting involved in another person's parenting, and she'd heard what Helen said about evil, yet she'd always believed it more important to be truthful.

But then how well had she protected her own daughter. On a night like this, it was impossible for her to keep her guilt from rising. Perhaps she had coddled her. Had she been stricter with Juliet, then perhaps she wouldn't have gone to that party. Or she wouldn't have taken up with Peter Nelson in the first place. Had she only been able to protect her. She began to cry. It was all so much, these highs and lows. She missed Juliet so much. And she missed her husband. She wanted her old life. She wanted to do what she knew how to do.

Kosi tiptoed over. He sat down alongside her. Automatically she stretched out her hand to pet her and he scratched her hard.

"Damn you," she cried out, and ran back to her bedroom. She closed the door. It was enough. He scratched the door, but she pulled the pillow over her head. She had no patience for him. She didn't want him. Finally, she slept, and she had a happy dream, and in some ways, those were the worst of all. Because you had to wake up. But she did wake up, and she had some cereal and a lot of coffee. Kosi sat on the couch, eyeing her, unrepentant. The phone rang and she thought it might be Agnes asking her where she was. She knew she was late for work, though they didn't punch a clock.

It was Walter.

"Maggie   Dove.   Please   come   to   my   office immediately."

"Is everything all right?"

He hung up.

So Reverend Sunday must have spoken to him about having her sub. He was going to have a tantrum. Perfect. Well, let him. It wasn't her fault that he was so inflexible. The 1950s were a long time ago and it was pointless to try to go backwards. While she dressed, she had an entire imaginary conversation with Walter, planning what she wanted to say. But as she started for the door, Kosi pounced in front of her. She assumed he wanted to get in one last swat before she left. But no, he had something in his clutches. She looked down at it, uncertain what she saw.

It was Charlotte, the tarantula. She'd followed Maggie home.

Chapter Twenty-Six

Maggie put the tarantula in one of her Tupper-ware containers. She used spaghetti tongs to pick it up. That spider had weight.

Then she put the Tupperware container into a Stop & Shop bag, so she wouldn't have to look at it, and she set out for the police department. She hoped that Walter would give her a little slack on the subject of Sunday School since she'd faced down a tarantula, though with Walter it was hard to say. He was just as likely to argue that the tarantula would never have found her had she not become involved in the first place.

Mercy Williams looked suspiciously friendly when Maggie got to the police station. She kept smiling even when Maggie handed her the bag and told her what was in it.

"What should I do with it?" Mercy asked.

"I would call Lucifer. He might want it back."

Then Maggie set off down the hall to talk to Walter, who she assumed would be sitting dejectedly at his desk, but not so. Walter stood right by the door and lunged at her the moment she walked in. On a good day he looked like Frankenstein, but when he was angry, as he was now, there was something almost pre-historic about him.

"Sit down," he growled.

He sounded so preemptory she was tempted to flop right down on the floor, but she got hold of herself and made her way over to the desk. She certainly hadn't expected him to be this upset. Perhaps Reverend Sunday wasn't as tactful as one might have hoped.

"I'll come right to the point," he said. "I've had a complaint against you."

"Against me!" Maggie said. She felt her jaw open and snapped it shut. "For what? By whom?"

"Grant Winfrey filed a harassment report with the police. He said you'd been following him."

"Oh dear," Maggie said. She started to laugh. "Oh dear. I'm sorry. Oh dear, I guess I was following him, but I'm a private detective. I have that right, don't I?" That was what Detective Grudge said, anyway. She'd taken careful note of it. The chief reason for law suits against investigators came out of rough shadowing, from surveillance conducted in an offensive manner, or by embarrassing someone. None of which she'd done.

"You are not allowed to follow someone if you make him feel unsafe," Walter said.

"He felt unsafe because of me?"

Walter didn't smile, but she thought he saw his lips tip up just the teensiest bit. "Why were you following him?"

"Because he wouldn't talk to me."

"Why did you want to talk to him?"

"I told you. Racine hired me to find out more about the circumstances of her sister's death. I know she and Winfrey had words and I wanted to ask him what that was about."

Walter put his large hands across the desk. Hard to remember that only last April, he'd hugged her to him and whispered, "My dear." Hard to understand why he was always so agitated over everything she did.

"And I told you that the matter of Domino Raines's death is closed. The coroner ruled it an accidental death."

"And coroners are never wrong?"

"You plan to prove the coroner of Westchester County is wrong."

"I'm not planning to prove anything," Maggie said. "I have been hired to get information, and that's what I'm doing."

"Not with Doctor Winfrey, you're not. I told him you'd leave him alone."

She really, really hated being told what to do. It activated a reflex in her that went right back to her teenage years. She stood up.

"I am a licensed private detective and I have the right to follow up with any questions that I want. I'm not harassing him. I'm not embarrassing him in any way. It is my right."

"Maggie," he said.

"Walter, I'm tired and I'm stressed and I don't want to argue. I'll see you in class on Sunday." She started toward the door.

"What?" he said.

She turned around. For the first time since she'd known him, Walter Campbell looked unsure of himself.

"Reverend Sunday spoke to you, didn't she?"

"She called," he said. "But I wasn't in, and then when I called back, she was at the hospital with Gemma Jones."

"Oh," Maggie said, feeling flustered. She knew this would hurt him and she really didn't want to. All the excitement of the past few days was catching up with her. Her eyes were starting to close. She'd had no sleep. It had been a rough night.

"Is it something important?" he asked.

There was no point in beating around the bush. Nothing she said was going to make this palatable to him. "She asked me to help you out with confirmation class."

"But you don't teach the confirmation class," he said. "You teach the six-year-olds."

"I know. But you've got a big class and she thought you could use some help."

Maggie would have expected to feel triumphant, but she didn't. He looked so hurt. She realized how important his position was to him. Suddenly she saw him as the boy he had been, probably teased for his height, trying to do the right thing, always working hard and not understanding why he was so unpopular.

"I'm sorry, Walter."

"I suppose you suggested it," he said.

"No, I did not."

"I suppose you'll be doing arts and crafts with them. Baking cookies."

"Believe it or not, I do actually teach things. Some people think I'm good at it."

He crossed his arms. "When I was a boy, we had to memorize the entire long catechism. All 196 questions. We had to recite all the books of the Bible at our confirmation."

"I learned that too, Walter. But times have changed. We don't do that anymore."

"We should!"

She shrugged. She loved the old catechism too, especially the first question. *What is the chief and highest end of man?*

Man's chief and highest end is to glorify God.

We have to be a church of our time," she said. "We have to be able to speak to the young people of today.

He stared at her mournfully. "It's a cruel thing, Maggie Dove, to undercut another Sunday School teacher," he said, and he turned his back to her.

Chapter Twenty-Seven

The man was infuriating. Maggie burst onto Main Street, plowing right into Daisy Stanton, who asked her to sign a petition for a dog park, which Maggie signed, although she didn't have a dog and didn't actually care. Yet it seemed important in that moment for her to have her name on a list. She wanted to make a mark. She walked past the candy store, paused, and then decided to go in and buy a Snickers bar. Her anger would burn up the calories, she reasoned.

Trudi Branch excelled at candy. Her family had owned the shop for generations. Maggie suspected that some of the candy had been there for generations, and yet it still tasted so good. Trudi organized the candies in a haphazard fashion, and yet whenever you looked at the shelves, you saw just what you wanted. Periodically people came in and told her to arrange the candies alphabetically, but Trudi wanted no part of that. A very long time ago, when Maggie was a girl and Trudi's mother ran the shop, Maggie bought a Coke in a glass bottle and accidentally dropped it. She still remembered the shock of hearing the bottle crack. Her family'd had little money. Maggie had a quarter to spend each week, and if the quarter was gone, that was the end of it, and she always remembered how Trudi's mother swept up the glass and then gave her another Coke. Funny the way one small kindness could stay with you for so many years.

"What's making you smile?" Trudi asked. She handed over the Snickers bar without Maggie asking. She'd been buying the same thing for a long time.

"I was thinking about your mother," Maggie said. Trudi looked like a nurse, Maggie thought. She had warm gray eyes, soft white hair, and she wore a chain bracelet that jingled. You could always hear her coming.

"A long time ago, she gave me a free Coke. It was a small thing, but it mattered."

"It's only the small things that matter," Trudi said. "That's what I've learned from working in a candy shop."

"You should write a book," Maggie said. "You could call it: Everything I know I learned selling candy."

Trudi laughed, and her charm bracelet jingled.

"I was thinking about your daughter just now," Trudi said. "I always think of her when I open up a new box of Take Fives."

"I'd forgotten how she loved them."

"In fact," Trudi said, "I always keep one set aside, just for her. You'll think me silly, perhaps, but it's my way of remembering Juliet."

Maggie felt her eyes start to mist. "I'm glad to know you remember something like that about her. I worry sometimes that the only thing people do remember about her was that she died in a car accident. She was so much more, but she'll always be The Girl Who Died."

"Not to me," Trudi said. "To me, she's The Girl Who Ate Take Fives, and who stopped by occasionally to buy her mother a Snickers bar because she knew how much her mother loved them."

"Thank you," Maggie said. "I'll be smiling about that all day. And crying."

Trudi smiled with her.

It was so peaceful in the store, Maggie thought. That was the beautiful thing about living in a small town— you felt like you were always in the presence of ghosts, and that could be a very good thing. Sometimes when she walked the same paths she'd walked for decades, she felt the people she loved walking alongside her. There was a verbena bush near the river park where she absolutely always heard her mother. People suggested that she move away periodically, buy a condo in Florida, start a new life, but she never wanted to.

"There are good ghosts, aren't there?" she asked Trudi.

"Of course."

The sun diffused as it came in through the window, which reminded Maggie of Lucifer and the library. It occurred to her that Domino had asked Trudi for special candy.

"You were friends with Domino Raines?"

"We knew each other a long time," Trudi said. Her bracelet jingled as she picked out a bag of M&Ms and tore it open. She shook out a few into her hand. "I guess that made us friends."

"You seem like very different people."

"We ended up very different," Trudi said. "But we started off more similar than you'd think. We both went to Cranston."

"I didn't realize that."

"My mother felt strongly that a private school education was better than a public one. She took out a mortgage on the house to send me there. She wanted me to become fluent in ancient Greek, which I did, and I also became friendly with Domino."

Some kids came in from the middle school then, jostling around, holding their quarters. Some things didn't change, Maggie thought. Kids were always exuberant. They made a lot of noise. They traveled in packs. They could be cruel. She wondered what Edgar would be like in five years' time. She tried to picture it but couldn't.

Maggie noticed Trudi position herself so her hands were covering a jar of loose candies. She was gentle, but she was also shrewd. They lived in an affluent area, but that didn't stop kids from stealing. That reminded Maggie of something she'd read in the book on sin that the reverend had given her—that larceny rates were higher at religious seminaries than anywhere else. When the author asked why, the seminary dean said, "Because we all believe in forgiveness. We're not worried about punishment."

"What was Domino like when she was young? Maggie asked, after the kids had gone. "I don't remember her at all."

Trudi never answered a question quickly. She always thought about it, so when she didn't say anything, Maggie knew to wait.

"She was loud," she said. "She always liked sugar straws--the purple ones. Her teeth were always a little purple. She always had a boyfriend, sometimes two. She wore a leather jacket that she loved. She got it when she worked at the gas station. She was one of the gas girls."

"What was that?"

"They pumped gas. You'd drive in and they'd sashay out and pump your gas. I applied for the job but didn't get it."

"Just as well."

"She wasn't a good friend. I mean, she wasn't someone you could trust, but she was fun to be around. She always knew where the parties were. Which kids had the best basements. Where there'd be liquor. Who had the cool parents."

"She sounds so normal," Maggie said.

"That's just it," Trudi said. "If you'd asked me to come up with one word to describe her, I'd have said 'ordinary.' But then she turned herself into someone who was really extraordinary."

"Was that why she left? Because she knew she was extraordinary, but felt she couldn't be that way here? In Darby?"

"No," Trudi said, looking toward the window, Maggie following her gaze in time to see Billy Kim maneuvering on his hover board. He rode it right in the middle of Main Street. A parade of cars waited behind him, some honking, which was what had drawn Trudi's attention.

"She left because she was run out of town. After the incident with the poppet."

"The voodoo doll?" Maggie asked.

"Yes."

"What happened there? I've heard only rumors."

"Domino didn't talk about it, so I'm not sure I know the full story," Trudi said. She settled herself back on a stool, and gestured to Maggie to sit down herself. A great honor. Very few people were allowed behind the counter. The world looked so different when the candy was behind you instead of in front of you, Maggie thought. One of her Sunday School students came in just then, and started when she saw Maggie near the cash register. She giggled and ran out of the store.

"I cost you a sale," Maggie said.

"She'll be back," Trudi said. "Peanut M&Ms."

"So, the poppet?"

Trudi nodded. "Domino was dating Tim Harrison."

"I heard about that," Maggie said.

"I don't think she liked him that much, but she liked the idea of going out with him because he had lived in Stern Manor. She liked the twist of fate. I suspect she liked toying with him, hinting that if they were to marry, his family would be back at Stern Manor. She could be cruel."

"Yes," Maggie said, remembering how she'd bit Passion's lip.

"In fact, she was going out with someone else at the same time."

"Grant Winfrey?" Maggie asked.

Trudi looked startled. "You've heard of him? Yes. Grant Winfrey."

So Domino was romantically involved with that doctor. Somehow, he didn't seem like Domino's type, Maggie thought, but then she only knew the worn-out version of the man. Time hadn't been kind to Tim Harrison either, come to that.

"Tim broke things off with Domino because he fell in love with someone else. She was a sweet girl—Laura was her name, I think. Loved Juicy Fruit. Bought a pack every day." Trudi closed her eyes. "She wore white Keds. I always remember that because I wanted a pair but my mother wouldn't let me get them. Anyway, Domino just laughed when Tim ended things. She said he was a loser, but I didn't think she really cared. She had so many boys who wanted her."

Trudi paused. Maggie found herself wondering if Trudi'd had boys who wanted her. She had a daughter, so there had to be a boy in the picture at some point, but Maggie'd never seen a man associated with her—or her mother, come to that.

"Then one day this poppet shows up in Laura's locker. There was a pin sticking out of its neck, and everyone's saying that Domino put it there."

"Did she?"

"She must have," Trudi said. Her long fingers pushed around the M&Ms on the counter. "It was the sort of thing she would do, and yet when she found out Laura'd died, I felt as though she was really surprised. She laughed about it. Said she hadn't realized how strong her powers were."

"She didn't feel badly?"

"No, I wouldn't say it was in Domino's nature to be remorseful. Though I do remember thinking she looked afraid. I wondered if she just thought to scare the girl and hadn't planned to kill her. She left Darby not long after. Didn't even graduate. I didn't hear anything more about her again until she got a part in a movie in Hollywood. She sent me a postcard. Then she went on and married Lucifer and became herself. The woman she is today."

"Do you think she actually caused Laura to die?"

"I know she believed she did."

"What about Laura's parents," Maggie asked. Suddenly it occurred to her that if anyone had a motive for hurting Domino it would be them, but Trudi shook her head. "They died a long time ago. Killed by grief."

There wasn't much to say after that. Maggie could only imagine how horrifying it would be to lose a child in such a way. To think that someone intentionally wanted to take your daughter's life. The fear and anguish they would have felt. Trudi gave her an extra Snickers bar when she left.

"For free," Trudi said, and Maggie took it for the present it was, though she swore to herself she would not eat it for a month, and then she set out for the office, except that as she started to walk, she felt too buzzed and decided instead to walk a bit on the aqueduct.

This aqueduct was a long path that ran from the Croton River in Westchester down to Manhattan, but a part of it ran right through Darby. Once its pipes carried fresh water to the city, but now it was just a long and peaceful swath of green, large parts of it so covered with shrubs and vines that it seemed primordial. Many of Darby's great mansions backed onto it, and without precisely meaning to, Maggie found herself walking in the direction of Stern Manor.

No one else was around, though it was a clear, fine day. The leaves were falling in bunches. They crunched underneath Maggie's feet, but periodically there'd be one bright red one, underneath the dead ones, shining brightly. Some of the leaves looked as though they had lip liner around their edges, which made her think of Domino. She'd never liked that look herself. Thought it made you look like you were bleeding, or that you were artificially constructed, and perhaps that was the point.

Maggie kept on walking, past the old aqueduct markers. She always liked to touch them, remnants of an earlier time. Trudi's words rang in her head, old friends lost. So many losses and yet so much continuity as well. She walked past a little rock painted yellow in order to stop bicycle riders from flying over it. She kept going and soon enough there was Stern Manor in front of her.

From this angle Maggie had a more comprehensive view of Stern Manor than you could get if you stood in front of it, though from any angle it was a forbidding place. The thing that struck you most of all was just how big it was. It extended back further than she'd realized. There were windows piled on top of windows. She could see the windows of Madame Stern's room, noticed curtains blowing out of them. Underneath that was a cupola. The whole building made her think of a hive. There was life inside it but it was hidden and the house was designed to look secretive, she suspected. All the windows were hidden by cornices. It was impossible to look in. Dominating the whole thing was the tower. It seemed to off center the house, Maggie thought. But then it was a discordant sort of place. It wasn't balanced. That was the point.

As she looked at it, Maggie thought over all she'd learned about Domino in the last week. She kept coming back to the question that had started off everything. Was she evil? Had Racine been right when she came to Maggie's office and explained why she wanted her, a Sunday School teacher and private detective.

It was all so complicated. Maggie lived in the modern world and the modern world was full of reasonable explanations. People were abused, they were sick, they were damaged. There were so many reasons for why people did what they did, and they made sense. So was there something deeper underlying all this? Was there an exterior force that moved people to do harm? Maggie believed in a force for good, so how could she not believe in its reverse.

She stared at Stern Manor and thought of the people who'd perished in its cellar. A human being had chained up other people and forced them to die. Something dark and ugly moved inside that house and moved there still. Had that very force turned against Domino? Had she been murdered by the very spirits she revered.

Maggie shivered. Could she really defeat such a force? She was a 62-year-old Sunday School teacher suffering from anxiety and self-doubt. It seemed a lot to put on her plate. But she wasn't alone she thought, and that was a comfort. She wasn't alone.

Chapter Twenty-Eight

Maggie planned to spend Saturday getting ready for her Sunday School class. She needed to come up with something stupendous. Domino's son Milo would be there, as would Walter, and she suspected neither one would be easily amused. She set out a pad of paper, she got out the curriculum, she began to write out ideas and the phone rang. It was Racine.

"I'm sorry to bother you at home on a Saturday," Racine said.

Maggie never understood why people said things like that. If you were truly sorry, you wouldn't do it.

"No problem," Maggie replied.

Maggie also didn't understand why she said things like that, given that it was so clearly a problem.

"I just wanted to see how you're coming with today's report."

Maggie had emailed Racine a report for each of the last four nights, but she hadn't realized Racine expected one on the weekend too.

"It's only 10:00," Maggie said, hoping to keep querulousness out of her voice. No one wanted a whining detective. Detective Grudge certainly never whined. He grunted. "Nothing's happened yet," Maggie pointed out.

"What time will you get it to me? I know I'm being a bother, but I rely on those reports and the one you sent me last night was short. And late."

Maggie was tempted to say many things. She'd discovered a tarantula and been yelled at by Walter Campbell and a slew of other things that would not be appropriate to put in a gold star report. She was also tempted to point out that this was her first big job as a private detective, and she was doing the best she could do, and if Racine criticized her any more, she would cry. But she suspected that this was yet another matter in which it would be best to say nothing. No one wanted to hear their private detective suffered from anxieties. No one wanted to know that it had been a very long time since anyone had expected something more of Maggie Dove than that she show up and be pleasant.

"What are you doing today?" Racine pressed on. "What are your plans?"

Maggie looked at the pad of paper on her desk, the stacks of curriculum, the cup of coffee slowly cooling.

"In fact, I was planning to stop by Stern Manor to speak to Passion."

"She's not here today. She's gone into New York City. She's never been there before. Why, did she tell you she'd be home?"

"No. No," Maggie said. "Then I think I'm going to talk to Tim Harrison."

"Tim." Racine laughed. "The garbage man? What do you think he can tell you?"

Maggie wondered if Racine even knew about Domino's romance. It must have taken place in Domino's last year of high school, when Racine was living in France. The two sisters were separated by fifteen years. Racine had not come back to Darby until after Domino left. When you thought about it, Domino and Racine had probably not been together for close to fifty years. What must it have been like for Racine to come back from France with her sister accused of murder and her father dead, because his death had come soon after the scandal?

"They were close when they were young," Maggie explained. "I'm hoping he can help me understand her."

"You think that what happened to Domino had its origins in something that happened that long ago."

"Her death happened less than two weeks after she arrived home for the first time in decades. Maybe that's a coincidence, but it seems unlikely. I think something happened."

"Okay," Racine said. "So when will you get me the report?"

"Six-thirty" Maggie said, which was as good a time as any to do something that she hadn't planned out at all.

"I'll be waiting."

She wasn't worried about finding Tim Harrison. There was no garbage pick-up on Saturday, so he could only be at D'Amici's. She'd talk to him and write up a report. She supposed she should change out of her pajamas, in that case. Her pajamas were like her regular clothes. Black pants, black top and a white shawl, but they were all softer. She went to her bedroom to put on her clothes. It had gotten chilly, a more normal version of November weather. She was just trying to decide between heavy black pants and middle weight black pants when the phone rang. She hoped it wasn't Racine again, and it wasn't.

It was Leona Faraday.

"Everything's a disaster," she said.

"What is it?"

"Have you looked at the menu for that Ghanaian restaurant?"

"Not yet."

"There are cow hoofs on the menu."

"That doesn't mean you have to order them. I'm sure there's something with rice."

"You know, there's a nice church up in Tarrytown that has a Dining Out Club and they're going for Italian food. Right in Tarrytown."

"That's nice, but we could do that any day of the week. Where's the adventure in it?"

"May I speak frankly?"

Which was another expression Maggie was not wild about. She would rather someone asked if she could speak kindly. "Leona, you can speak frankly, but it's not going to change anything. Reverend Sunday has chosen this restaurant. She's excited about it. She wants to introduce us to her culture. To not go would be an insult. We will just have to attend, taste the food and be pleasant."

"Well," Leona said. "You've become a different person since being a private detective.

"I hope so," Maggie said.

She went back to getting dressed. She fluffed up her white hair and put on her pearls. She hadn't had breakfast yet, but she figured as long as she was at D'Amici's she'd get a bacon and egg sandwich. She was looking forward to that when her phone buzzed again.

"Yes," she said.

"Hey, Maggie Dove," Helen said. "Do you have a minute?"

"Always," she said, and sat back down. She kept a careful eye on Kosi as she sat. He'd been quiet since she shut him out of her room last night, but she didn't trust him.

"Everything okay?" Maggie asked.

"I don't know," Helen said. "I've been thinking about that tarantula. Don't you think it's odd that it showed up at your house?"

"I just figured it followed me."

"There are 6,000 people in Darby, more or less. Why would it follow you?"

It was a reasonable point. "I suppose I was so dumbfounded to find a tarantula in my living room that I didn't stop to think about what it meant."

"I think it's a warning," Helen said.

"About what? I haven't done anything."

"You must have."

Maggie was dumbfounded, though it made sense. She knew something and didn't know what she knew. Why else would someone put a tarantula in her house? She felt frightened. She'd been to a witchcraft store; she'd followed a strange man. What if there was a coven after her?

Helen said, "You don't have a security system, do you?"

Maggie eyed Kosi. "Nothing formal."

"I have some friends I can get hold of. Let me bring them over. We'll get the house wired up. We'll make sure you're safe."

"It seems like a lot."

"You're precious, Dove. Anyway, why take chances?"

Indeed, Maggie thought. She didn't go out the rest of the day. She spent the afternoon with the men and women who showed up with Helen. She was fascinated by the transformation in Helen when she was with her co-workers. Normally so exhausted and beleaguered, with her cohorts she was dynamic and confident. It made Maggie realize how much of a toll Edgar was taking on her.

When they were done, Maggie's front door looked like a launch pad. Red lights beeped. "Just remember to put the code in when you get back in the house. And if anyone is holding a gun to you. ..well, that won't happen," Helen said.

"You have a code in mind? Helen asked.

Maggie was going to use "Juliet." That was the code she always used, but something different seemed called for. She typed in *Grudge*.

Only then did she remember that she hadn't sent Racine a report. It was 6:24. One minute to go. She typed up a one-line report: *Big news coming! Will send more information tomorrow*. That seemed reasonable, Maggie thought, as she stood by her computer, wondering if Racine would respond. Nothing. That was good news, wasn't it?

Chapter Twenty-Nine

Maggie could see that Walter wasn't in a happy frame of mind when she walked into the confirmation class. He seemed to be doing an imitation of a very large sulking child. He stood up as soon as she arrived, moved from the head of the table to sit at her right hand.

"This is the teacher I was telling you about," he said.

"Good morning," she said to class.

They eyed her. One girl smiled. She was head of the Girl Scout troop, God bless her. One of those sweet good-natured children. The rest of them looked at her suspiciously; Milo, Maggie noticed, was engrossed with his phone.

This was the closest she'd been to Domino's son. He was so thin and pale as to give off a blue aura, his veins adding the one true color to his frame. Under his eyes were bluish streaks. His long fingers fidgeted, reminding Maggie a little bit of the tarantula and its wandering legs. He wore a black suit and a thin black tie; she wasn't sure if he wore it for mourning or fashion. More than anything, he seemed isolated. Although every person in the class was hyper aware of him, although he had a circle of girls around him and probably always would, he seemed very alone. Without his mother, he would be lonelier still. Maggie wished she could reach out to him, but they were hardly on the same level. She was a middle-aged Sunday School teacher and he the coolest boy ever to walk into her class.

She knew everyone else there, although of course she'd known them as six-year-olds, which was a completely different proposition. Then they'd been enthusiastic and wanted goldfish and juice and hugged her and now they looked at her warily, except for Walter, who looked at her implacably, as though hoping she would fail. One thing Maggie knew for sure was that no matter how cool kids were, they liked to have fun. So, she brought out a secret weapon: her box of crayons.

"I'd like to get to know you a bit, and I wonder if you would do this for me. Pick a crayon that speaks to you," she said.

"Speaks to you," one boy repeated. Gemma's son, she thought. When he was six, he had such separation anxiety that his mother had to hold his hand all during class.

But he chose a color. Black, of course. Red went fast, then green, and then the box got to the end of the table and the prettiest of the girls handed the box to Milo and blushed. "For you?" she said.

They all waited to see which color he would choose. He had a strong sense of the dramatic for a 13-year-old. Outside two blue jays began to fight, chasing each other around the oak. Maggie wondered what she would do if Milo didn't take a crayon. That would throw everything off. The mood would die. Fortunately, he eyed the crayons seriously. Then he picked pink.

She noticed the boys look at each other. A different boy they would have teased, but not this one. She could almost see them all nod and decide to accept it. Then the moment broke and they all got to work and there was coloring and laughter. She listened to them talk, waiting for the moment they forgot she was there and could be natural.

"How about you, Walter?" Maggie asked.

He seemed to fight an internal battle, which played out on his normally granite face. But he picked one, aquamarine.

Then she went around and had each one talk about why they'd chosen the color they had. She was surprised, as she often was, by how willing they were to speak. The good-natured girl chose green, because it made her think of the Girl Scouts. The pretty girl chose violet, because she loved lilacs. Johnny Taylor chose black because it reminded him of a nun. There was always one. Walter chose aquamarine for the sea and because he liked sailing. Then they came to Milo, who'd sketched out an elaborate heart made of lace.

"It's for my mother," he said.

"So, Mrs. Dove," Johnny Taylor asked. "What does this have to do with confirmation class?"

"Ah," she said. "Thank you, Johnny. Let's think about that. We're working on our faith statements, which is how we understand our relationship with God. Which relates to how we see ourselves in the world. What do we believe? What do we love? Who are we? I believe that God created us all, but He likes us to decide who we want to be, and thinking about colors, is just a first step into that. Does that make sense?

They nodded, all except for Milo, who was back on his phone.

"The more you love the world and the colors around you and who you are, the more you can love God, I believe."

They talked about that for a while, and then she pulled out the official confirmation curriculum and they read from that, and then class was over. She wanted to make sure she had a chance to talk to Milo, and she asked him to stay for a moment, but Walter refused to leave. He bustled around, tidying up, and she wondered if this was a ploy to stop her from talking to Milo, but then she realized he had something on his mind. He stalked over to Maggie. He looked her in the eye and said, "You're a good teacher." She knew it cost him to say that and she appreciated it. She doubted she would have been so graceful. Finally, Walter left and she was alone with Milo.

"Thanks for staying," she said.

He shrugged. His shoulders slumped forward as though in prayer, but she knew he was simply on the phone.

He was only thirteen, but was the child of a rock star. Which meant he was a child of privilege and probably old beyond his years. He'd just watched his mother die. He had been at Stern Manor that night. What must it have been like for him? He was a child raised on dark energy, who watched his father imitating devils and his mother doing whatever she did. Presumably he grew up hearing about witches and damnation and yet he wanted to come to church. No one forced him to come to confirmation class. Perhaps when your parents were Lucifer and Domino Raines, the only way to rebel was to choose Christianity. He was strong. She could tell that much just from the fact that he was here. He'd survive.

"I was very sorry to hear about your mother," Maggie said.

"Were you?"

And he was honest, she thought. Direct.

"Yes, I was. I won't lie and say we were best friends, but she was a very vivid spirit."

"You lost your daughter." That came out of nowhere. She was surprised he even knew. Was it something people still talked about?

"Yes."

"She was young. Like me."

"She was 17. A little older than you. She was in a car accident."

"She was speeding."

"No, she was stopped at a stoplight. There was a truck coming toward her and he couldn't stop. It had been raining and he skid."

He nodded. Those fingers were whirling around. "It wasn't her fault?"

"No," Maggie said. "It was an accident. Bad luck, I guess you could say."

He nodded at that. She noticed the cuffs of his suit coat were short on his arms. They were too small for him. She was surprised he didn't own one that fit and she wondered if perhaps Domino's financial troubles went deeper than she'd let on.

"Why do you ask," she said. "Why do you want to know about Juliet?"

"I don't know." He shrugged, then said, "If you do something bad in another life time, it can come back and bite you in this lifetime."

"Are we talking now about your mother or my daughter?"

He shrugged.

"I don't believe that," Maggie said. "That lets out the possibility of atonement and forgiveness. I don't believe you're punished for everything you do. This is what grace is all about."

"My mother used to say she deserved to be punished. She said she was wicked."

Interesting parenting strategy, Maggie thought.

"Do you think your mother was wicked?"

"I don't know."

She knew he wanted to tell her something, but didn't know what, worried that if she didn't ask the right question, the moment would disappear. But what was the right question? She thought of something Detective Grudge said about confession. Why do people confess? Why will they do it even if they wind up going to jail? Detective Grudge postulated it was because secrets and guilt are a burden most people don't want to bear. Confession can be a release, even if it gets you in trouble. What the detective has to do, Grudge said, is find a way to make it possible for a person to confess. She wished, in this moment, however, that Grudge had been more specific. Then she had a sudden intuition.

"Did you argue with your mother on the day she died?" Maggie asked.

Milo's eyes flashed. He jolted, as though electrocuted. Then he looked at her like she was a mind-reader, though in fact it was the only thing that made sense. What was a 13-year-old likely to feel guilty about?

"Yeah."

"What happened?"

He curled inward, as though trying to protect himself. She didn't press him. It was clear to Maggie that he wanted to tell her. Instead, she sat back in her chair, and gave him space.

"She wanted me to go to the balcony with her."

Maggie forced herself not to jump on that statement. *Let him talk. Let him be.*

"She said we were a dynasty and she wanted everyone to see me. But I didn't want to. I wanted to get something to eat. I was hungry."

"It's not uncommon for teenage boys to not do what their mothers want them to do."

"If I'd gone up there, I could have stopped her from falling over," he cried out.

"Maybe," Maggie said gently, "or maybe you would have fallen over yourself. There's no way to know."

Domino hadn't asked Lucifer to come up with her though, Maggie thought. When she'd seen him, she'd handed him the tarantula. Was that because she was mad at him? But he said they were intimate. Was he lying? She trusted him because they liked the same books. Perhaps she should probe further.

"Did she see your father after that?" Maggie asked.

"She saw Passion," he said. "She was there. Hovering. Then I left. I don't know what happened after that."

Maggie thought of where the stairs to the balcony were, which was right off of the main entry way. A small, compressed spot. Passion was there, and Milo, and at some point, Lucifer. It was a lot of commotion, and meantime Domino had time for an encounter with a broomstick. She must have been disoriented. Would it have been possible for someone else to squeeze past her and then wait on the balcony for her to arrive? But Racine would have to have seen something. Everything came back to Racine being the murderer. She had motive, she had the disposition, she had the opportunity. She was there. But she had not pushed Domino. Hundreds of people watched that encounter. She came close. She remembered how Domino beckoned toward her, but they did not touch.

Unless, perhaps, someone put a spell on her. Was that possible? Unless someone magnetized Racine somehow, causing her to give off a repulsive quality that would force Domino off the balcony.

"Did your mother mention someone named Grant Winfrey?"

"She said he was stupid."

"So, she wasn't afraid of him?"

"No. My mother wasn't afraid of anything. She said he couldn't do anything to hurt her."

"She thought he might want to hurt her?"

He shook his head. "She always said she was more powerful, but maybe…" He paused and looked down, and Maggie hoped he wasn't thinking about that broomstick. That image, combined with guilt, would be a devastating thing for anyone to carry, but most especially a 13-year-old boy. "Maybe she was weakened."

He looked like one of those creatures who'd been drained of blood.

"Chickie, I've felt guilty for years that there wasn't something I could have done about my daughter. I've lived it over and over in my mind, what I could have done to save her. And I could have. I knew she was going to a party and she would be breaking up with her boyfriend and she'd be upset and so she'd probably have something to drink. I could have told her not to go to that party and she would have listened. I loved her. I didn't want her to die. I had no idea my actions would have ramifications like that."

He closed his eyes. He looked like he was about to fall asleep. How vulnerable he seemed, though she knew he was stronger than he appeared.

"I told her I hated her," he whispered. "I told her she embarrassed me. I said my life would be better if she wasn't in it. But I didn't mean it."

"Of course not," she said. "Listen to me, your mother was one of the toughest people I ever knew. You being mad at her was not going to cause her to despair. She would have known you were just venting. Am I right?"

He nodded. "She laughed at me. Said I reminded her of herself."

"You see!"

He crossed his arms. She noticed the pretty girl hovering around outside the classroom. He'd have someone to comfort him. "You'll find out what happened to her, won't you?"

"I'm trying," Maggie said, which was as much as she could promise.

Chapter Thirty

Monday morning Maggie borrowed Helen's car. She figured a white Subaru would be less noticeable than a red Audi, though she was slightly appalled at the condition of Helen's car. There seemed to be remnants of every snack Edgar had eaten in his young life. Boxes of Juicy Juice. Empty yogurt bottles. An entire collection of Captain Underpants books. When the car moved forward, everything in it moved backward, so there was a steady cacophony as she drove. Maggie didn't consider herself a neatness fanatic, but she did prefer not to have an old ball of gum roll under her feet when she braked a car. One thing was certain: if called upon to perform a citizen's arrest, she would not put Grant Winfrey in the car.

Not that she planned to do a citizen's arrest. There were levels of assertiveness Maggie knew she would never reach.

She pulled the car into the parking lot at the doctor's office, positioning herself so that she had a view of the front door, and also of Grant Winfrey's car, parked two aisles down. Then she settled herself in to wait. She hadn't brought along a book because she didn't want to be engrossed with one of the Karamazovs and have Dr. Winfrey go sneaking by. Neither did she think she should play Candy Crush on her telephone. She'd brought a thermos of coffee, but she wasn't drinking any. Detective Grudge recommended bringing along an empty bottle for bodily needs; since she didn't want to use that, she decided it was better not to ingest anything at all. She just hoped he didn't work late on Mondays. Daylight Savings Time had just ended and she didn't like the idea of following him around in the dark.

She would have put on the radio, but Helen said the car had a quiffy gas meter that sometimes said the tank was full and other times said it was empty. Best not to turn on the car, she reasoned, as it would be foolish to follow someone and not have the car move.

"How do you know if the tank actually is empty?" Maggie'd asked.

"I keep filling it. I just did it the other day. I think. Don't worry Dove," she said, "you'll be fine." Those were words that always struck terror into Maggie Dove's heart, but she needed to get this done.

No, all she could do was sit and watch and think. There was a time when spending a few hours alone thinking would have been torture. Her mind would have been filled with sorrow. But now Maggie found herself engrossed with the problem at hand. She tried to visualize the scene with Winfrey, when she finally caught up with him. It was the same principle as teaching Sunday School, she supposed. You prepared and you thought everything out, and then quite often things followed your anticipated trajectory, though not always.

She kept trying to understand the relationship between the two sisters. That seemed the heart of it all, and it was so mysterious to her. As an only child, she had no experience of siblings. She couldn't figure out how siblings apportioned responsibility. There often seemed to be one sister who took on all the responsibility, and another who shunned it. Racine went to France and had a magical time. So much so that she wore a beret all these years later. But then she surrendered everything when her mother needed her. Domino went off and found fame and love and motherhood, and seemed content to ignore her mother all these years. Had she felt guilt? Had the wounds from her childhood been so painful that she'd felt she couldn't come home. Yet, Domino had not seemed like a wounded person. That wasn't her persona, but you didn't know what wounds people had.

Maggie kept picturing her going up the stairs to that balcony. She'd handed her pet tarantula to her husband. She'd fought with her son. Her mother was in bed. Her husband's lover was near, but she could well have gone off with Lucifer. Was she alone when she walked up those stairs, or was Racine alongside her, or perhaps someone else? That was the problem with Domino, Maggie realized. There was always so much distraction around her that it was hard to figure out the truth of what was going on.

It was almost 5:00 when Maggie saw Grant Winfrey walk out the door and to his car. She couldn't believe so much time had gone by without her having to stop in at a restroom. Epic.

Grant Winfrey looked around, but she was pretty sure he didn't see her. Still, she waited a moment before turning on the car. She knew he wouldn't be able to dash away. There'd be too much rush hour traffic. She put on a baseball cap. Detective Grudge recommended small changes that could disguise your regular look. She also took off her pearl earrings.

Fortunately, he was staying straight on Broadway. She kept three cars between them. She hoped the increasing darkness would provide even more of a disguise. She noticed the indicator light said there was no gas, but she hoped that was just a fluke of the tank. She couldn't stop now.

They kept going north, into Tarrytown, past Main Street, and farther, past the Sleepy Hollow cemetery, which was where Domino was buried. He didn't stop, for which she was grateful. She didn't relish the idea of chasing around a witch in a dark cemetery. Thankfully he kept going north. Now it was quite dark, and as they went further north, there were fewer lights. Fortunately, he turned onto a side street and pulled right up in front of a small house. He stopped so suddenly that Maggie was forced to go around him. She got to the end of the street, waited for a beat, and then turned around and parked two houses away.

So he had come home. Only then did it occur to her that she could have just looked up his address. Well, it was all a learning curve, she supposed. Anyway, here she was, and now, what to do? She knew that people felt more comfortable on their home ground. Perhaps he would be more willing to talk to her here. She started up his walkway and had a rogue memory of Juliet selling Girl Scout cookies, Maggie always sitting in the car while she went house to house, to make she was safe. And now here was Maggie about to meet someone who was decidedly not safe.

She rang the bell quickly, not wanting to give herself a chance to turn around and run for the car, which was her first instinct. She tried to assume her least threatening look. She'd put the pearls back on and a little lipstick. She tried to twinkle. He opened the door and immediately his face contorted in fear.

"You!" he said.

He went to slam the door closed but she dropped her handbag in the opening. Another one of Detective Grudge's recommendations.

"Please," she said. "I mean you no harm. I'm just looking for information about Domino."

"Leave us alone," he said. He started kicking at her bag.

Us, she thought.

"I wish I could make it clear to you that I really am not looking to get you, any of you, into trouble."

He kicked at her bag, kicking her in the process.

"Leave us alone," he cried out, slamming the door shut, and then she was alone, on his front stoop. She stood there for a moment, then picked up her squashed bag. She wasn't quite sure what else to do. She felt she had proven definitely that he didn't want to talk to her, but beyond that she was stymied. Perhaps the best thing would be to work around that. Winfrey had gone to school with Domino. Other people had to have been in class with him. Maybe if she found a yearbook and looked through pictures, she could figure out who else they associated with. That was the only plan she could come up with, and it felt like a good one, and so she went back to the car, which would not start.

"Dear God," she whispered. "Must this get worse?"

She noticed Winfrey's curtain twitching. She imagined the poor man terrified of what she planned to do. She would have called Helen to pick her up, but what was the point of that? She had her car. So, she called the Darby gas station. Jasper answered the phone.

"What'd you do, Dove?"

Some years ago, perhaps thirty, she'd been sitting in her car reading a book and had accidentally drained the gas. Ever since then, Jasper assumed she'd done it again.

"I'm up in Croton. Can you get me and my car?"

"You bet," he said, and so she sat there waiting for him to arrive, she and Grant Winfrey divided by a curtain and a lot of fear. She had a lot to write in her report that night, but none of it was going to make Racine happy.

Chapter Thirty-One

The next day the weather forecaster predicted a bad storm coming. Ever since Hurricane Sandy, when a good portion of the village flooded, and people lost power for weeks, everyone in Darby was jittery over storm predictions. Maggie, along with 1,000 other people, more or less, decided to go to the hardware store and buy batteries. She'd just bought the last of the C batteries, when she saw Passion walking down Main Street.

Passion walked like she'd had years of ballet lessons, feet turned out, posture straight. Maggie put the batteries in her bag, paid, and ran out the door to catch her. But before she reached her, Passion turned into one of Darby's five hair salons. One Maggie had never been in before. Immediately Maggie scooted inside and sat down alongside Passion, who smiled at her blankly. No recognition of her at all, although Maggie had met her at Stern Manor, on that horrible occasion in the cellar. Maggie felt a tad offended. Granted Passion must have a lot on her mind, and Maggie was old enough to be her grandmother. Still, one liked to be recognized. One did not want to feel invisible. Maggie knew she was being foolish, because actually her invisibility was working in her favor. Passion would not have talked to her otherwise. Might as well make the most of it. She assumed her most dithery expression.

"Did I hear that girl call you Passion? What an unusual name."

Passion smiled at her genially, as though Maggie were a turtle crossing the road. Unlike Grant Winfrey, she didn't find Maggie a threat.

"I know," she said. Maggie noticed her lip was still a little swollen. There was a bruise where Domino had bit her. "It was my mother's choice. She wanted me to have an unusual life, and so she gave me an unusual name."

"Did it work?" Maggie asked.

"Oh yes," she said, grinning. When she smiled, she was beautiful in a way that only youth could be. "It worked better than she could have imagined. Matter of fact," she said, conspiratorially, "I've been living at Stern Manor. Do you know it?"

"The house where that lady died."

"Yes," she said. "Domino Raines. I was the last person to see her alive."

"Really!" Maggie said. That was exactly what she wanted to know about. "Where was that?" she asked.

Passion looked startled by the question and Maggie thought perhaps she should take a step back. She felt odd sitting in this new hair salon. The colors were different. Here were all earth tones and candles, unlike

Iphigenia's black and white motif. Maggie was definitely more of a black and white person.

"You're friendly with the family?"

Passion huffed a laugh. "Yes, Domino and I were very close. She was like a mother to me."

"And what were you to her?" Maggie asked. She couldn't help herself. One could only pretend to be dithery for so long.

Passion smiled. She didn't seem embarrassed at all. "You've heard the stories," she said. "I know, in a small town like this gossip gets around."

"It was just gossip?" Maggie asked.

Passion eyed her curiously, but clearly, she wanted to talk. A girl named Passion who traveled as the girl-friend of a married man was not a girl who wanted to hide her light under a bushel, Maggie thought. If in fact it was appropriate to bring a Biblical allusion into this conversation.

"People are so judgmental," Passion said. "You try to be creative. You're not hurting anyone. You just want to explore the meaning of everything, to try something new. You know?" She looked at Maggie and must have concluded Maggie did not know. "Anyway, what business is it of anybody's what we did? It's between us."

"Now I guess it's just between you and Lucifer," Maggie pointed out. "With Domino gone and all."

"That's true," Passion said. She didn't try to pretend she mourned Domino. Maggie liked her for that.

Just then the hairdresser moved them over to a set of maroon chairs, settling Maggie next to Passion.

"Did you make an appointment, dear?" she yelled at Maggie.

"No," Maggie said. "Is that all right?"

"No worries," she said. "Well hook you right up with Ursula."

"Fabulous," Maggie said. She didn't think she actually needed anything done to her hair. She'd only seen Iphigenia a few days ago, but she didn't want to interrupt her momentum with Passion.

"Still, he and Domino were married a long time," Maggie said. "Wasn't it thirty years?"

"He doesn't miss her at all," Passion whispered. "He's been trying to get rid of her for years, but she wouldn't go. He wants to have more children. He wouldn't have stayed with her at all. Except, well, you know."

"He needed money."

"It's just wrong," Passion cried out "He loved me. What we had was perfect. She'd had her time with him. She had decades with him, and now it was my time and it wasn't fair that she hung on to him. I told Lucifer that when I'm her age, I won't expect him to stay with me. I'll understand if he wants to put me aside for someone young and new. It's only natural. But for now, it's my time with him."

"Lucky for you she died then," Maggie pointed out.

"I know," Passion cried out. "That's what I keep thinking about. It's almost like karma. She was always taking about that, the Rule of the Three, and that what you send out comes back three times, and now look what happened."

"Are you also a witch?" Maggie whispered.

"No," she said. "I told them I didn't want any part of that. My mom's a Sunday School teacher."

"I am too!" Maggie said.

For the first time, Passion looked at her. Closely. Maggie'd never before felt those words convey such power. She figured this was the moment to press her point.

"When did you see Domino?" she asked. "Did you see her when she went up to the balcony?"

Passion blushed. "I did see her right before she went up," she said. "But then I left."

She looked so embarrassed. Maggie couldn't imagine what as troubling her. She hadn't struck her as a person with major shame issues. She tried to picture what it was like. Domino there. Lucifer. Passion probably trying to insert herself.

"Did Lucifer give you Charlotte?"

He'd made her feel like an errand girl. Dismissed her. That's what she was embarrassed about.

Ursula came then and began tugging away at Maggie's hair, and Maggie didn't even look. Didn't want to know. She had short white hair. How much could the stylist do?

"I hated that stupid thing," she snapped. "Always made think of Domino with those black hairs sticking out. What sort of pet is that? When I get married, I'm going to have dogs. Golden retrievers. Beautiful ones. They're the best. And lots of children."

She had reason to kill Domino, but not opportunity. Not if she was wandering around Stern Manor with a tarantula.

"It's a very pretty picture," Maggie said. "Are you planning to get married soon?"

For the first time Passion blushed and looked girlish. Maggie wondered how old she was. Twenty-five? Younger? "I can't say anything yet, but it's going to be special. He's just waiting for the right time to propose."

Maggie thought of Lucifer assuring her that Passion did not expect to get married. You could change all the rules and do whatever you wanted, but it didn't change the fact that everyone wanted to feel special, and chosen.

"I hope it all works out," Maggie said, and she did, because this child was so vulnerable, and thought she was tough, but Maggie suspected she'd soon find out that she wasn't that tough at all. Or perhaps she was misreading the situation because she always sympathized with young, hopeful girls.

Just then the stylist swooped in and moved Passion to a different station. Maggie noticed almost immediately she began chatting with her hairdresser, and it looked like that conversation was following a similar trajectory. Maggie wondered if she could sit down with her and have the same conversation all over again and if Passion would even remember who she was. She sat there, lost in thought, thinking about all she'd learned. For a person who had died accidentally, who her sister hoped had committed suicide, Domino had a lot of enemies. More than just people who disliked her. There seemed to be several people who actively wanted her to die. The problem was that the only person who seemed to have the opportunity to kill her was Racine, and that was the only one it could not be.

Not if Maggie wanted to avoid Agnes killing her.

Maggie looked up then, surprised to see that the hairdresser had completely changed her hair. It looked fabulous. She couldn't get over it. All wispy. She smiled at her reflection, and then, just as quickly, watched her face fall. She couldn't keep it like this. To do so would be to betray Iphigenia, and she'd been going to see Iphigenia for two decades, plus which she was her friend. She'd cut Juliet's hair. There were ties that went beyond anything else…and yet her hair did look so nice. She quickly paid and snuck out the back door, so as not to go on Main Street. She took a back route home. She would go home and stay there for the night. There was no reason to go out anyway because of the storm. She'd enjoy the way she looked for a few hours and then she'd take a shower and no one would be the wiser. There was no point at all in upsetting Iphigenia, she thought, as she tiptoed back into her house. Her friendship was worth too much.

Chapter Thirty-Two

Soon the wind started rising, its sound whipping against Maggie's house. Maggie's poor little oak tree danced wildly under its assault, branches flinging themselves back and forth. Occasionally one broke off and Maggie saw it go flying by her window like a broomstick. Unfortunate image.

She went throughout her house, setting out flashlights and candles, getting ready. She actually liked storms, because unlike most disasters that hit you, you had time to prepare. You knew what was coming. You didn't know precisely how bad it would be, but at least you didn't usually get completely blindsided. Plus, there were so many wonderful storm images in the psalms. "The God of glory thunders, The Lord is over many waters." She'd created a lot of good Sunday School lessons out of that one.

That done, she made herself some avocado toast, poured herself a glass of white wine, and then went upstairs, ready to watch the storm. She had a window in her attic that allowed her a slight view of the river. There was still enough light that she could see the waves churning. She settled back to watch. Kosi leapt onto the window sill. She imagined he liked storms too, though it was impossible to say. He might just want to block her view.

She had a lot to think about.

She needed to get together a gold star report for Racine. She'd fallen behind, and was surprised she hadn't called. There was a lot to say, but Maggie wasn't convinced Racine wanted to hear any of it. She couldn't prove Domino killed herself. If anything, Domino must have felt triumphant when she walked on to that balcony. She would have seen Lucifer treat Passion like an errand girl, handing off the spider to her. She'd had a fight with her son, but Maggie couldn't imagine that her upset her too much. She was a woman with a lot to live for, and a woman with a lot of enemies. Plenty of people wanted to kill her, Maggie just couldn't figure out how they did. She needed to take a closer look at the balcony. It had been closed off last time she was at Stern Manor, but perhaps that had changed. She would check tomorrow.

Maggie wasn't sure what she thought of Passion. There was something naïve about her that was both touching and disturbing. The older she got, the more Maggie struggled to figure whether she thought naiveté a virtue, or not. She approved of innocence, but didn't you reach an age when you shouldn't be quite so innocent. Wasn't it the responsibility of an adult to see the world as it was?

You might want to change it. You might disagree with it. But was it right to just blindly assert that the world was a particular way when all evidence pointed to the contrary? Maggie did not believe that Domino didn't mind sharing her husband. And she also didn't believe that Passion would be willing to surrender him when she was 40. It reminded her of that Somerset Maugham story when he plans to live in paradise for ten years and run through all his money and then kill himself. And then ten years go by, and he has a change of heart.

Kosi began batting at the window, then Maggie's phone rang. It was a different young woman. A woman who perhaps saw the world all too clearly.

"Hey Dove," Helen said. "Just checking in. How are you?"

"Not bad," Maggie said. "Hunkering down. Just ate some avocado toast."

"Nice. Hey, I hear you're looking mighty gorgeous."

"How do you mean?"

"New hairdo, right. I hear you look like a young Lana Turner." Helen howled with merriment, but Maggie felt disheartened.

"Does everyone know?"

"I don't think the President knows," Helen said. "Would you like me to call the White House?"

"Oh dear," Maggie said. She could only imagine what Iphigenia would have to say.

"I'll go tomorrow and talk to her," Maggie said, but then she recounted her talk with Passion, and told Helen about what she'd been thinking. Helen thought Passion would wind up marrying Lucifer. She'd get pregnant. "Mark my words, Dove. Girls like that have one tool and they're not afraid to use it."

Maggie was surprised at the harshness in Helen's voice, and wondered what set of circumstances led to her pregnancy with Edgar. She wished Helen would tell her, but now was not the moment.

They talked for a while more and then Helen had to out and find some batteries. Maggie went back to her wine and her thoughts and the storm, until Agnes called.

"You're in deep doo doo," she said.

"I will apologize to Iphigenia tomorrow," Maggie protested.

"Good luck with that," Agnes said. Maggie tried to shift direction by telling Agnes about her conversation with Passion, and it worked. She thought they might be able to offer her a special discount "because that girl is surely going to need some marital detective work in the future."

Maggie laughed. That was the thing about Agnes. Bad as she was, she always made her laugh.

"You okay in that house of yours, Maggie. Cherrelle and I can come over, if you like."

"No, don't drive around in this. I'm fine. I'm just going to sit here and wait it out."

Joe Mangione gave her a buzz soon thereafter, and Leona Faraday called to tell her this was going to be the worst storm ever. "A complete disaster. You okay, Maggie Dove?"

By the end of the hour, and five different phone calls, Maggie felt so loved she didn't know what to do with herself. As always, when she was feeling loved, she wanted to turn around and pass the kindness on and so Maggie thought she'd call Racine. The storm must be hitting Stern Manor hard, given that the mansion stuck out so far into the river. Bad as it was at her house, it would be worse there. The rain was flying at her window like pellets. One of her gutters dropped off and swung back and forth like a noose.

Maggie called Racine's number, but got an out of service message. Must have a black-out. There was nothing to be done, then. Maggie would try again in the morning. She settled back in her chair, the wine and the excitement and emotion exhausting her. She fell asleep and dreamt of Juliet on a boat and then an awful crack of lightning exploded outside her window. Bits of lightning seemed to crackle in her eyes. Then there was another blast and all the lights went out.

Maggie checked her phone: 2:18.

She stood up and stepped on Kosi, who had settled by her feet. She decided to stay where she was, pulled a shawl over her and fell back asleep and didn't wake up until late the next morning. Still no lights. She hoped it didn't take too long to fix the electricity. She couldn't shower because the water pump didn't work. But avocado toast worked just as well for breakfast as dinner, and given that her freezer was defrosting, she thought she'd stop by Stern Manor with a bread pudding and see how everyone was doing.

That was not officially part of the gold star service but few people minded a guest with bread pudding.

She decided to walk there. The air smelled clean, but the sky was the color of a bruise, black and blue and edged with yellow. There were branches flung everywhere, twisted and contorted. It looked like a battlefield. She walked along the river. Her beautiful blue river had turned brown overnight because of all the sediment rising up from the bottom.

As Maggie expected, when she neared Stern Manor, she saw no lights. The whole mansion seemed blanketed in darkness. The granite facing looked imposing, built to keep people out. Maggie rang the doorbell, which didn't work, of course, and then she knocked on the door. Nothing. Perhaps they were all still asleep. Maggie pressed in Racine's number on her cell phone, but Racine didn't answer, and yet Maggie was sure she heard the phone ringing inside. Racine might just be ignoring her, of course, but Racine had been so relentlessly insistent on being contacted that it was to imagine she wouldn't answer.

Maggie stood there a moment more. She looked up at the tower. Domino had fallen to her death from that tower not long ago. She had to do something. She pushed open the door and called out.

"Hello," her voice warbled. "Hello."

No answer. Nothing. She tried phoning Racine and once again heard its ring; she headed in that direction, toward the stairs. First, she had to walk down the long hallway, wood-paneled and solemn—as she got closer to the end, she saw a bit of white on the wood. She ran toward it´and found Passion's body lying at the foot of the steps.

She was dead. Her large blue eyes stared blankly. Her mouth was still contorted in a scream. Quickly Maggie called 911 and told them to get right over and then she did CPR, though she knew it would do no good. Once again, she was transported back to Marcus Bender's body on her lawn, and then before that, to her dear daughter's body. Each death called up another. Each horror built on the one that preceded it.

Passion's hair still smelled of the hair salon. She smelled of peach and cleanliness and youth, and now she was dead. Maggie began to shake, but then she heard another sound, one that sounded like a kitten. Maggie ran toward the noise, up the stairs, and there she found Racine, hunched over and whimpering.

"Racine," she said, crouching down beside her. "Are you all right? What happened?"

She clutched her beret in her hand s like a baby. Maggie'd never seen her without it and it was startling. There was a large bald spot in the middle of her head, but Racine seemed unconscious of it. This proud woman didn't even notice how exposed she was, and

Maggie wanted to take the beret and plant back on her head, but she thought she'd scare her.

"Racine," she said. "What happened?"

"It's too late," Racine moaned.

"What's too late?" Maggie asked.

"We're cursed," Racine said. "This place will kill us all."

She had no chance to go further, however, because at that moment Milo and his father came wandering in from another part of the house. The police car and ambulance and fire truck pulled up. The door flung open. Walter Campbell was there.

Chapter Thirty-Three

It should have been pandemonium, but it wasn't. Walter stood perfectly still, for a moment, for two moments, and everyone around him stayed still too. Mercy stood behind him, silently, holding a camera. Even Milo and Lucifer didn't move. It was as though someone clicked pause on a remote. And then Lucifer began to keen and he hurled himself toward Passion, and Walter caught him in midstride.

"Stop," he said. "Stay."

Doc Steinberg ran around them, knelt down by the body.

"Can't you help her?" Lucifer cried out. "Is there anything we can do for her?"

Doc Steinberg shook her head. "No, she's been gone for a few hours."

"She can't be dead. She just went to get a glass of water."

Lucifer clawed the air, desperate to escape Walter's grasp and reach Passion, which surprised Maggie. She'd thought his grief over Domino was sincere, but it was nothing compared to this display of emotion. Perhaps

Passion was not as naïve as Maggie thought. Maybe he really did adore her. Maybe he did plan to marry her.

"Dad," Milo said. "Come on."

He'd always be the boy forgotten, Maggie realized. Always the one who had to remind his parents he was there.

"She went to get a glass of water. She asked me to get it, but I was tired. Then I must have fallen back asleep."

"We'll take your statement soon," Walter said. "But for now, we have to investigate the crime scene and I need you to go in another room."

Tim Harrison and Joe Mangione had come in with a stretcher, though Walter put his hand up, telling them to wait. Maggie wondered how Tim must feel being back in his old house. He stared down at the pattern on the floor and smiled at it as though it contained special meaning for him. Maggie wondered, if you had a great enough shock in your youth, was it ever possible to recapture the emotions you had then? She began to feel cold.

"Crime scene," Lucifer cried out. "What do you mean a crime scene? No one would have hurt Passion."

"It's just procedure," Walter said. He'd yanked Lucifer over to the other side of the landing, so that he couldn't see Passion, and now Walter stood in front of him, blocking his view.

"Until I know otherwise, I have to assume this is a criminal act. We can't risk losing important information. Now please, let me go about my business."

Maggie cringed, thinking of how cavalier Peter Nelson had been that April night on her lawn, so confident Marcus died of a heart attack that he hadn't even put up crime scene tape. No wonder Walter got so mad.

"Did you touch her?" he asked Maggie.

"I tried CPR when I got here. But I could see she was dead."

He nodded.

"Harrison, would you take Mr. Raines and his son to a room and wait for me to debrief them, and Ms. Stern, I imagine you'll want to get back to your mother."

"She's all alone," Racine said, jumping to her feet. She seemed to come out of her trance, looked at the beret and plunged it on her head. She began running up the steps.

"Maggie, would you please go with Ms. Stern? I'll want to talk to you in a bit."

She didn't think she'd ever seen Walter that calm.

"Walter, how long is her body going to be here?"

They both looked at Passion, flung out at the bottom of the staircase. Her hand stretched forward, which seemed right to Maggie. She was a forward-looking girl. She was preoccupied with the future.

"It will take a little time," he said. "We have to take photographs and sketch the scene."

"I'd like to stay here while you do that."

He shook his head. "I can't allow that Maggie. It's a complete violation of all the rules."

"Walter, she's someone's daughter and now she's dead. If I were her mother, I would want to know that someone sat by her when the police were here. You know I didn't kill her. Would it hurt to be kind?"

"Did you know her?"

"Not well," Maggie said, "but I might be the closest thing to a friend she had here."

He crossed his arms.

"Please," she said. "I know it's irregular. But I think it's the right thing to do."

He was a man who would always want to do the right thing, she suspected, even if it meant breaking the rules. In fact, she realized for the first time that Walter didn't care about rules at all. Except for his own. That's why he was teaching the Sunday School class in his way although he knew it would get him in trouble.

"You can stay, but you have to stay out of the way. Sit over there."

He pointed toward a hard-backed chair tucked into the corner. Maggie went and sat down. She watched as they went about their business. She was glad to see they were gentle with Passion. No joking, the way they did on TV. Mercy took photos. Walter sketched out a map. Doc Steinberg spoke into her phone. There was something almost religious about all the murmuring.

"We're going to take her away," Walter said. "We've spoken to her parents. They're flying in from Texas. They'll be here tomorrow. Come on, let's see what information we can get. You doing okay?"

"I just saw her," Maggie said. "Just yesterday. At the hair salon."

"How did she seem?"

"She seemed really young," Maggie said, and she replayed the conversation with him. He took out his notepad and wrote down notes.

"She planned to marry him?" Walter asked.

"Yes. Definitely. Do you think this really is a crime scene? Was she murdered?"

"Doc doesn't think so. Doesn't see any bruises, beyond the ones you'd expect. Nothing to suggest it. Probably just a tragedy. Wandering around in the dark. These old houses have a different building code than we have now. You'd never have a staircase like this anymore. It's a death trap really. Stairs so close together. So easy to fall."

He went on talking, thinking out loud. He nodded toward the EMTs, who were removing the body, and then he began walking up the steps, treading carefully. "Haven't found a flash light. She could have gone to get a glass of water, and then been startled when the lights went out. She'd be trying to make her way back to her room, lost her way and fell down these steps. Easy enough to imagine, and it happens enough."

"Seems awfully coincidental though."

"Not really," Walter said, walking across the landing and then pausing at the outside of Madame Simone's bedroom. "People are more likely to get into accidents when they're tired and confused. It makes sense that, after witnessing a violent death, Passion would be off balance.

Walter waited for a beat. He looked at her carefully. Maggie suspected he was the only person in town who didn't know she had a new haircut. "Why are you here, Maggie Dove?"

"Because I wanted to bring them a bread pudding. I don't even know what I did with it now. I was worried about them and I called last night and didn't hear anything and so I thought I'd come by and check up on them."

"And bring her a bread pudding."

"Yes, that's exactly right," she said. How to explain that she had been touched by the kindness other people had shown in reaching out to her, and she wanted to respond in kind. Also, her freezer was defrosting.

"That's all?" he asked.

"Yes," she said. "That's all."

He sighed. He was a big man and when he sighed it felt a little bit like the wind was changing direction.

"Let's see what we find out here," he said, and then went into Madame Simone's room, which looked transformed from the last time Maggie had been there. Then it had seemed so charming, with all its little details and knick knacks, but now it looked cluttered and a little tawdry.

"Ah," Madame Simone said. "Look who got a haircut. Very flattering."

"Thank you," Maggie said, though it hardly seemed the moment.

"Turn your head. Let me see your profile."

"Madame Simone," Walter said. "I have some questions to ask you and daughter about a death that has taken place in your house."

"That woman did not belong in my house. I did not want here. I didn't ask her here. She was an embarrassment to my daughter. My son-in-law has a lot to answer for."

"Mama," Racine said. "Please don't get upset. Not now. I can't bear any more tragedy."

"Did you hear her fall?" Walter asked.

"I heard nothing," Madame Simone said. "I couldn't hear anything over that storm."

"What about you, Ms. Stern. Did you hear anything?"

"She didn't hear anything either," Madame Simone said. She smacked her hand against her covers. "She was here. With me. Looking after me. I was hungry and I wanted some tea, but Racine didn't want to leave me alone. She would not let me suffer."

Maggie tried to imagine the two of them in that storm, the old lady increasingly querulous, Racine trying to take care of her. What a nightmare life that woman led, Maggie thought. Did she have any idea when she returned home from France, to take care of her mother, just what she was giving up? Maggie doubted she'd have the patience for it herself, though her mother, a laughing woman, would never have demanded it. She died too soon. It could also be a tragedy to die not soon enough, Maggie thought.

"Would you tell me, please," Walter said to Racine, "how you found the body? I assume you did find her. Please let your daughter talk," he cautioned Madame Simone, who clenched her jaws closed.

The room seemed to crackle. It was all so over-heated. The whole family dynamic was overheated, Maggie thought. For the first time she wondered why on earth Racine had stayed here all this time. What was in it for her? People did things for reasons. They didn't just decide to throw away forty years of their life for nothing. Something motivated her.

"There was an explosion and I woke up. I thought it was a gun firing. I ran in to check on my mother, but she was asleep. I thought I would go downstairs and get some tea, but when I got down the steps, I found her."

"That was in the middle of the night. You didn't call the police then?"

"No. I couldn't move," she said. Maggie thought of her sitting on the stairs, without her beret, and she believed her. "I thought if I didn't move, then maybe she would come alive."

"She might have come alive if you did move," Walter said. "You might have been able to save her."

A breeze gusted in right then, blowing the curtain open. Maggie jumped up, intending to pull the window closed, but Walter got there first, shutting it for her. "I have it," he said.

"I know that," Racine said. "I know that now. But with the storm raging, I thought it was coming for… but I thought it got her first."

"Racine didn't do anything wrong," Madame Simone said. "She shouldn't have been wandering around like that. She got what was coming to her. Passion."

"My mother's exhausted," Racine said. "Please, you have to let her rest for a while."

Walter didn't press the point. Perhaps he too felt defeated by the atmosphere. Instead, he nodded and got up and said he would be in touch later that afternoon. Then he went back down the stairs, Maggie following. For just a moment the two of them were alone, by the front door.

He was the sort of man who would protect you from anything, she thought. No raging storm, no quirk of fate would bother you. Come the apocalypse Walter would stand strong, and she realized, as she breathed his scent, that there was something tremendously appealing about that. It was like landing at a safe harbor. You might not want to be there, but how could you bring yourself to leave.

She looked up into his gaze, reading there concern, and she knew in that moment, that if she did surrender, she'd never get herself back, and she'd fought so hard to get herself back. She liked where she was, but oh what a tempting harbor he would be. He represented everything she'd lost, everything she'd craved for so long. Security and safety and love. But in order to get that, she'd have to give up her hard-won independence, and she didn't think she could do that. It seemed like it would be a sin after all the people who struggled so hard to get her here.

"Are you okay?" he asked.

"Yes," she said. "I'm fine."

Chapter Thirty-Four

Maggie intended to leave Stern Manor and go to the office and report in to Agnes and Maggie, but as she started to walk in that direction, she paused for a moment to admire the copper beech tree. It was a truly majestic tree. Leaves the color of cinnamon. Many of them had blown off in the storm, but enough hardy ones clung to the branches that it retained its beautiful shape. Maggie'd always loved the way that tree flamed out in in the fall. It was like a gift. One day it would be its normal brown color and then suddenly it burst into color. Like a surprise party.

She didn't like surprise parties, actually—too surprising—but she did like this tree, and this particular one was a magnificent specimen. It must have been fifty feet high. It stood so proud. Admiring it, Maggie thought that maybe what she liked so much about trees was their independence. They stood alone, even when in a grove. They were battered and occasionally hacked down, and yet there was always something dignified about a tree. You never saw a pitiful tree, except for the Charlie Brown Christmas tree. She aspired to treehood, she thought. A worthy goal, and she was smiling, thinking about that, when she noticed someone sitting under the tree, lounging on a pile of leaves.

Tim Harrison.

Thank God he was sitting, she thought. She could not bear to discover another body lying prone under a tree. He must have sent the ambulance on ahead and decided to stay behind.

"Hey, Miss Maggie Dove," he drawled. "How you?"

Tim had bright blonde hair, bleached from spending so much time in the sun. Although he didn't have a dog with him at the moment, he had that sort of rumpled look she associated with dog lovers. She noticed several bits of dog hair on his shoulder.

"I'm okay. How about you?"

Maggie scrunched down alongside him. She hadn't sat in a pile of leaves in a while, not since she'd jumped in a pile of leaves and got stung by a bee. A cautionary tale. At the same time, she felt a conversation with Tim Harrison would go better in a pile of leaves. Not the sort of man you could talk to across from a desk.

"Spent many a night sleeping under here, me and the squirrels. They love the nuts, you know?"

"I didn't actually know this kind of tree had nuts."

"Beechnuts," he said. "I could live under here."

"I think I like a roof myself. But I take your point."

He patted the tree's trunk. "Poor girl's sensitive. Didn't like the storm last night."

"How can you tell?"

"She told me. Her little leaves whisper in my ears." A slight breeze swirled and a few of the leaves floated to the ground. She wondered if Tim knew about LSD and ergot. She wondered where Domino got it from. Would you ask your old lover to provide you with hallucinogenics? She suspected Domino would.

"Tim, you know how Domino died, don't you?"

"Yeah," he said. "Broomsticks."

"Ergot," she said. "Have you ever used that?"

He tilted his head as he looked at her. His eyes were milky as an old dog's. "Tried to make it once. Had a recipe for it, but I couldn't do it. Highly toxic. Not for the amateur."

"So she wouldn't grow it herself?"

"No. You have to buy it from someone. You'd have to be a Ph.D. at MIT to do it on your own."

"Where could you buy it?" she asked, though even as she asked, the answer clicked into her head. From a doctor, of course. "Grant Winfrey."

"Yeah."

"You know him?"

"Used to. Before he became a big success. We went to school together. We were like the Three Musketeers."

"And you and Domino went out?"

"We went out, yeah. For a while. She had powers, you know? She could stand on a street corner and say, there, and you'd go ring the doorbell, and you'd find the party."

"Were you serious about her?"

He nodded. "I gave her a ring. Family heirloom." Maggie remembered the delicate antique ring on Domino's hand. She'd thought at the time that it didn't look like a ring Domino would wear. She seemed a black onyx sort of person, but now she understood. It was a trophy.

"My mother went to talk to Leonard Stern about it."

"About what?"

"Getting the ring back. She told him that ring was the only valuable thing my family had left, but he said that if it was important to us, I shouldn't have given it to Domino. He told my mother that that's why we were poor. Because we gave our money away. And that's why they were rich. Because they hung on to theirs. She'd gone to California by then." He shook his head.

"And that was the end of it?"

"No, I went to California to ask her for the ring back. Then I wound up in jail."

"Why?"

He slumped against the tree. "I tried to kill Domino. With a knife. I was crazy back then."

The scar on her arm.

He looked tired, she thought. One of those people who flamed out in their youth and never reached that peak again. Profligate people. She thought of Peter Nelson, another one who didn't take care, though he got a second chance. You never knew when life would give you a second chance. Maybe you had to go look for it.

"My brother died here," he said. "On the lawn."

He seemed to pull himself together then, and he spoke directly to Maggie. "I hate this house. I wish they would have burned it down. I couldn't wait to leave here when I was a kid. Used to hear voices in my room. Had to sleep here, to get away from them. The day my father sold this house to Leonard Stern was the happiest day of my life, and look what happened. The curse went on to them."

"You think that's why Domino died? Because she was cursed?"

"She called me. She wanted me to come over and talk about old times."

"Did you?"

"No."

"But you did come to the Halloween party?"

"I knew she was going to die," he said.

"How did you know?"

He smiled softly. "The tree told me."

He stood up then and put out his hand. "Come on Miss Maggie Dove, let me help you back to town."

A man without irony, she thought. Also a man without much sense. Also, a man with a pretty strong motive.

She knew she should probably stop by the office, but she also felt she should visit with Kosi. Cruel as he was to her, he seemed to like it when she paid attention to him. In that respect, he was like Madame Simone, she thought. A diva. She figured she could write up her notes at home. It wound up taking much longer to do than she anticipated, so it was not until the next morning that she got to the office and saw the craziness that had erupted there.

Chapter Thirty-Five

First of all, there were track and field medals all over the walls, even more of them than the bowling trophies. Maggie glared at Agnes, who was whispering into the phone, but then she noticed Helen cackling and realized Agnes wasn't the culprit.

"I was a track star in my day," Helen said. "I figured why should Agnes have all the glory?"

"This is starting to look like a sporting goods store," Maggie said.

She didn't want the agency to be a joke. The line between pitiful and loveable was a narrow one; she'd crossed it herself. And the more she got involved with this agency, the more strongly she felt she wanted to be respected. She didn't want anyone laughing at her.

"Too much?" Helen asked.

"I think you could take them down."

"And the bowling ones too?" she asked.

It was the same with Sunday School, Maggie thought. You always had to be careful not to favor one child over another. Sometimes she thought she only had one child because she didn't want to deal with sibling rivalry. Sometimes she regretted that awfully. So many times. But then she thought of how perfect her relationship with Juliet had been. She did it the way she wanted to.

"I'll talk to Agnes," Maggie said. "But who is she talking to?"

"The Lady Cherrelle," Helen said. "She's been doing this for half an hour."

"I love you more," Agnes murmured into the phone. She giggled and pressed the phone against her lips. "No, no, no. I love you more."

A pounding sound came from the dentist's office. Maggie hoped he wasn't murdering one of his patients. She hoped he wasn't having sex against a wall. Somehow, she could never be with Agnes without thinking of sex in all its possibilities, and what did that mean? Walter was safety and Agnes was sex and she was a very confused Sunday School teacher.

Agnes giggled again. She was wearing a red silk blouse and cream pants. She looked like she'd bolted right out of the 1980s.

"No, me first. Me first." She swiveled her chair and bounced a bit. When she noticed Maggie, she frowned.

"Gotta go, babe. Gotta go."

But then she began giggling again and meanwhile Archie the postal worker had shown up at their office. He carried a huge package that read *Agnes Jorgenson* on it.

"There we go," Agnes said, finally ending her conversation. "Guess what Cherrelle told me."

"Would you sign for the box?" Archie asked. He was a very timid man. He didn't like talking to people, which was not the ideal personality for a postal worker, Maggie thought, given that he spent his day going from person to person. But he was very polite, and when she gave him a Christmas bonus, he always wrote the most lovely thank-you notes.

"What's this box?" Maggie asked. There was no return address.

"Supplies," Agnes said.

"Are you thinking there will be an apocalypse?"

"Just wait and see," Agnes said, zipping it open with an X-Acto knife. There was no hesitation to her. Having slit the box open, she began pulling out one item after another. Infrared goggles. A long tube that allowed you to see around corners. Invisible ink. And on it went.

She began piling up her things, stacking them on the bookshelves. She arranged everything alphabetically. So different than Trudi, Maggie thought, who seemed to let intuition guide her. Agnes always liked a system.

"So do you want to know what Cherrelle told me about Passion's autopsy?" Agnes asked, as she tucked a decoder onto one of the shelves.

"Is that what you were talking about?" Helen asked.

"Yes, and guess what, they're saying it's accidental death. No sign of foul play. No unexpected bruises. Looks like she slipped on the steps, put out her hands but couldn't stop herself."

Maggie thought of that girl at the hair dresser and how excited she'd been. "That's what Walter was saying when I was at Stern Manor. He said that it looked like an accident to him, but he had to be sure."

"Oh Walter, is it?"

Maggie ignored her. Sometimes if you ignored things, they actually did go away.

"What happens now?" Helen asked.

"Nothing," Agnes said. "Parents are on their way up. They'll bury her and that's the end of Passion."

"I think I read a novel with that title," Helen said. "Though that one ended on a boat. Or was it a ship?"

"Are you all right?" Maggie asked. Helen had laid her head on the table.

"Great."

"The thing is," Maggie went on, keeping an eye on Helen as she spoke, who definitely did not look great, who had dark purple smudges under her eyes, "we still have the job from Racine. This doesn't change that. Our priority has to be to figure out what happened with Domino. I'm going to try to get Grant Winfrey to talk, and Agnes, you should go to Cranston and look through the yearbooks and see what other contacts Domino might have had. Helen, I'm thinking we should also look into her financial history."

"Well look at you, Maggie Dove," Agnes said. "You're a regular Humphrey Bogart."

"I'm simply saying that just because Passion died, sad as that is, doesn't mean that our original mission has changed."

"Dove with a mission," Helen murmured.

Just then Archie the postal worker knocked on the door. "Come on in," Agnes yelled. "It's a public office. You don't need to knock."

"I forgot to give you this," he whispered, and handed a certified letter to Maggie. "Would you sign for it, Mrs. Dove?"

"Of course," she said.

She signed, then opened the envelope, and when she did, a check fell out. Agnes swooped on it. Maggie'd never seen her move so fast. Perhaps it was all the track and field medals.

"Five thousand dollars," Agnes read out. "It's from Racine."

Maggie read the letter that came with the check. *I am officially informing you that I would like to terminate your private detective services,* Maggie read. *Thank you.*

"Oh well," Agnes said. "She can terminate away if she's going to give us $5,000."

"I think that's the third time she's fired us," Helen pointed out.

"This can't be right," Maggie said.

"Don't feel guilty," Agnes said. "It wasn't anything you did."

"I wasn't feeling guilty. I just can't believe she's firing us." Maggie thought of how Racine had looked just last night. So worried and frightened. Why would she be jettisoning the one group of people who were on her side?

"There's still so much to discover," Maggie said. "I still have so many questions."

"I'm going to go to the bank," Agnes said.

"I've got to stop by the school," Helen said. "Edgar's teacher wants to talk to me again."

"What happened?" Maggie asked.

"Nothing serious," Helen said. "Just an issue involving a hamster. He wouldn't share it, though he did offer to cut it in half. Not that he did, of course."

"Want me to come?"

"No," Helen said. "I've got this one covered."

Agnes looked in the mirror and fluffed up her hair. Then she smiled at herself, a wide-open smile to check her teeth.

"Don't worry, Maggie," she said. "We've got some marital investigation work coming up. It's going to be nasty."

And with that they were both gone, leaving Maggie alone in the office. She felt aggravated. She wanted to talk to Racine, but knew she should stay put for a bit. This was not a situation that required a hysterical response. She began looking over all her notes, trying to figure out who she needed to talk to and what questions she should pursue. She wondered if Madame Simone had asked Racine to fire them. She'd been so querulous last night. Maybe she didn't want to share Racine's attention with anyone. What could she say to Racine to get her to hire her again?

She noticed then that the light on the VCR was flashing. She kept forgetting to look at those tapes. Maggie got the remote and clicked start. The transmitter was voice-activated, so the tape went in fits and starts, showing Racine getting into bed. Not moving. Then Racine getting up in the morning.

Maggie skimmed past all that. She felt uncomfortable watching Racine, particularly having seen her without her beret. She zoomed through the last week of October, but then on the first of November she noticed something strange. Racine went to bed, but a few hours later, in the dark, someone was walking around her room. The picture quality wasn't good, so all she really had was a ghostly image of a woman walking around in the dark. Of course, it could just be Racine. But Maggie thought she could see the outline of Racine in her bed.

The next few nights nothing happened, but then on November 6, the figure reappeared. It looked like she was going through the drawers, looking for something. For a horrible moment, Maggie wondered if this phantom figure was a ghost, one of the murdered slaves who'd come back to haunt Racine. But then she looked more closely at the color of her hair and realized it was Passion. The young woman was sneaking around Racine's room in the dark, but why?

Could she be sleepwalking? Maggie had an aunt who sleepwalked, and they used to find her in all sorts of strange locations. Passion had been walking around the night that she fell and died. Then a more sinister possibility suggested itself. Could she have seen some-thing in her sleep-walking, some fact that registered, and did that put her in harm's way?

Maggie was reflecting on that when she noticed a couple walking down Main Street. She'd never seen them before. The woman was heavyset and wore a black dress and black coat. Her bright blonde hair was care-fully blow-dried. Her husband walked slowly alongside her. Maggie could see the glint of his wedding band even from a block away. It had gotten chillier. November was starting to settle in, but Maggie knew the chill in their expressions had nothing to do with the weather. Here were Passion's parents, come to retrieve their daughter. Maggie went out to greet them.

Chapter Thirty-Six

Maggie realized as she walked up to the couple that she had no idea what Passion's last name was. Someone must have spoken it at the crime scene, but she didn't hear it. So, all she could do, when she reached them, was say, "You must be here about your daughter."

"Yes," Passion's mother said, looking at her hopefully. "Did you know her?"

"Yes," Maggie said, glad she could answer honestly.

Darby rush hour swirled around them. Buses were going down Main Street, picking up children to take them to school. Commuters were creeping up behind the buses, trying to get to their train on time. Garbage trucks were out, picking up recycling, and then there were the high school students with their new licenses, veering off and doing erratic things.

"My office is right over here," Maggie said. "Would you like to come in and have a cup of tea?"

"I'd love that," Passion's mother said. "We've been on the road since we got the news and we met with that tall policeman. But we have to wait for a bit for them to release her. I'm sorry. Does that make sense? I can't quite hear what I'm saying."

"You're doing fine," Maggie said, touching her arm for a moment, knowing that there was nothing to say. Nothing to do except to try and remind her that she was still part of the human race. It was horrible that as much time as she'd spent grieving herself, she couldn't think of anything better to say, but really there was nothing.

"Come with me. My name is Maggie Dove."

"I'm Lila Cooper and this is my husband, Douglas. How did you know Passion?"

"We went to the same hairdresser."

"Oh, she loved that about New York. How skilled the hairdressers were. She showed me a picture of that last styling." Lila pulled out her phone and began running her finger over it. She had long orange nails, and she pulled up a picture of Passion at the hair salon.

"She always sent me a picture whenever she changed her hair style. She knew I'd like to see it."

"We didn't want to stay at that Stern Manor," Douglas said. "Wanted to get some air."

"Of course," Maggie said sympathetically, and brought them into her office. "Here we are."

They gazed around, taking in the large slab of the table, the chairs, and all the medals. "You must be very successful," Lila said. "You're a detective?"

"Yes," Maggie said. She was going to qualify it, but then realized she didn't have to. She actually was a detective.

"That's amazing," Passion's mother said. "And at your age."

"It's a growing field for women," Maggie said.

"Ah."

They had a small coffeemaker that served as a hot water maker and she began to brew some tea. Their mugs were pink and emblazoned with their logo. *Trust issues? Call us.*

"We've never been to New York before," Frank said. "Always wanted to see it. But now that I have, I don't like it."

"No," Maggie said. "I wouldn't think so."

"It was such a big house," Lila said. "Stern Manor. I always hoped she'd have a chance to live in a place like that. She used to have a doll house that looked just like it. Douglas made it."

"She was a good girl," her father said. "That Lucifer told us they were getting married. He said he loved her very much."

"I always knew he'd leave that woman for her," Lila said. "Passion worried that he was insincere, but I told her, you hang on. No man can turn away from you. I told her that," Lila said, picking up the tea cup and then setting it down because her hands shook so much.

"If it's a comfort, she was very happy last time I saw her," Maggie said.

"Was she?"

"Yes," Maggie said, remembering how she'd glowed. "She was very beautiful."

"She was a happy baby," her father said. "That Lucifer told us they were going to get married."

Maggie thought it was kind of Lucifer to tell them that, whether he'd actually planned to marry her or not. He'd certainly looked brokenhearted.

"I always knew she'd have a big life," her mother said. "That's why I gave her that name. I knew with a name like that she'd draw attention. I wanted her to travel and meet amazing people, but she surpassed all my expectations."

"She was like that," her father said. "Always surpassing."

"She's got three sisters, but they're not doing anything much. None of them are like her. She was our shooting star."

"Icarus," he said. "I'm an English teacher. Mythology."

"Accidental death, they're ruling it. She didn't have any drugs in her system," Lila said. "They figure she tripped in the dark. Looked like she didn't have a flashlight and the house was pitch dark and it was unfamiliar to her. But she didn't have any drugs in her."

"I'm glad," Maggie said. What a relief it must be for this girl's poor parents. "By any chance, do you know if your daughter sleepwalked?"

"No, she didn't do anything like that," Douglas said. "She was a good girl."

"They said you get really bad lightning here, and that might have startled her," Lila said.

"She was always afraid of lightening," her father said. "Even when she was a little girl. Didn't like it. She'd come into our bed and stay with us."

"She had on a silk gown," her mother said. She sighed. "She would have been such a good wife to him. Not like that other one. That witchcraft and voodoo and all the other stuff she was in."

"Passion didn't like that Domino. She didn't like her friends either. All those witches." Passion's father shook his head. "She wouldn't go to any of those coven meetings. She was a good girl."

"That Trudi," Lila said, "trying to tell her that there were different kinds of witches and different covens she could go to."

"Trudi?" Maggie asked.

"That was her name, right?

Trudi. From the candy store. The woman she'd known for her entire life, the woman she'd been chatting with just the other day, the woman who knew her weakness for Snickers Bars? That woman was a witch?

Of course, it made sense. She should have seen it. She knew Trudi went to school with Domino. She must know Grant Winfrey too. If she was part of Domino's circle, if she was her friend, then it made sense, but Maggie felt staggered. She wanted to go to Trudi's shop, but she couldn't leave these people just yet. She had to force herself to stay present. Still, her mind was racing.

"She was having an argument with that first wife and she kept trying to pull Passion into it, but she wouldn't get involved."

"She was strong-minded," her father said. "She didn't go with the flow."

Just then his phone buzzed. He looked down at it, and his face paled. He put his hand on his wife's arm. "She's ready for us," he said.

They both staggered to their feet. "We've got to get back to the police station," he said.

"Of course."

Maggie looked into Lila's face and saw her own face reflected back at her. "I've been there," she said. "It's very hard."

"Yes," she said, and they both head out the door. Maggie paused for a bit. She said a prayer for them. She tried to right herself, and then set out to the candy store to talk to Trudi.

Chapter Thirty-Seven

Maggie found Trudi in the midst of unloading a candy shipment. She had boxes and boxes of candy all around her. She jumped, startled, when Maggie burst in, but then she smiled at her. The same smile Maggie'd seen for years. Only now she looked different to Maggie. Sinister. Had she always had that mole on her chin? Trudi, a witch.

"Trudi," she started to say, but then stopped. What could she say?

But Trudi seemed to know immediately what Maggie had discovered. Something tensed in her. Her gentle face tightened, her eyes hardened. She looked toward the door, then back at Maggie. The very air around her felt charged. Maggie thought of how she'd felt during the lightning storm the other night and this sensation was similar. She felt frightened.

"I've just spoke to Passion's parents. They've come up to get her body. They told me you asked Passion to join a coven."

"That's true," Trudi said. She eyed Maggie warily. Grant Winfrey had looked at her in the same way, as though worried Maggie might physically attack. As though scared of her.

"Your friendship with Domino goes deeper than a shared interest in candy?"

"Yes," Trudi conceded reluctantly.

"Trudi, I want to understand. I consider you a friend, or I have. Two people are now dead, and I keep hearing they died accidentally, but everywhere I turn I run into witches. Domino threatened to put Racine under a spell, and for all I know, she did. And now I hear you wanted Passion to join a coven. I want to understand what's going on."

"Your kind is always looking to blame witches for everything. You accuse us of Satanism. You say we are in league with the devil."

"Your kind," Maggie repeated. "That's not fair, Trudi. You know me. You know what sort of person I am."

Trudi took some deep breaths.

"All I'm trying to figure out is what really happened to Domino."

"Why do you care?"

"Because people are blaming Racine for her sister's death and I don't like to think of an innocent person being blamed. It offends me. It's wrong. And it will ruin Racine's life, and it seems to me she's sacrificed enough of it."

"Domino fell over the railing," Trudi whispered.

"Yes, she did. But when she fell over, she made a lot of people very happy, and that makes me wonder if there's anything someone could have done to make her fall over the railing."

"You mean a spell?"

"I don't know. Is it really possible?"

Trudi ran her hand through her white hair. Her bracelet jingled softly. It was a sound that had always brought Maggie comfort, that she associated with chocolate and friendship. Trudi walked over to the door and put up the Closed sign. Then she beckoned for Maggie to follow her into the back office. They walked through a room filled with shelves of candies, stacks of bottled water and cans of soda. Beyond that was another door. Trudi took off her bracelet, and Maggie saw that one of the charms was a key. She used it to open the door, and beckoned for Maggie to follow her inside.

There Maggie found herself in a small windowless room no larger than a closet. Against one wall was an altar. It was actually a tree stump that had been carved with drawings, and then had legs attached. On top was a candle, an incense burner, two dishes and two naked figures. The male figure had his arms crossed in front of him and wore a horned hat. The woman had long flowing hair and her arms were stretched wide, welcoming.

"These are my gods," Trudi said. "This is who I worship. I cannot tell you their names. Those are only for those who belong to know. But I can tell you that they represent nothing evil. Wicca is a celebration of nature. We believe in taking care of the environment. We try to attune ourselves with the natural rhythm of life forces marked by the phases of the moon. We value intelligence. We value sex as pleasure. But we mean no harm to anyone. In fact, one of our principles is opposition to oppression."

"That may be what you believe, Trudi, but did Domino believe the same thing?"

"The Devil is a Christian invention," she said. "There's no mention of him before the New Testament."

"Trudi, you know as well as I do that there's evil in the world, and that's not a Christian invention. I'm willing to concede that you don't want to harm anyone, but what about Domino? What did she intend to do? Is it possible she put a spell on Racine?"

Trudi looked at the altar. Maggie noticed a calendar in the corner with the phases of the moon on it.

"You must promise to speak of this to no one. Do you know what would happen if this news got out, Maggie? People are scared of witches. They would burn me out. My family has been here for generations, and it wouldn't matter. I'd be closed within a week. There was a store only one town south, it was a pagan bookstore, and when people found out who ran it, they had to close."

Maggie knew the truth of what she said. "Trudi, I don't wish to cause you harm. I won't tell anybody, but I have to know. Do you think it possible that Domino could have put Racine under a spell?"

"We don't use spells for evil purposes. We use them only for healing."

"But do spells exist that someone else could use?" Maggie pressed. "Someone less ethical."

Trudi shook her head. She kept looking toward the door.

"Is it possible Domino put Racine under a spell to get her money?"

"Domino was always drawn toward the darker part of witchcraft. She was attracted by the power of it. She liked hostile magic. It was all a game to her. I told her that when you attempt to draw on those dark forces, you are the one who is opened up to harm. You bring the destructive force into yourself. You're letting loose more violence into the world, and the world doesn't need that. I tried to explain to her that in the end it would not be Racine who she hurt, but herself."

"But she didn't agree with you?"

"She wanted things. She wanted control. She didn't understand the beauty in our way. I believe, in the end, that when Domino went over that balcony, she was pushed by the destructive forces she'd unleashed on her sister."

"I believe," Trudi said, "that Domino wound up killing herself."

"Bad karma, you mean?"

"Yes, this is what we believe, that whatever energy you put out into the world, whether good or bad, will return to you three times. Not exactly, of course. If you kick a cat, your leg won't break in a later life. But some deep hurt will occur."

"So you mean that someone who suffers in this life is paying, somehow, for something bad they did in a previous life." Maggie felt her chest tighten.

"Doesn't that explanation make more sense than to think it was random?"

"No," Maggie cried out. "It makes it even worse. People are already inclined to villainize people who are ill or suffer. Now if you have to believe that it really is your fault, how much more terrible would that be?"

She paused. This was not a place for a religious argument. She had to stop personalizing everything. If she was going to be successful as a private detective, she had to figure out how to distance herself, how to get past her own emotions. Wasn't this something she was learning—that it was time to start thinking about the whole world and not just herself.

"What about Grant Winfrey? How is he involved in all this?"

Trudi would say no more. The very mention of Grant's name shut her down. Maggie felt sure he knew something important. She had to meet with him. As she left the candy store, she thought of the calendar she'd seen on Trudi's wall, and the fact that the date of the full moon was circled. She suspected there was a coven meeting that night and it was in the woods. It was worth a try. Maybe if she tried meeting Grant Winfrey in a situation in which he felt comfortable, he would be more likely to talk to her.

But first she needed to see Racine and see if she could persuade her to hire them again.

Chapter Thirty-Eight

That conversation did not go well.

Racine wouldn't even open the door. She spoke to Maggie through a window, and just kept shaking her head.

"No," she said. "No more."

"Racine, you wanted to find out what happened to your sister and I feel like I'm making progress. I don't think you should stop right now."

"You want more money," Racine said.

"No," Maggie said. "You've been more than generous. I just want you to know that there are still avenues to pursue and I plan to look into them.

"But the case is over. Domino's dead. Passion's dead. There's nothing to investigate. There's nothing to do."

"I think there is more to learn. I think there may have been more to Domino's death than even the police realized. I'm not positive. I can't make promises, but you hired me to get you information and I think there's more to get. I just wanted to let you know that I'm eager to keep working on this." She cleared her throat. "You do want to clear your name?"

"No," Racine said. "It's enough. I should never have started investigating this in the first place."

"Has someone threatened you?" Maggie asked.

Racine shivered. "No," she said. "I want to go back to the life I was living. I want to take care of my mother. We keep to ourselves. What do I care whether people think I'm a murderer or not? I just want to take care of my mother."

"Do you feel like you're in danger?" Maggie asked.

She found herself looking around, just as Racine was doing. The house itself seemed like it was going to collapse onto her.

"No, no, no," Racine said and slammed down the window.

"I feel like I've let her down," Maggie said when she got back to the office.

"You did nothing of the kind," Agnes said. "She wouldn't have paid you if she felt disappointed. You're our top money earner, Maggie."

"Only because the same person kept hiring and firing us."

"Baby steps," Helen said.

"We have other business to take care of," Agnes said. "I'm working on persuading Hal Carter to hire us to watch his wife. That would be a big one."

"I don't want spend my days following around poor Gretchen Carter," Maggie snapped. "Racine is in trouble. Something is going on with that woman and she needs our help."

"She doesn't want our help."

"She says that," Maggie said. "But I'm not convinced it's true. I think she desperately needs our help."

Agnes looked at her. She had a turban wrapped around her head. Maggie's mother used to wear something similar on days between going to the hairdresser, but she hadn't seen one in years, which reminded her of Iphigenia. She really would have to stop by. It was ominous that she'd been up and down Main Street several times and Iphigenia had not hurled herself at Maggie once.

"I'm not sure it's legal to work for someone who doesn't want you to work for them."

"Then I'll hire myself to investigate what happened."

"Investigate what?" Agnes said. "What else do you want to find?"

"I can't stop until I speak to Grant Winfrey. I think he's going to be at a coven meeting. Let me go to that at least and see if I can talk to him."

"This is a complete waste of time," Agnes snapped. "We're here to provide a service, which we've done. Now leave it alone."

"I'm not going to leave it alone until I'm sure it's done."

She looked into Agnes's eyes. How to explain to her that she felt a sense of responsibility? That the whole reason Racine hired her was because she felt Maggie had a special understanding of evil. While Maggie didn't think that was true, she did think some deeper form of transaction had taken place between them. Racine trusted her, and when people trusted you, you owed them something special, didn't you?

"You know, Agnes, you're always telling me that we need to have a gimmick for our agency. We need to have a niche. Well, what if our niche is that we genuinely care about our clients. That we truly want to do the right thing by them? I think we should have a higher ethical standard," Maggie said. "I think that's what makes our detective agency different. You talked about appealing to the women's audience, but I think our appeal should be greater than that. We do more than provide a service. We provide help.

"Something is wrong with Racine," Maggie went on. "I don't know what it is. I don't know if she's a killer or if someone's trying to kill her. I don't know if there are witches after her. All I do know is that I am not going to turn my back on someone in trouble, and I don't care if Racine fires me ten more times."

Agnes looked stunned into silence for the first time since Maggie knew her. Never had Maggie before noticed that one of Agnes's teeth turned in a little bit, but never before had Maggie seen Agnes stand so still.

"Agnes, just let me go to this coven meeting. Let me see what's going on, and then I promise you I'll drop it."

Agnes still said nothing, but Helen began to laugh.

"An ethical private detective agency. Oh my God, Maggie Dove, now I've heard everything."

Chapter Thirty-Nine

The coven meeting was days away. Maggie needed to prepare for her Sunday School class, but felt jumpy. Restless. She kept pacing around and without fail, every time she stood up, she stepped on Kosi's tail. She was beginning to think that some force was leading her to hurt the cat, and it bothered her. They were caught in a cycle of pain, both of them aggrieved with the other. There had to be a way to break the cycle.

Maybe Kosi needed a treat.

She called Helen. "I'm thinking of going to the pet store. Do you think Edgar would like to come?"

"Please, please, please," she said.

"I'll be there in ten minutes."

The pet store was a wonderland. They were having a rescue-cat adoption afternoon, featuring tons of cats, all of whom seemed much friendlier than Kosi. Maggie and Edgar watched a dog trainer with a bunch of puppies and both found they wanted to adopt a golden retriever, but Maggie, as the responsible one, felt they should hold off. Edgar immediately bonded with a gecko. The nice salesperson said he could have it for only $20. Maggie called Helen and asked her what she thought.

"Thank God it's just a lizard," she said. "I thought he'd bring home a golden retriever."

As they waited for the lizard to be packed up, Maggie heard a distinctive voice and turned to see Reverend Sunday admiring one of the iguanas in a cage. Reverend Sunday wore a gray sweater and gray slacks, a sort of casual version of her usual outfit. She seemed a beacon of calm in the middle of the insanity that was the pet store on a Saturday afternoon.

"Hello," she said when she saw Maggie and Edgar. "I like to come here when I'm feeling homesick for Ghana. I look at some of these little fellows and they remind me of what I used to see on my lawn."

"You had things like this at your house," Edgar asked in awe.

"Yes, but much bigger," she said. "There were also pythons and cobras and the black mamba, which is the most venomous snake in Africa."

"Didn't they attack you?"

"No, we left them alone and they left us alone. Are you ready for tomorrow night," she asked Maggie.

"Yes, I've got the limousine ready."

"No trouble?" the reverend asked, though from the way she raised her eyebrow, Maggie suspected she knew exactly how much trouble there was. Furthermore, Maggie suspected she picked this restaurant for the exact purpose of making trouble. She was staking a claim to who she was. Maggie had just done something similar, she supposed, in standing up for Racine.

"What brings you here?" Reverend Sunday asked.

"I'm getting a gecko," Edgar shouted, "and Maggie Dove needs to get a present for her cat because she hates him."

"You hate your cat?"

"I wouldn't use the word 'hate,'" Maggie said, drawing Edgar to her. She would have put her hand over his mouth but she worried he'd bite it. "It's more that I dislike him intensely." She explained how she'd come to adopt the cat after his owner died. "I know he's grieving for her, and that grief is making him irascible, but it's hard living with someone who dislikes you, so I thought I'd get him a treat. See if I can win him over, because I have to say, that cat is killing me. I never know when he's going to pounce."

Reverend Sunday nodded. She was not a woman who gestured a lot, and yet in that slight incline of her head, she conveyed a lot of meaning. She was thinking about something.

"Have you considered praying about it?" she asked.

"Praying about the cat? No," Maggie said. "I can't ask God to bother Himself about a cat."

"Why don't you let God decide what He wants to bother Himself with?"

They started walking toward the checkout. "It just seems like with the Middle East and terrorism and everything else, God has enough on his hands."

"Ask him," Sunday said. "He will answer you."

Maggie felt silly about it, and put it out of her head. She took Edgar home and helped him get the gecko set up, which was a process. They had to find the right place for his tank, and they had to warm up a rock. Fortunately, it ate dry food so they didn't need to buy frozen crickets. Helen seemed especially quiet. Edgar ran over and asked her to look at the gecko, but she just patted his curly head and went back to staring into space.

"Everything okay?" Maggie asked.

"Yes, Maggie Dove. Don't you fret."

That night when Maggie went home, she prayed over Helen—and then, so long as she was there, she prayed over Kosi. *Dear God, please help me find a way to deal with this cat. With Kosi*, she said, using his name. It seemed good to be specific. Then she fell asleep and woke up an hour later with Kosi scratching at her arm. An hour later he scratched her face. She couldn't get back to sleep that time, worried he'd scratch out her eyes, and so she lay awake worrying about that and then other things, and then thinking about Racine, and when she finally woke up, it was almost time for church.

"I have definitely proven that prayers to God about cats do not work," she muttered to Kosi, to God and to Reverend Sunday.

She looked in the mirror and sighed. She had such dark circles under her eyes. When she was young, she used to put on concealer, but it would take plaster to get rid of these, and she figured she'd just make believe she was French. Somehow that led her back to thinking about Racine, and how she never talked about the time she spent in France. Ten years was a long time. Maggie wondered if she'd had to suppress that memory now that her life was so different. She was thinking about that when she stepped out the door and almost stepped right on to a kitten on her veranda.

"Now who are you?" she whispered, peering down.

It was a little gray thing, curled up on her front steps.

Automatically Maggie looked around, wondering if some larger angry mother cat was nearby, but no. It seemed to be just this little kitten, who was all bones and fur and who collapsed so warmly into her arms.

"Oh Lord," she whispered. "I ask you for help with one cat and you give me another."

There was nothing to do but to bring the kitten inside. There were coyotes outside and a host of other dangers. It made little mewing noises as Maggie set the little creature down in her living room and pondered what to do with this new development.

And then Kosi came meandering in and at the sight of the kitten he stopped. His tail began lashing against the air. He made a slight rumbling sound, but the kitten wasn't scared. Immediately it went bounding to Kosi and rubbed its head against him. Kosi stood still. He looked up at Maggie as though struck dumb, and he then he licked the kitten. Maggie watched them for a while, to make sure Kosi wouldn't eat the smaller cat, but instead Kosi lay down, and the little kitten curled up alongside of him. Maggie thought how odd it was that a person—or a cat, in this case—could be so jammed up with love and unable to get it out. Until some little creature showed it the way. She remembered Edgar's love for her had just about changed her world. She'd felt so cold and all alone until that wild boy wrapped his arms around her. He brought new life to her, and he brought Helen into her life. Helen was not quite a daughter, but she was the next best thing.

That morning, after Sunday School let out and all the kids were running around outside, Maggie went to the library in the church, where she knew she'd find Helen. She always liked to nap during the service.

"You look exhausted."

"Phone calls from Syria. There's a seven-hour time difference. It threw me off."

"Did you have that teacher meeting the other day?" Maggie asked. "How did that go?"

"Oh God, don't even ask me about that. They make him sound like *he's* the bad seed."

"Somehow I doubt that," Maggie said. She knew Edgar's teacher, a good-natured young woman who'd gone to Columbia to get an MA in child education. She was serious teacher, but Maggie knew she treated Edgar kindly.

"They want to do all sorts of tests, and put him on medicine, and have meetings. It's overwhelming."

"I'll go with you."

"No, I'm not doing any of it. He's a boy. He's a boy who's got to learn to adjust. He's just going to have to toughen up. That's all. He's strong and intelligent. He simply needs self-control."

"Sometimes kids need a little more than that," Maggie pointed out.

"Not my kid," Helen said. She shook her head. "Sorry, Momma Dove, but that's it."

She looked so resistant, Maggie thought. So solitary, so isolated and so frightened. She looked like Racine, when you got down to it. Both of them desperately needing help, and both were resistant to receiving it. Maggie thought if she just knew the right combination of words, she could unlock both their defenses. But she didn't know it. She felt frustrated with herself.

"I'm not going to tell you what to do," she said to Helen. "You're his mother. But if I promise to sit quietly and not offer advice, will you tell me what's really bothering you?"

Around them Maggie could hear the sounds of the church: people talking, getting cookies and coffee. The choir director was playing on the piano, working with the teenagers on a song.

"As you have probably gathered, I wasn't married to Edgar's father. I didn't know him, truth to tell. We worked on a mission together. I can't go into details, except to say that he was famous for his skills. We were in Syria, the only two people around. We had a moment, you could say. I don't regret it, but I never expected to have Edgar."

"Is he someone you could ask for help?"

Helen brushed back her hair. On her hands was written the word "dinner."

"He was an assassin, Maggie. He was the man they went to when they needed a hard task done. Not long after that, when we were on a mission, I saw him do something truly evil. I can't tell you what it was, but it was bad. I was shocked. I thought I'd seen everything, but not that.

"I switched to working for the CIA then, where, you'll laugh to hear this, at least there were rules, and it was then that I found out I was pregnant. That evil, Maggie, is inside of Edgar. I hoped it would never flourish, but now, when I look at him, I see his father and I worry it will come out. He looks exactly like him, and when I get these school reports, I'm afraid that that darkness is flourishing inside him. I don't know what sort of man he's going to become and it scares me."

"No," Maggie said, grabbing Helen's hand in her own. "That boy is not evil. He's trouble, he's a headache. He should probably take Ritalin. But he's not evil."

"Can you promise me that, Maggie?"

"Yes, I can promise you, because one thing I know is that goodness is stronger than evil. It always is. Goodness will triumph with that boy and he'll grow up to be a good man."

"I wish I had your certainty."

"It's not certainty," Maggie said. "It's faith. That's something completely different, but it's powerful, Helen. It's more powerful than anything."

"I hope you're right," she said, and then she heard the sound of Edgar's footsteps, and she automatically clenched her stomach, preparing for where he would hit her, but decided it would be better to tackle the situation head on. So she turned and ran at Edgar instead, almost toppling him over. But it worked. No pain.

She stayed and talked with him for a bit, but then Maggie had to go. Because this was the day she always visited the most ancient member of the church, and one of the most inspiring people Maggie knew.

Chapter Forty

Since taking over the helm of the church, Reverend Sunday had initiated several new programs, and one of them involved visiting homebound members once a month. She argued that these souls tended to slip between the cracks. That once they stopped coming to church, people forgot them, and so every Sunday she paid visits and this second Sunday in November was Maggie's turn to accompany her. They were going to visit Ella Standards, who was 91-years-old.

She lived in a small house not far from the church. It was a home filled with pictures. The walls were covered with photos of her children and grandchildren and great-grandchildren. She'd been a great knitter in her time, and every single piece of furniture had an afghan on it. Sarah, her aide, wore a pink afghan. Sarah came from Ghana, which was a great source of joy to Reverend Sunday.

"How is Ella?" Reverend Sunday asked as Sarah guided them to the bedroom.

"Good," she said. She smiled at the very old lady, who was sleeping peacefully. Ella slept most of the time. She was very pale, but her face wore a slight smile. She clutched a little brown teddy bear that had a little knit jacket on it. Her Bible was by her bed. Her breathing seemed shallow. Reverend Sunday held her hand and prayed with her for a while. Often the sound of the familiar words would rouse Ella. Maggie was always touched by how those words could have such power, but not today. Ella was in a sound sleep, and after while the reverend said, "Maggie, I'm going to visit with Sarah for a bit."

"I'll stay here with Ella," Maggie said. "You two go and chat."

She settled herself into a chair. She had *The Brothers Karamazov* with her. She was almost at the end, and was content to sit there reading. The fact was that she'd been running around so much, that being in a room with this well-loved woman would be peaceful.

Reverend Sunday and Sarah went off to the living room. Maggie knew they liked to talk about their memories of Ghana. She could hear their laughter, and she settled in and began to read, when all of a sudden, Ella opened her eyes.

"Maggie Dove," she said.

"How are you, my friend?" Maggie asked. She clasped her hand. Ella had always been one of her favorites at church, an elegant woman who was always the first to greet strangers. She was very well-organized and had run the annual Attic Sale like a military operation. Once she caught someone stealing and had chased him down with an umbrella. She was a pip, as Maggie's husband liked to say.

They discussed Ella's health for a few moments, or lack of it, and then Ella asked how Maggie was doing. One of the nice things about being with old people, Maggie thought, was that they made you feel so young. In Ella's eyes, Maggie was a young mother and always would be.

Then Ella moved on to subject that was always foremost on her mind. "Is the church budget balanced?"

"A small deficit, I think."

She shook her head disapprovingly.

"How's church attendance?"

"Pretty good. Lots of new families."

"And this minister. She's all right?" She searched Maggie's face.

"Yes," Maggie said, and she told her about how they were all going to a Ghanaian restaurant with the Dining Out Club. Now that she thought about it, it occurred to Maggie that Ella might have started the Dining Out club many years ago. "I wish you could go."

"Soon enough I'll be dining with the angels," Ella said. She nodded at the chair in which Maggie was sitting. "My grandfather's been starting to visit. He sits right there. I think he'll be the one to guide me over. I'll say hello to Juliet for you."

"Thank you," Maggie said.

Ella closed her eyes. She looked like she was dozing off, but then she opened them.

"What's this I hear about you having a detective agency?"

"It's true," Maggie said. "I'm working with two other women. Solving mysteries."

"In Ferris's old offices?"

"Are they? I don't know." Everything in the village had belonged to someone else at some point. You would have to build your own house, as Agnes had done, in order to claim something for your own, and even then, people said her land belonged to somebody else. It was Miller's old farmland.

"You're making money?"

"Yes," Maggie said, with a smile.

"Good for you. You're working on the case about Domino Stern?"

"That's right," Maggie said, laughing. "Ella, I think I'm going to hire you. You have better sources than I do."

"I've been seeing Leonard," Ella said. "He comes to visit."

"Leonard Stern?"

"He comes to me. Sits right where you do, though of course he's much bigger. I always liked big men."

Maggie knew enough about the dying to know that they existed in a place out of time. They lived in a dream-like state. She also remembered that Ella's husband was quite short.

"He was the great love of my life."

Life was full of surprises. Maggie tried to think it through. Ella Standard was 91, which was the same age as Madame Simone. Maggie had never connected the two of them. Madame Simone had always seemed a force unto herself. A woman closely knit to her husband and daughter. She never thought of her having competition.

"What was Leonard Stern like? I've heard stories."

"Don't believe the stories. People are jealous of a man like that. You want to know what he was like? He was alive. He was vibrant. He was romantic. Unlike that wife of his, who just married him to come to this country."

"Didn't he love her?"

"At first, he did, I guess. You know, she told him she was a countess, but that wasn't true. She lied. She just wanted to get out of France, to marry a rich American. Once she got here, she didn't care about him. She was looking for a servant. Not a husband."

Maggie thought that seemed to be a theme with Madame Simone. She treated her daughter the same way.

"We fell in love. I don't excuse myself, but it was real."

She started to cough. She gripped Maggie's hand, and forced back the pain. A woman who could force back a lot of pain, Maggie thought.

"He was going to divorce her, but then she became pregnant with Domino. When he told me, I thought Simone was lying, but not that time. All those years she refused to have another child, and then suddenly she wants one." That explained the fifteen-year difference in ages between Domino and Racine, Maggie thought. Having seen how strong-minded Madam Simone was,

Maggie could well believe she used whatever weapon she had to hang on to Leonard.

"He was trapped," Ella went on. "And that little girl, she was a monster. A carbon copy of her mother. Self-absorbed. They both made his life hell. The only good one was Racine. He encouraged her to leave, to get out of there. He sent her to stay with family in France. Oh, she didn't like that, Madame Simone didn't. But he had to protect her. Domino was dangerous. He worried she would kill Racine.

"It was such a comfort to him to know she was flourishing in France. But then everything collapsed. He died, on April 15. Heart attack, and not long after Domino attacked that girl. With that voodoo doll. She left and then Simone couldn't wait to get Racine back. She called and Racine dropped everything and came."

"But why?" Maggie asked. It had been the question she'd been puzzling over. Why had Racine given up everything for her mother?

"For love," Ella whispered.

Then she closed her eyes, and slept.

Maggie sat with her a while longer. Was it that simple, she wondered? Had Racine given up everything because she loved her mother? People did make great sacrifices for love. She'd seen it. Yet she didn't completely believe it. She thought of how worn and gnawed Racine's lips were. Those lines. Something serious was eating its way through Racine. Maggie needed to get through to her, but she wasn't sure how.

Chapter Forty-One

Finally, it was the night of the Diming Out Club. The limo awaited. A long stretch limo that seated twenty and was stocked with liquor and nuts. All hesitation vanished. The crowd was ready to pile in and go.

Except they couldn't leave just yet, because Cherrelle was late.

"This is terrible," Leona Faraday said. "We have a reservation for twenty. We can't be late."

"She's in trouble," Agnes said. "She'll be here as soon as she can."

Agnes wore a black lace dress and high heels and her hair mounded with gel. Maggie wore her usual black dress and pearl earrings, but it was Reverend Sunday who was a revelation. She wore a stunning two-piece green dress. A beautiful snake-like pattern swam across it and at the top, on her shoulders, there were light epaulets that mimicked the material. She'd draped a dark yellow cape over shoulders. She'd also put on dark maroon lipstick and she smiled. Up until then, Maggie hadn't realized how serious she always was.

"Agnes," Maggie whispered. "We really have to go. I don't want this to be a disaster."

"I don't know what's wrong with Cherrelle," Agnes said. "What if she's breaking up with me?"

"Why would she do it now? Tonight?"

"She's mercurial."

"I don't suppose you could just wait for her and then drive her."

"To the Bronx. In the dark. In the rain?"

It had started to drizzle softly.

"What's up partners?" Helen asked. She alone had not dressed up for the occasion. She wore jeans and a white T-shirt, but Edgar, happily, was with a new babysitter. So Helen seemed relaxed, though she did keep checking her phone—whether that was because she was worried about Edgar or Syria, Maggie wasn't sure.

Things were just about to get really bad, when all of a sudden, a Mercedes came tearing into the parking lot. It shot into a spot, and out of came a thin, middle-aged woman. She had white hair and pearls.

"Cherrelle," Agnes cried out and ran to greet her. "You're here. Oh my dear," she said.

Cherrelle looked at her good-humoredly. "Calm down, Agnes. Good Lord."

Everyone sighed with relief and then they all piled into the limo. Walter went first, to fit himself into the back, and his wife followed. Then came the various Faraday sisters, who were preoccupied with Cherrelle.

"Doesn't Agnes's girlfriend look like Maggie Dove," the loudest of the Faradays said.

"Shhh," Walter said.

Helen was engulfed in laughter and couldn't move, but Maggie kicked her and Iphigenia was there, though Maggie noticed she hadn't spoken to her. She must still be upset about the haircut. She hadn't had a chance to apologize.

"Is that a bar cart," Agnes cried out. "Let's pop some champagne. This is going to be a fabulous night."

"Let me do it, silly, you'll blind everyone." Cherrelle grabbed the champagne bottle and popped the cork.

"She's got hands like a chicken farmer," Leona Faraday said.

"Bubbly," Cherrelle said, smiling at Maggie.

By the time they got to the restaurant in the Bronx, they were all feeling much more cheerful. It was a small restaurant, with a giant buffet. There was peanut butter soup and roasted fish and roasted chicken. There were also a cow's feet, which everyone avoided., and huge vats of rice, toward which everyone gravitated. It was all so colorful and spicy and Reverend Sunday was laughing and telling stories.

Maggie found herself sitting next to Cherrelle, who was quite entertaining. She had a font of stories about what it was like to work at the Coroner's Office. Some of them quite lurid, including one about a death that seemed accidental but wound up being declared a murder when a broken mirror was discovered in the basement. Sort of a complicated story, but Maggie enjoyed it and she was laughing, when she happened to glance over and saw Agnes glaring at her.

Agnes on a good day looked angry. Maybe it was the way her brow covered her eyes. Her face looked perpetually clenched. But now she seemed to be radiating heat. The sight of her brought Maggie back to the day when she'd fumed about her turning down Racine. A similar expression flickered across Agnes's face.

"Are you all right?" Maggie asked.

"How dare you flirt with my girlfriend," Agnes yelled.

"Agnes," Maggie said. "I'm not flirting. I'm just talking."

"You always have to be the best," she said. "Everyone always has to like you more."

Cherrelle jumped into action just then. Put her arm around Agnes and tugged her away. Fortunately, everyone had been so busy talking they didn't notice. Or they were being kind and just kept talking. But Maggie felt shaken. She clenched her fists. Every time she felt like she knew the rules, they changed. Nothing was what it seemed. She was getting too old to do all this. Life was so messy and uncertain and painful. She never meant to hurt Agnes.

When she got back to her house, she sank into her living room, two cats at her feet. She looked around her tidy room, at the desk she'd made herself a long time ago, at the photographs on the wall and the maps that had once belonged to her husband. She felt safe here. In the twenty years she'd mourned her daughter, she'd known the rules. She was in charge of the rules. There was no one else to worry about. In fact, although she'd been depressed, she'd felt perfectly content in her house up until her neighbor went and got murdered on her lawn.

Life just took such courage and she wasn't sure she was up for it.

She looked at the little cat curled up next to her, and at Kosi, who had survived a fair amount himself.

She noticed one of her Detective Grudge tapes on her desk. She so loved being a private detective. She couldn't just surrender. She had to fight for what she wanted.

"Hello," Agnes said, voice muffled when she picked up the phone. Maggie knew she'd been crying.

"How are you, friend?" she asked.

"Oh, Maggie. She's going to drop me. I just know it."

"She's not, Agnes. She seems very fond of you."

"I'm going crazy," Agnes said.

"I am too," Maggie said. "But I cannot go crazy without you at my side."

Agnes laughed.

They talked for a long time, and Maggie felt much better. At the end of the conversation Agnes said, "Are you still planning to go to that coven meeting tomorrow night?"

"Yes," Maggie answered, warily. She hoped this wouldn't provoke another argument.

"I'm going to come with you," Agnes said. "We're going to do this together."

"Fabulous," Maggie said, and she meant it.

"But I think I'm going to take some Xanax."

"Fabulous," Maggie said.

Chapter Forty-Two

They agreed to meet at sunset at the large rock that marked the entryway into the woods. Maggie figured the witches would come later in the night, but that would give them a chance to hide and get into position. Her plan was that she and Agnes would stake out a spot, wait for the witches and then follow them. It all sounded perfectly reasonable until you actually said to yourself: *I'm going to follow witches into a dark wood*. But Agnes would be there, and Maggie was grateful for that.

She considered alerting Walter, but rejected that idea. He would stop the whole thing. She didn't tell Helen either. Her babysitter had quit after she got home from the Dining Out Club. It turned out Edgar had tried to close the garage door on her head. There was no point in adding further stress to Helen, and Maggie certainly did not want to bring Edgar along. She could deal with witches and she could deal with Edgar. But she didn't think she could deal with them both at the same time.

Maggie got to the rock first. She'd worn black sweat pants and brought a flashlight. Detective Grudge said there was no piece of equipment more important for a detective. Following his advice, she checked to make sure the batteries were good. They were.

A family of deer wandered by. They stood, neatly arranged by a rock, almost as though they were arranging a tableau for her. She loved their stillness. She was always surprised by how big they were. They were like those plant-eating dinosaurs that roamed the earth, chewing leaves and essentially harmless unless you got between a mother and her baby.

Watching them made her think of the four members of the Stern family. She thought of what Ella had said about Leonard Stern pushing Racine to go away. She thought of how the family collapsed in a month: Domino caught up in a scandal and Leonard Stern dying. Racine's entire life twisted sharply in one month's time. Maggie couldn't help but feel sympathy. There Racine had been, in France, happy, and then all of a sudden that life ended and she began one of service to her mother. The odd thing was Racine did not seem bitter. She seemed anxious, intense, and even frightened. But she didn't seem angry.

Suddenly Agnes appeared. She dropped in so suddenly it was as though she'd parachuted onto the rock. She wore camo gear and she carried a heavy back pack. "Night vision goggles," she explained. "And a bunch of other equipment. I also brought coffee and some cookies for you, Maggie. I figured we'd have to kill some time."

Maggie was never one to turn away a cookie, and so they sat companionably eating cookies and drinking coffee.

Darkness fell. At one point, Agnes shook a pill onto her hand and smiled, "Xanax," she said. "It really helps."

Maggie patted her hand. It was nice to see her so calm, though she wondered if right before staking out witches was the perfect time to medicate yourself. Still, the less hysteria, the better.

The sky began to darken and the moon to rise. It was a giant moon, as big as the sun, and almost as bright. The woods erupted in sound. The birds seemed to be shrieking at one other. An owl hooted and the crickets screamed. Something small dashed by Maggie's feet, startling her. The stars began to come out. Hours passed. She expected Agnes to fuss, but she stayed calm. Very calm.

"I suppose it's possible the witches aren't meeting tonight," Maggie felt obliged to point out. "Or they might have a different path into the woods."

"Don't worry," Agnes said. "They'll show up. I have confidence in you."

She moved and Maggie could hear the pill bottle jangling. She felt like all her senses were on alert. She was so focused on listening that she didn't even feel cold, though the night certainly was cooling off. She and Agnes settled into a companionable silence, and then suddenly, toward midnight, Maggie heard an unusual sound—the whispering of feet scraping across leaves. The witches were here.

"Put on your goggles," Agnes whispered. "And let's go."

Chapter Forty-Three

Following witches in the woods turned out to be easier than Maggie had thought it would be. What with all the animal sounds, they didn't have to worry about being overheard. The goggles weren't even necessary. The moon lit their way.

Maggie walked along familiar trails for a while, and then the witches reached a large split rock and veered deeper into the woods. Maggie could still hear the thrum of the parkway, which was reassuring, as they kept moving forward. And then they arrived at the circle she had found a week earlier. She was right. It had been their meeting place.

Maggie and Agnes watched from behind a rock as the witches went about their business. A tall man in a long robe emerged from the group. He wore a headdress with two horns sprouting from it and he carried a sword with him. *Grant Winfrey*, Maggie thought. Although he was disguised by his clothes and headdress, it seemed like an incredible coincidence that there would be another man of his height, another man that sloped the way he did. The witches around him chanted as Grant walked in a circle, dragging a sword through the dirt, lips moving as well. Maggie couldn't understand what he said, but the rhythm of his words twisted through her heart. She felt her blood rise in sync to the music.

Then one of the women walked out and put four candles around the circle--marking the directions of a compass, Maggie suspected. She remembered the way Domino arranged the candles in her own circle, in the cellar. This didn't feel as ominous to Maggie, though, maybe because it was outside. Then another woman stepped out and began sprinkling liquid on the ground. Maggie smelled incense. She began to feel uncomfortable watching them. It felt like a violation.

She hadn't realized how solemn it would be. She didn't share their beliefs, but she understood reverence. She respected it, in fact. She'd often felt she had more in common with religious people of other faiths than with people who didn't believe anything at all. She understood the desire to make sense of this world, a quest that had animated her entire life. She also respected the desire to live your life according to a set of rules.

"I have to tell them I'm here," Maggie said. "I should tell them before things go too far."

"Okay," Agnes said. Her voice sounded almost slurred.

Maggie took a deep breath. She removed the goggles and cleared her throat. She didn't like drawing attention to herself and she knew she'd startle them. "Excuse me," she said, as she walked into the clearing.

Immediately they all jumped back. There was Trudi, looking angry, and Grant Winfrey, who quickly ripped off the horned headdress and held it behind his back.

"What are you doing here?" Trudi cried out.

Like the others she wore a long gown that looked handmade. She had a circlet in her hair and she wore a deep black necklace.

"I'm sorry to interrupt," Maggie said, "and I didn't mean to scare you. But I wanted to talk to you, Grant, and I thought it might be easier to have this conversation in the presence of the coven. I thought you might feel more comfortable that way." Maggie wondered where Agnes was. She'd thought she was behind her.

"You followed us here?" Trudi said.

Maggie ignored Trudi, focusing on Grant, who looked terrified.

"Please," she said. "I just need to find out what happened to Domino, to try to understand why she killed herself, if she did. That's all. I'm a private investigator, and I don't want to get any of you in trouble. I just want information."

"I had nothing to do with her death," Grant said.

Finally, Maggie thought. Finally, he was going to speak to her. Finally, he was going to do something besides run.

"But you did argue with her?"

The coven moved closer to him, offering him support. Maggie counted fourteen people in total. She wanted to make sure Agnes was close, but didn't dare interrupt this moment. She assumed Agnes was watching, getting ready to pounce if Maggie needed her. She hoped so.

"If I answer your question, will you leave me alone?" Grant asked. He looked deflated, like a runner who'd been running a very long time.

"Yes," she said. "I promise."

At that, he seemed to lean back into the circle, as though placing all his weight against his fellow witches. "Yes, I knew Domino. I met her and Trudi in high school, at Cranston. We were in the same chemistry class. I was good at chemistry. When Trudi invited us to join the coven, I thought it would be fun, but I got pulled into it, and then I started hearing about how ergot could improve the experience. I wanted to see if I could make it myself.

"It was a challenge. If it was a little bit off, it could be lethal. But I liked the challenge—I was a whiz kid, you see.

"I spent months trying to get it right, to grow the *Claviceps purpurea*, to isolate the ergot compounds, to find a safe combination, but after months of work, I did it. We found using it exhilarating, but after high school, I stopped doing it. I went to college, then to medical school, and then I began to pursue my career. I lost touch with Domino. Trudi and I were still going to the same coven meetings, but Domino moved away and went to California and married Lucifer. I didn't expect I'd ever hear from her again."

He was panting. It was as though he'd kept the words inside him for so long that he couldn't stop them now that they were coming out. An owl hooted and rustled in one of the trees overhead. The moon shone into the circle.

"One day, out of the blue, Domino contacted me. She called me and said she'd joined a coven in California. It was different than ours. Black magic. Hard core," he said, with a ragged laugh. "The thing was that they needed ergot, but she couldn't find any as good as mine. She liked mine best. She wanted me to make some for her."

He puffed up his cheeks and blew out.

"I said no. I hadn't made any in a long time, and I didn't want to risk it. My career as a doctor was going well. I could get arrested. I could kill somebody, but when Domino wanted something, she was ruthless. She told me I didn't have a choice. She would report me. She didn't care if she got into trouble. She was famous for getting into trouble. But if word got about me, I'd be ruined."

"You continued making the ergot for her?" Maggie asked.

"I had no choice. I kept begging her to find another supplier, but she said no one's was as good as mine."

"This must have gone on for years," Maggie said.

"Decades," he said. "It haunted me."

Maggie thought of how disorganized his office was. Fear and anxiety had a way of filtering down into all aspects of your life. This poor man had been distracted for decades.

"But when I heard she was coming back to Darby, I figured that finally I would have my chance. I would talk to her, or her husband. I would give them the formula. I would train someone else. I just had to make it stop."

"So that's why you went to see her?"

"Yes," he said. "But she wouldn't meet with me. She said there was nothing to discuss. I knocked on her door and tried to get in, but she wouldn't talk to me."

That must have been the day Maggie saw him on the property, she thought.

"But on the night of the party, I finally got hold of her."

"And she said no?"

"She said yes," he cried out. "She said she didn't need me anymore. Then she told me I was a fool, and that she would never have reported me if I'd just said no in the first place."

He clasped his hands together. Poor man, Maggie thought, to be so trapped by his fears.

"I ran out of there, I was so relieved. I knew she was laughing at me and I didn't even care. I went back home and destroyed all the equipment, and then, you were at my door. You were following me. I thought she sent you. It seemed like the kind of game she would want to play."

"I am sorry," Maggie said.

"I was so glad when I heard she died," he said. He looked at the people around him, all covered up. "We Wicca, we don't mean anyone harm. We worship the earth. We celebrate love. We're a gentle faith."

His nerves were shot, she thought. He reminded her of one of her students who'd been posted to Afghanistan and came home war-weary and jumpy. But did that mean he was innocent? He had such a good motive to kill Domino. She'd destroyed his life. But how could he have got out on that balcony. To have hidden there would have required courage, and this man had lost his. Had he murdered her, she couldn't see him doing it in such a flamboyant way.

"You'll leave me alone," he said.

She nodded. There was nothing more she could get from him.

"Yes," she said, beginning to step back. But she froze when she heard a low rumbling sound. "What is that?" Trudi asked. Grant began to shiver.

"It's nothing," Maggie said, though she recognized what it was. It was Agnes snoring. She'd fallen asleep, standing against a tree.

Chapter Forty-Four

Maggie woke Agnes and they started for home. She had no other avenues to pursue in her investigation. Maybe what everyone said was true. Maybe Domino, high on ergot, had fallen off the balcony. Passion, startled, had fallen down the steps. Maggie had been so eager to find cause and connection, but perhaps that was due to nothing more than her desire to prove herself as a private detective. She had so hoped her first big case would lead to something. But now she didn't have a client, she didn't have a witch to track down. It was hard to justify continuing on.

Slowly they made their way through the woods.

"How many of those Xanax did you take, Agnes?"

"Just two," Agnes said. "I feel great though. I haven't felt this relaxed in years."

"It's very nice that you're so relaxed, but I think it's a bad idea to overdose on prescription medicine."

"I didn't overdose. I just doubled the dosage."

"Agnes, don't do that anymore."

"Okay," Agnes said, smiling.

Something about Agnes reminded Maggie of a story a friend of hers had told her about her mother. She had always been a difficult woman, but then she developed Alzheimer's and her entire personality changed. She went from being mean and querulous to being a kind and gentle soul. Maggie had wondered if that gentleness had been inside the old lady all along, and whether there might have been a way to bring it out earlier. That made her think of Madame Simone.

They might as well take a route that would bring them past Stern Manor, she figured, as long as they were wandering around in the dark, and as long as Agnes was so cheerful. She wanted to see it one last time. Soon she would move on to following around poor Hal Carter and checking up on his marital indiscretions. But for now, she wanted one final view of her first real case. She wanted to see Stern Manor in the dark. She wanted to see if it looked different to her, now that she knew more of its secrets.

They paused for a moment to look at the house, and that was when Maggie saw a ghost in the window.

Chapter Forty-Five

Maggie wasn't sure she believed in ghosts, but she knew one when she saw it. The white billowy creature hovered at the window, then disappeared. Racine and Madame Simone were alone in the house, Maggie knew. Lucifer and Milo had moved out.

"We have to check what's going on there," Maggie said. "Are you up for it, Agnes?"

"Of course," she said, smiling genially. "What do you want to do?"

Maggie couldn't get used to this new more pleasant Agnes. Was it unethical to prefer your detective partner sedated?

"Agnes, we might be in danger. How are your reflexes?"

"My reflexes on a bad day are a thousand times better than yours, Maggie Dove. Now come on," Agnes said, tilting backward against a tree for a moment, closing her eyes and then opening them quickly. "Let's go."

At the front door, Maggie hesitated. It was now 1:00 in the morning and it went against every principle she had to wake up people in the middle of the night. She'd always been so law-abiding and thoughtful.

But she'd seen a ghost, and Racine and Madame Simone were alone with it. Perhaps the house really was evil come to life. Maggie pressed her finger to the doorbell. The whole house shuddered with the noise. But no one answered.

"I think we have to go in," Maggie said.

"Duh."

"Hello," Maggie called out, opening the door.

No answer. They both started up the stairs. Maggie clenched the railing as they made their way up, and suddenly she heard Agnes go clattering down behind her.

She ran down to grab her, but fortunately Agnes was loose enough that she hadn't hurt herself.

"What happened?"

"I felt like someone pulled my leg."

"You walk in front of me," Maggie said.

When they got to the top of the stairs, Maggie saw a light on in Madame Simone's room. She walked to the door and knocked, but there was no response. Pushing the door open cautiously, she found Racine sitting by her mother's bedside. Madame Simone's eyes were closed. She looked pale and still. Racine's whole posture was of grief.

"Has she passed?" Maggie asked, briefly wondering if perhaps the ghost she'd seen was Madame Simone's spirit.

But the old lady opened her eyes at Maggie's question. "Not yet," she said.

Agnes sank into one of the soft chairs, and Maggie approached Racine. "Are you all right?" she asked. "Has anything been going on here?"

Racine shook her head. Lines of stress clawed her face. Her eyes looked sunken. She seemed to be deteriorating under Maggie's eyes. She even smelled of decay. In some ways, Maggie thought, she seemed closer to death than Madame Simone, who stared at Maggie with her bright blue eyes. Madame Simone shivered then, and Maggie realized how cold it was in the room. She noticed the open window and looked to Agnes to ask her to close it, but she was asleep. So Maggie went to shut it herself.

It was a large window that opened out, like doors, over the river. Maggie couldn't help but pause for a moment to admire the view. The full moon shone over the new Tappan Zee bridge. The bridge looked ghostly itself, as though it had floated there from another time.

She leaned forward then to tug the windows closed and as she did so she felt movement behind her. She thought she saw a white reflection in the window. Whipping around, Maggie saw Madame Simone standing in front of her, but not Madame Simone as she'd ever seen her before. Gone were the merry blue eyes. Instead, they were hard. There seemed to be a blue color emanating from her. Even her teeth looked different. She looked feral.

"It's almost over," Madame Simone said, smiling sweetly. "You're the last of it and then it's all done."

"What's done?"

Racine still sat by the bed. She began to whimper. "I didn't know. I didn't know."

"What's going on," Maggie said.

"You just need to jump," Madame Simone said. "Just jump out the window."

"I'm not going to jump out the window," Maggie said. She looked over at Racine, waiting for her to pull her mother away. Because although Maggie weighed more than Madame Simone, and although she was younger, there was a mad strength in Madame Simone's eyes. And there was the open window behind her.

"Domino jumped when I told her to," she said.

Domino. Maggie shivered. She'd seen the red beret, just like everyone else, and assumed that it was Racine up there on the balcony. Could it have been Madame Simone? Was this what Domino saw that made her jump. Domino high on ergot, seeing this vision, hearing it whisper her to her death. Or, even worse, seeing her mother and knowing she wanted her to die.

"Why would you want your daughter to kill herself?"

"She wanted to take money away from Racine. That wasn't fair," Madame Simone said. She put out her hand to Racine, and as though in a trance, Racine walked over to her and held it. "Racine is the only one I've ever loved. She's the perfect daughter. I always knew she'd do whatever I asked. She's like her father. Not Leonard. Not that horror. But her real father. Eric. He died. He left me alone and then Leonard came. So proud of rescuing me. So large and gross. Just like his daughter. All he wanted was to separate me from Racine. He wanted me to devote myself to Domino. What did I care about Domino?"

Maggie remembered what old Ella Standards had said. Had Madame Simone conceived Domino as a way of securing her position? Had she hated her from the moment she was born?

Madame Simone grabbed onto Racine's hand so tightly that Racine staggered forward.

Agnes snored.

"He wanted to keep me from my daughter. Well, I took care of that. I took care of him."

"How?"

She leaned toward Maggie. "Ergot, of course. Dangerous stuff if you don't get it quite right, and it can look just like a heart attack."

Racine began making a keening noise.

"Then I put that doll in that girl's locker. I knew she'd die and Domino would be forced to leave and then Racine could come home, and nothing would separate us. Why did she have to come back here? Why couldn't she have just stayed away?"

Racine must have known, Maggie realized. That's why she'd been so desperate to keep Domino away. Not to protect her mother, but to protect her sister.

"Then she brought along that foolish girl, with all her plans, so obvious to see. She wanted to get rid of

Domino and then she'd push Racine out of this house. It wasn't fair."

"Passion," Maggie whispered.

"I left one of my little balls on the top step. She tripped right over it. She flew."

She laughed at that. Agnes coughed a little. Maggie thought she might wake up, but she didn't.

"Racine," Maggie said. "I think this has gone far enough. Your mother's sick. She needs help."

"No," Racine said. "I can't do that. She's my mother. All she's done, she's done for me."

Maggie could feel a breeze blowing in from the window. She had dressed warmly for the woods, but that decision restricted her mobility now. She thought she could take on Madame Simone, but not her daughter too. She wasn't even sure she could take on one person. She was a 62-year-old Sunday School teacher. What was she doing fighting down an insane murderer and her daughter?

"Racine, you still have a life in front of you. You could travel. You could go back to France. You could sell this place and go somewhere new. You can have a life."

"You're like the rest of them," Madame Simone howled. "You want her to leave me. She will never leave me."

"Racine, whatever she's suffered, remember how you came to me and said you felt evil, and you did feel evil. But you couldn't tell me where it was coming from. But you can stop this."

"I can't," she said. "I can't."

"Push her," Madame Simone said.

Racine started toward her and Maggie began to recite the 23rd psalm. Those beloved words popped into her head and she said them as loud as she could. "Yea, though I walk through the valley of the shadow of death, I will fear no evil…" She looked directly at Racine. "I will fear no evil."

Racine stopped.

Madame Simone looked at her daughter and then ran at Maggie, grabbing her around the neck. Her hands were like claws. Maggie couldn't get them loose. She pried at them, conscious that every step was taking her closer to the window.

"Help," she called to Racine. "Please."

She staggered right on the edge, and then suddenly Agnes was there. She grabbed hold of Madame Simone's hands. The old woman was thrown off balance. She slipped, fell forwards, and out the window. She screamed all the way down.

Chapter Forty-Six

Two days later, Maggie went back to work. She had a bandage around her neck, but beyond that, she was unscathed. She stepped into her office and was struck immediately by the change in its atmosphere. There existed a heaviness that hadn't been there before. She noticed that Agnes had taken away the trophies and Helen had removed the track medals. It looked like a detective's office, which it was.

"You know what threw me off," Maggie said. Agnes brought her some coffee. Poor Agnes seemed to feel that the only way to atone for almost sleeping through Maggie's near-murder was to keep bringing her coffee. Maggie figured anything that made Agnes feel guilty was a good thing. She needed something to suppress her a little.

"It was the prodigal son," she explained. "That's what confused me. I've always loved that story. I've always identified with the joy the father would feel at having his lost son come home. I could even understand the young son going off and wasting all his money. I just never stopped to think that a parent might not be happy to see her child."

"The limitations of parables in private detective work."

"I guess so."

"She must have hated Domino," Agnes said.

"Maybe she was frightened of her," Helen said. She was playing with a pen, rolling it up and down her hands. Maggie noticed she'd written the word, "Edgar," on her palm. Maggie knew she had yet another school meeting to go to. "You don't always know who your children are going to be. Do you suppose she really killed Leonard Stern?"

"Walter wants to exhume the body. It's been in the Stern vault all this time, so he thinks there may be a trace of poison remaining."

"She was a monster," Agnes said.

"She was very selfish," Maggie added. "I knew that. I saw that all along, but I guess over time it became something toxic. It started off as a survival skill, a defense mechanism, and then it turned into something aggressive, something poisonous."

"Do you think Racine really would have let her kill you?"

Maggie thought of the way Racine had looked. The way she'd stopped when Maggie said the 23rd psalm. She thought of how people get themselves twisted around into a terrible place.

"I hope not," she said.

"What do you think will happen to Racine? Will they arrest her?"

"She must have known for years that something was not quite right with her mother. That's why she always kept her apart from people. But I don't know if she realized quite how bad her mother was. It's scary when nightmares come true. Much easier to imagine it's all just a bad dream."

Agnes cleared her throat. She was wearing a velour pant suit, which for Agnes was restrained.

"Maggie, I've been thinking about this a lot, and I'm going to let you decide."

"Okay," Maggie said, stunned. Agnes must be feeling really guilty. "What?"

"Do you think we should give Racine the money back?"

She opened up her pocketbook and pulled out a check for $10,000, made out to Racine Stern. "This represents all the money she's given us over the last two weeks. What do you think?"

Maggie's first impulse was to say yes. Of course, they had to give the money back. How could you charge a client when you'd accidentally killed her mother, even if, in fairness, her mother tried to kill you first? But then Maggie paused. She thought of Detective Grudge. She looked into Agnes's and Helen's solemn faces. Racine had hired them to do a job, and they had done it well.

"You know what," Maggie said. "I think we earned that money."

Agnes jumped to her feet and began pumping her hand. "Finally," she cried out. "Finally." She ripped up the check. "I didn't dare dream."

Then Agnes took out her checkbook again. "I'm going to make it out to you," she said.

She set the checkbook down on their huge slab of a table and started to scrawl out Maggie's name. "You can keep it."

"No, we're dividing it three ways. We're a team right."

"I feel a group hug coming on," Helen said, and they were in the middle of a huddle when Walter came in. He hit his head on the top of the door frame and swore, and then stared at them in his typical bemused fashion. He looked around.

"This is the office. Very nice."

"Sit down, Walter, why don't you?" Agnes said.

"I thought you'd want to know that the court didn't charge Racine with anything. She's going to sell Stern Manor though. I understand she wants to move back to France."

"Good for her," Maggie said. "She needs to start over."

"At her age," Helen said.

"I'll have you know, she's only eight years older than I am. That's not so late," Maggie said. "You can start your life over at any point you want."

Walter cleared his throat. "I came by for a reason," he said.

They all waited.

"I have a referral." He held up his hand, stopping Agnes in mid-swoop. "Don't get too excited. It's just some subpoena work, but I thought you could use the business."

"Thank you, Walter," Maggie said, ridiculously touched.

Somehow, she'd arrived at this amazing place. She had two partners, she had a nutty little surrogate grand-child and she had the chief of police referring work to her. She knew private detectives weren't supposed to weep. She felt sure Detective Grudge never did. But she did wipe away a little tear. She was so thankful.

Chapter Forty-Seven

Senior Friends Day arrived and Maggie felt nervous. Would it break her heart to be around so many real grandparents? She'd become braver about so many things. She'd embraced her new life in a way she could never have anticipated. Still, there were times such as this, walking into the same elementary school her daughter had attended, seeing some of the same teachers, that she felt she would sink.

But this wasn't about her, she reminded herself. This was Edgar's day, and Edgar was, as always, enthusiastic. He wore a suit and tie and he gave a presentation about her. He'd made a poster of her life. He'd pasted on pictures of Maggie as a young author, her house, the cats, Juliet as a baby, and then a photo of the two of them at the apple orchard. She was covered in apple sauce and grinning like a lunatic. He gave a report about her and then he said, "My grandma is a private detective and she just chased down some bad guys and she pushed a lady out the window."

"Not pushed," Maggie felt compelled to say. "But I was there."

"She fought and she won."

When he was done, everyone applauded. Edgar bowed, then came over and curled against her.

After all the presentations were over, Maggie chatted with all the other grandparents, who marveled at her experience. They were both floating as they walked down Main Street. That's when Maggie noticed Iphigenia's hair salon. She'd not apologized to her. She had to do it, and started in that direction, when Iphigenia flew out. "You look terrible," she said to Maggie Dove. "I hear you almost died."

"That's true."

"Still, you can't let it affect your hair. You'll come by tomorrow?"

"Absolutely," Maggie said.

They continued a little further and Trudi came out from the candy store. She handed Maggie a Snickers bar and Edgar a bag of Sour Patch Kids.

"Thank you," she said. Then she whispered in Maggie's ear. "Thank you for not reporting us."

They'd not gone much further when they ran into Reverend Sunday. She seemed to be coming from Maggie's house. "I put a casserole on your porch," she said. "Rice and beans."

"Thank you," Maggie said, and then she told her about how she'd recited the psalm when Madame Simone attacked her. "I think it made Racine stop."

"Of course it did," Reverend Sunday said. "Do you not know your powers, Maggie Dove? And you too little

Edgar. You will grow up to be a powerful man, some day. If you use your powers well."

Maggie couldn't help but think about what Helen had said about his father. It had been on her mind ever since that conversation, an undercurrent to everything he said and did. She knew better than anyone that life could be hard and could twist people around. It had happened to her for a long time. It happened to Madame Simone. She had started off a beautiful young woman and turned into something monstrous. But Maggie believed that with her love, and the love of his mother, and the love of the community, and the love of the detective agency, this boy would grow up to be something fine. He had his father in him, but he had his mother too. And he had Maggie Dove, and she was starting to realize she was a much tougher character than she'd ever realized.

"What say we go watch a Detective Grudge video," she suggested, once they got inside the house. "I think there's one that shows you how to search through garbage."

"Yes," he cried out. "Yes!"

THE END

Acknowledgements

Turns out it takes a couple of villages to write and publish a novel, and I'm very grateful to the people who populate mine.

Especially:

Keri Barnum of New Shelves Books, for her creativity and hard-work. Anna Gray, also of New Shelves, for her work on social media graphics and Maggie Dove book trailers.

Mila (milagraphicartist.com) for the beautiful book cover and Amit Dey for interior design.

Paula Munier, Amy Collins, Gina Panettieri and the rest of the fabulous team at Talcott Notch Literary. I could not ask for better advocates.

Dana Isaacson, for believing in Maggie Dove.

Alex Steele and Gotham Writers and all my friends/students. There's no better resource (or joy) for a writer than spending hours talking with other writers.

The mystery-writing world, which has been so much cozier than you would think. Special shout out to the kind souls at Mystery Writers of America, Malice Domestic and Miss Demeanors (missdemeanors.com) Also to Linda Landrigan and Jackie Sherbow, who've given Maggie Dove a chance to tell her stories at *Alfred Hitchcock's Mystery Magazine*.

My beautiful little village of Irvington-on-Hudson, which is not exactly Darby, but shares certain trees.

The Irvington Presbyterian Church, which has been a place of grace and hope for me. Special shout out to the IPC book club, which has shown me what readers look for when reading a book. Also hugs to Chris and Rhett Omark, who have been Maggie Dove superfans from the start. Enthusiasm matters!

Chris Canning and Patricia van Essche designed a magnificent website for me. www.susanjbreen.com

My circle of friends, most especially Melinda Feinstein, Terry Gillen, Leslie Mack & Robin Freedman, and Kay O'Keefe.

My family of Breens, Bucks, Lujans, Murcotts, Turchettes and Zelonys (especially my brother, Robert Zelony). Special hugs for Rosey Singh and my friends at the Good Shepherd Agricultural Mission.

My treasures: Tom Breen and Lucy Gellman, Kathy and Alex Brennan, and Chris Breen. My loved one, Will.

And my dear husband, Brad. Who is everything.

About the Author

Susan Breen is the author of the Maggie Dove mystery series, originally published by the Alibi digital imprint of Penguin Random House and now rereleased by Under the Oak Press. Her first novel, *The Fiction Class*, also published by Penguin Random House, won a Westchester Library Association Washington Irving Award for "readability, literary quality, and wide general appeal." Her short stories have been published in *Best American Nonrequired Reading*, as well as an assortment of magazines ranging from *American Literary Review* and *The Chattahoochee Review* to *Alfred Hitchcock's Mystery Magazine and Ellery Queen's Mystery Magazine*. She has a story forthcoming in the anthology *Murder Most Diabolical*, introduced by Walter Mosley. Susan teaches novelwriting and does editing work with Gotham Writers in Manhattan. She lives in the Hudson Valley with her husband, two sweet dogs (cockapoos) and two slightly opinionated cats. Her three children are flourishing elsewhere. You can find more information about her at www.susanjbreen.com.

Made in United States
Orlando, FL
11 December 2024

55449120R00195